UNSUITABLE OBSESSION

Part One

TRISHA**FUENTES**

Outskirts Press, Inc.
Denver, Colorado

Thanks for reading *Unsuitable Obsession*, an original novel written by Author, TRISHA FUENTES. Look for the continuation of Amber & Eduardo's Love Story in *Broken Obsession*, coming soon! Other titles and eBooks available by visiting the author's website at www.theardentartist.com

Outskirts Press, Inc.
http://www.outskirtspress.com

ISBN: 978-1-4327-3275-2

Library of Congress Control Number: 2008936617

PRINTED IN THE UNITED STATES OF AMERICA

Dedication

To my Father Figure, Larraine; never have I known a woman like you, you are a true emotional survivor. I hope I've made you proud, Mom, and to my Dad, Fred...I understand now, I truly do. I love you both.

To the Rico, Lugo, Cruz, Fuentes and Nava Families: Thank you for allowing me to step into your world of deep adoration, family conviction, high regards and utter respect for your kin. Thank you for all the amazing childhood memories.

To my sister's Tamara and Monica: May you always feel complete and loved to the fullest extent with the men in your lives. For you two were not as nearly as fortunate as I was to have experienced so many influences.

To my daughter, Erika: Oh how I envy you! You have your whole life ahead of you and know exactly what you want; study hard and keep chasing your dreams for they can come true!

To my own green-eyed monster, Lou: Thank you for the thrills of sharing your exciting life, the ups and downs and everything in between. Thank you for the boys and the passion you show me daily, ***te amo mucho!***

To my three brother-in-laws: This is only fiction.

Prologue

"It started out innocent…playful glances, a gentle pat on his arm. We were cordial with each other, cracked a joke now and then—"

Dr. Hayward stopped her at that point. "No—no Amber, I want you to explain ***how*** it happened."

"Explain? How it happened?" She repeated.

"Yes dear, can you do that for me now?" Dr. Hayward asked hopeful.

Amber closed her eyes. Can she do that? How could she ***not?*** The images in her mind practically strangled her to death she couldn't help but think of anything else. "...I found myself ***undeniably*** attracted to him. And that's not an excuse for what I've done, it's the truth."

"I don't want you to create an excuse Amber; I want you to tell me the truth. A truth statement." Dr. Hayward explained, restarting his dictating machine.

Amber felt her throat close up. She choked back tears and tried to focus on the ceiling tiles above her. "When he was in the same room...I couldn't think of anything else but how to get him to ***touch me***."

"That's good Amber, keep going." Dr. Hayward stated optimistic.

"...He was one of those men whose smile alone could build up a woman's appetite to gratify her. He was so incredibly gorgeous; no woman was able to deny his charms. Any woman who was around him was instantly mesmerized. And not just to me, he had that deep affect on the opposite sex.

He was charming, affectionate, considerate...conceited, spoiled, intelligent, fashionable—***Good Lord***—he was perfect. He was my...he was ***my***..." Amber could hardly mouth out the word, bent over in anguish as her tears bit against her eyes.

"Amber, you need to say it now, he was ***what?*** You can you know, you're safe here. No one else is going to hear you. We're not in front of a group like you requested, you're with me." Dr. Hayward clicked his dictating machine off once again. "Now, tell me ***how*** it happened, let's go back to the day when you felt you needed to end the relationship." He then started the device again.

Amber stared up at the wall and wiped away the moisture from her face. End it? Yes, to put it quite bluntly, she did end her despair. Cut it so severely she would have a scar for the rest of her life.

CHAPTER**ONE**

A Scar for the Rest of Her Life

Amber's life was intertwined with her husband's family. Rather, her husband's family ruled her entire existence. She doesn't mind it though; it was what she always wanted, a family, ***and a real family***, with lots of relatives unlike her own. The tight knot that was the Sanchez Family was a far cry from the Fitzgerald's. "The Family", was what she referred to it, with all its deep-rooted Latin-American traditions. The drama a clan that size would unfold! She always craved relatives like them and relished in the fact that she was part of their exclusive unit.

Her father, Sam Fitzgerald was a mere teenager when he had Amber. He didn't know how or ***want*** to know how to be a father. He'd rather explore the world on his motorcycle than learn to be a parent of any kind. Giving up the challenge to Amber's mother, Sheila, Sam Fitzgerald walked away from his children when they were very young. Amber never truly understood why her father thought it was so effortless to just leave like that. And, after the divorce, Amber never understood why her Daddy never picked them up on scheduled days to see him. How can a parent ***just do that?*** What on earth would possess a parent to just ride away from that kind of responsibility? That deep horrific consideration was now hers to swallow. She ***would*** leave her husband and kids for the man she now loved. If only he'd do the same. Good Lord, could this be the same exact reason her own father left her mother?

"...Are you going to calm down now?" He asked

exasperated, arms still around her body in a tight grasp. He wasn't going to let her take off yet, not until he gained his way.

Amber was breathing heavily, she wanted to compose herself, she did, but relaxing would only mean to continue the misery. ***"Please leave her,"*** she asked one last time.

He was worn out with the subject and closed his eyes in disappointment.

His silence only fed her decision. She could either go on through life the way she was living, or she could end it, no longer feel the pain.

With all her might she pulled away from him and pushed his unreceptive body into the wall. Amber ran out of the doorway and hiked down the narrow hallway—ignoring his calls for her return from the staircase above.

Don't look back Amber, don't look back!

She ignored his demands. In the corner of her eye, she caught a glimpse of the pool nearby. Kids splashed in the water—a big, fleshy man did a belly flop off the diving board. She hid her face from their view, her failed attempt at being decent. ***Yah decent...I don't feel decent, I feel like trash...***Sprinted down the staircase, reached her car, pressed the keyless entry and unlocked the door. Flung her body into the driver's seat and pulled down the vanity mirror. ***Why do they call it a vanity mirror anyhow?*** All she saw lately when she looked in the mirror was a cheater—***an adulterer***—a woman deceiving her husband with another man, excessive rather, a woman cheating on her husband with her ***brother-in-law***.

She screeched away from the motel. Tears flowed down her face, warm, frightening tears. Oh how could she continue on with this charade? It was so hard and tiresome to keep up with all the lies. But he was so magnetic, so elusive, the man she always wanted, but didn't settle for. He was the opposite of Victor Sanchez, contrary in every way. Oh she knew it was vile, immoral, insincere, and every wicked word you could think of. And heck, she even liked her sister-in-law! Leticia Sanchez (her sister-in-law) was everything her in-laws cherished. That dedicated Latin woman with strong Catholic beliefs, amazing morals with similar family history. Salt of the Earth. Who cooked a fantastic Mexican meal; from the top of her enchiladas right down to her perfect pinto beans. Amber could not cook, nope, not one little bit. All she was skillful at was getting the timing just right on a Lean Cuisine. Damn, she had that down to a science! Amber was just the opposite of Leticia. Leticia was this long leggy brunette; with gorgeous green eyes she inherited from her mother and grandmother. That respected trait that The Family always talked about, like she was some patron saint that no one else could tarnish. Amber was always fighting her feeling of being envious of Leticia—even though she shouldn't be, Leticia was allowed to build a life with the man that Amber now loved. Leticia got to eat breakfast with him, watch him shower, go away with him, and create a daughter.

Amber drove herself to the nearest drug store, bought what she required and then drove to another motel. Once in the parking lot, she sat in her car sobbing. ***Oh how could they do it?*** All those years of lying, deceiving the people that they truly loved, swallowing her pride, hiding their secret affair, face to face with the family that she admired, loved.

He doesn't want me enough to leave her...I can never leave my husband...If nobody can leave...then no one will win...

Amber got out of the car. Stumbled to the front office and checked in. She reached the motel room, fudged with the keys for a moment then opened up the door. So, so despondent, she tossed her purse onto a chair next to the window and plopped herself onto the bed with a thud. Amber then rolled over on the bed and spread her arms out wide, feeling the length of the mattress and cried.

She would teach him a lesson. Send him a message that he'd never forget. All she wanted from him now was to show her how much he cared, that's all...just ***show*** her. Prove it. He said he would never leave Leticia, yelled at her when she asked him to. Said he would never put his family through that sort of shame. Said, "It would be a scandal". The Family would never allow him to go anywhere without the humiliation, it would be far worse for him than it would be for her. So why continue the affair? Why be such a willing participant? ***WHY?!***

Amber continued to cry in anguish on top of the sheets. It was the bed they used to make love on, the one she prayed to forget. She wished there was still some scent of him, but all she smelled was starch and bleach.

Amber started when her cell phone rang. Amber believed it was her mother calling and pulled herself up from the bed, "Hello?"

"Amber you OK? Where the hell are you?"

It was Eduardo. She doesn't want to speak to him. Never wanted to hear or see him again! She hung up on him and threw the cell phone clear across the room in defeat. The bell rang again…That relentless Van Halen "Jamie's Cryin" cell phone jingle, over and over and ***OVER AGAIN.***

Amber continued to bawl, her heart ached for some sort of relief. She went to the cell phone, screamed off the top of her lungs. "You son-of-a-bitch! Who the hell do you think I am? I'm not some bimbo of yours! I'm your fuckin' sister-in-law for ***crissakes!*** You need to show some respect!" She twirled herself around and threw herself on the bed once more. The phone continued to ring. She couldn't take it anymore. She ran over to it this time and answered the damn thing. "What? ***What!***"

"Amber where are you? Come back, let's talk—"

Amber cleared her throat. "No Eduardo, it's over, ***done.***"

"NO! Wait!"

"No Eduardo, you've said all you had to say, all I care to hear...I wanted you to leave Leticia but you can't...It's over! I'm done with this...someone has to teach you a lesson!"

"What? Amber please—"

Amber was distraught, desperate and beside herself; she wanted to distance herself from all her sorrow and ripped open the back of the cell phone and removed the battery. No more rings, no more calls, no more interruptions!

Amber dragged herself over to the writing desk. Opened up the drawer and pulled out the writing paper and pen the motel had provided and eyed the Bible sitting neatly in the corner. It doesn't faze her…not one little bit.

She began the first letter, one to her husband, Victor. Oh how she ***believed*** she loved him! He was her rock. Her sponge.

Her confidant. She would thank him for allowing her to feel so at ease with his family. Thank him for introducing her to relatives so full of love and passion for one another. Thank him for Adrian and Valentina, her son and little girl. Apologize to him about his brother. The next letter was a combination, one for her mother and her sister, asking them to take care of her children. Make sure that Valentina—her four year-old—knew what it was like to become a lady, a woman in this world. To show her pictures now and then so that she wouldn't forget her mother and to make sure that Victor still remembered he had a son, Adrian, who was still in Junior High and would need a strong male influence after she was gone. Then finally, to Eduardo, a farewell to him, a finale of sorts. A heart-felt love-letter to the man who stole her heart the day she met him.

It was a complex relationship, their clandestine affair. Watching him from afar, desperately containing herself from not wrapping her arms around him and never letting go. It had been a constant battle at family gatherings, keeping up the charade. ***Sister-in-law*** slash ***brother-in-law*** first and foremost. Pretending to be attracted to her husband, continuing to have intercourse with him while fantasizing he was really her brother-in-law. Trying to figure out what lacked in her marriage, trying to figure out what went wrong and what happed to them when Victor was such a great guy! It had all been so fatiguing—strenuous to extreme—having to continue to be the guiltless girl, the deserving girl of incomparable love. Fifteen years of rationalizing; give and take and bending over backwards. It was all so laborious. She wanted to be unrestricted, no longer thinking of how to attack her feelings; she wanted to surrender to them.

Good Lord, what did she do? How did she let it go on for so long? Her dutiful husband never having a clue. And her kids...***oh God***...it was so difficult to have them...her daughter, Valentina, with her face so round and pudgy and beautiful...her son, Adrian, all grown up, such a young man! Would they miss their Mommy? Oh God, they would…and Eduardo…Oh God, Eduardo...would he miss her as well? Would he? Good Lord, ***she...loved...him...so much!***

Amber slowly submerged herself in a tub of hot water. It

was soothing on the contrary—but not gratifying enough. She eyed the sharp razor, so shiny, small, and quick. All she had to do now was slash her wrist. It would be immediate. Quick. And then it will be all over. Done with. No scandal in the family. Nothing to verify. No more having to watch Leticia and Eduardo hug, no more Christmas' with The Family, or Thanksgiving dinners, birthdays, weddings. No more family gatherings. No more hurting and deceiving Victor.

Amber reached for the razor blade. Shiny, small, quick.

Through her weeping, she grasped the razor and raised her left wrist.

Quick...Oh...Good Lord...Quick...I can never leave Victor...Eduardo doesn't love me enough to leave her...Doesn't want me enough to show me…I don't wanna do anything but go away…run away…Please God, please let it be fast, Oh God, I don't even wanna breathe!…Eduardo doesn't want me…Oh God, why doesn't he want me? Why doesn't he love me enough to show me? Oh God, Eduardo doesn't want me…Daddy never wanted me either...Oh God...Oh God...Oh God…

Amber
Fifteen Years Earlier

As long as I could remember, I always knew something special was going to happen to me. When I was ten, I would cling onto that small hope that no matter how bad a day I was having, there was still something gigantic to expect just around the corner.

I'm still waiting...

Where do I begin? I'll be eighteen in a couple of months having just started my senior year in high school. I'm one of those kids who started school late. No, not because my Mom was some kind of idiot, but because my birthday happened to fall late in the year (born in December and you had to be born before November) my bad luck in order to start kindergarten. I was tossed in with other kids much younger than me, but yet since I was so shy, I always wondered who would be my friend for the day. I was oftentimes intimidated. I became a good artist by the age of seven. I'd rather hide in a corner with my crayons and drawing pencils than conjure up any effort to find someone to play with.

I grew up in the San Fernando Valley, a small humble neighborhood in Southern California. I have an older sister, Molly, and I love her to death. Molly graduated last year and I miss her companionship. Molly was a song leader and I thought since being associated with her friends, all her popular connections would befriend me, but not true. I'm oftentimes alone, walking around with my head down, anticipating a friendly hello and I suddenly find myself grouped among the other Caucasian kids who aren't considered fashionable because we can't afford trendy clothes. Recently, I've heard that word "stoner" whispered behind me in the hallways, but I'm not a stoner, I'm just insecure, I've never even tried drugs, well, OK, yes, I have tried marijuana, once in fact, and got really sick afterwards. But just because I'm not some stylish chic-chick, I'm considered a stoner? I'm more like someone who is stuck in the 1970's, but I'm labeled a nobody in the mass hysteria of New Wave.

Did I mention clothes? I can never keep up with the trends. High heels, miniskirts, ruffled shirts, flashy jackets, rows and rows of bangles on my arms—who can afford all that? My mother takes my sister and me to the swap meet (sometimes rummage sales) to buy our clothes. My mother is not able to afford retail or mall type clothing; it was second hand jeans, sweaters, tennis shoes and T-shirts for the two of us. I'm oftentimes embarrassed or ashamed even envious I don't own any of those shiny high-heeled pumps the popular girls are wearing today in the 1980's. Although I try to fit in, I never do. Girls my age tease their hair—the wilder, the better—have perms; I wear mine straight and long passed my shoulders. Young women today wear a lot of make-up: eye shadows of purple, turquoise, magenta, cinnamon, I choose none. I'm a plain simple girl, wearing plain simple clothes still anticipating the day for my something special to happen.

I'm also very tall. I tower over those petite fem. fatales strutting around campus with their elevated footgear. I'm also a jock-***ette***. A girl who loves to play sports, get dirty, feel the thrill of throwing a runner out at first base. ***Yeah, baby.*** I'm the catcher on the girls' softball team and I love to wear that mask over my face, eyeing patrons in the stands unable to see my eye contact. I stand erect and high behind that plate, all five foot eleven of my sturdy frame. I consider myself lean and fit, with strong tone legs. And in my sport, I'm a force to consider, and although I reign on that diamond, I unravel the moment I take off that uniform. Those short mini-skirts are far too intimidating and my self-esteem withdraws instantaneously.

***Trailer Trash*.**

If you want to really hurt someone deep, call him/her Trailer Trash—Caucasian with little or no money. That remark definitely lingered like garlic, and through life I was led to believe that being broke ***was*** Trailer Trash. Although my Dad gave my Mom the house when they divorced, my Mom is always struggling with the house payment and we girls oftentimes suffer for it. Or maybe it was low self-esteem. Yah, I have to admit I have low self-esteem. Boys just want to use me and I never had a best friend.

Boys...let's talk about them. I hate them. All of them. They should all be locked up in cages—Smelly Apes that they are. No, just kidding, I don't hate guys; I'm rather fond of males. Since my Dad left me at such an early age, I've always felt the need for comfort, for some big strong man to wrap his arms around me and chase all the nightmares away. Sad to say, I've had my share of promiscuous loser boyfriends. Being passed around, not really getting to know any of the guys I've happened to kiss. I lost my virginity to a senior at sixteen, a one-night stand and unplanned pregnancy I'll always regret. Low self-esteem will do that to a girl; not having a Father Figure will do you in as well. I guess I'll always feel like that little girl searching for a capable influence to guide me into solace and keep me safe and warm. I tilted from one juvenile slack to the next never being able to hang on long enough to keep a mature relationship.

The Smelly Apes only want one thing from me and that's to unhook my bra. Did I mention I have a nice rack? My assets seemed to form at an early age. By fifth grade, I was already into a C-cup. By Junior High, my assets (that's what I call them because that's really all I've got going on for me) formed into a nice pair of D-cups. Naked, I bet I could measure up to someone who had breast implants. Playboy, watch out. Mine are just as plump, just as perky, nipples just as high. I'm proud of my breasts. So much in fact, I know I can always count on them to be my channel in taking away a Smelly Ape's concentration. Neighborhood primates always seem to stare at them before noticing my face. Kissing Smelly Apes would never stop short of my mouth; they always seemed to want to tear down my bra. What was the fascination anyhow? Didn't they want to know how the game went that day? Those silly monkeys, don't they want to know what I'm thinking? How I'm feeling? Those boring, single-minded chimps, watching them gawk at me, as they seem to ***talk down*** to my chest. Trip or bump into something, never taking their eyes off my assets, inspecting them as I walked alongside, hearing them shout obscenities because of my figure. At the beach, sun bathing near a pool, at the supermarket, any public place. I know men stare at them. Smelly Apes, males, all men, even all my Father Figures! Feeling their eyes lowering to my sweater, T-shirt, softball uniform; noticing all my Father Figures watching me walk away, checking out my bottom, such parental inspiration. ***What creeps! I'm your step-daughter for crying out loud!***

Did I mention that I'm still waiting?

I'm a romantic. In love with love. Always with my head in the clouds, determined to meet my sweetheart whether right or wrong. In love with old movies where the men were admired, fought for what they believed in and swept his lady off her feet. I believe my soul mate is walking this very earth right now and is searching for me as well. And when we see each other, I expect to see shooting stars, hear the sweet sound of violins and savor electricity dart through my veins. I'm not partial to any one physique really, but I do require that my arms wrap around his body and meet. He has to have a persuasive personality and be stern in his attitude to calm me. Bring me home. Console me when times are rough, and believe me, times have been pretty stormy.

And I'm still waiting...Waiting to be swept away (or blown away) whichever comes first.

CHAPTER**TWO**

Careful What You Wish For

"What the hell—" Amber expressed with utter objection. Amber was in the dark room processing negatives into pictures when a beam of the light penetrated through the darkness.

"Oh man, I'm sorry; I didn't realize anyone was in here." Victor apologetically gives to her.

"Well, ***I am,*** now close the darn door!" Amber shouted back at him. Battling through courses, Amber took Photography 101 as an elective to help bring her grades up her senior year.

"Sorry, so sorry...I just need to get some film from the shelf really quick, I won't be in your way, I promise." Victor replied, reaching around her, pushing her body unintentionally into the chemicals.

Amber rolled her eyes. He smelled good, the air in the little room suddenly filled with Old Spice. She continued to process the picture, gently swishing the photo back and forth.

Victor walked over to her side and sneaked a peek at what she was doing. Transforming through the chemicals was an image of a guitar player on stage, head back in the waves of ecstasy performing a solo on his electric guitar. Victor looked in closer, couldn't believe his eyes. Eddie Van Halen! "Awesome! How'd you get that?" He quipped in awe.

Amber doesn't look at him, "It's mine—I took it." She tapped the picture against the edge of the bucket then gently clipped the photo above her on a nearby string of other photographs of the same rock star. "And don't go telling

Mr. Whitman that I've been using the school's chemicals for my own gain."

"Are you kidding me? Van Halen is my all-time favorite band! Can you make me a duplicate of that?" He asked of her, squinting and focusing, trying to figure out what she looked like in the dark.

Amber leaned over and turned on the light. Victor strained, tried to focus. Amber tried as well, and when she did, there was a boy, no taller than her staring back. He was Mexican, she realized, and cute with dark brown wavy shoulder-length hair, brown curious eyes with subtle shades of an introductory mustache just above his lips. His outfit resembled hers; pulka shells around his neck, Levi 501's, and Good Lord! That wonderful insignia of the letters ***VH*** on his T-shirt! "VH" of course (for any hard core fan of the group) meant ***Van Halen.***

Victor's mouth dropped open wide, fell in love with her at first sight. "Victor Sanchez," he pronounced, extending out his hand.

"Amber Fitzgerald."

Victor couldn't help but gawk. He'd seen her in class from afar, but Amber Fitzgerald always seemed to be unapproachable walking around with her head down all the time. He never imagined she'd look this stunning up close. Long jet-black hair that shined brightly even in the dim light, a smooth complexion enhancing incredible oblique eyes, Mexican? No, American Indian, he realized. Radiant those eyes, hazel almost, suntanned skin. And her smile, such straight white teeth, unlike his own; her smile could melt a tortilla chip. "Did you see them the last time they were here in LA? Did you take those at the concert?"

"Yep," she smiled again, realizing he was just as big a fan as she. "Front row seats. My Dad felt guilty for not picking me up one weekend and bought me the tickets." Now why ***on earth*** did she just confess that to him? She never offered personal information to anyone before, especially to Smelly Apes!

Victor collected the delicate info and decided not to pursue it, he was just too stoked that this ravishing girl was as crazy about Van Halen as he was. "That's awesome...my cousins and I went last year, followed them all the way to Portland, came back with tons of posters and T-shirts, this is one of them." He presented, pulling down his shirt for display.

Amber grinned and turned her body around, flaunting her backside and lifting up her mane. "I got this shirt actually ***signed*** by David Lee Roth back stage, it's at home...I wear this one to school though."

Victor was bowled over! ***"Awesome!*** Have you eaten lunch yet?"

Amber turned sharply around and bore into his eyes. Warm, brown and sincere, she'd never met anyone quite like him.

They sat together in the cafeteria, not paying attention to the other kids doing double takes at the mismatched twosome. They talk about everything: school, cars, part-time jobs, dogs, cats, and then finally ***family.*** She informed him about her sister and Mom—failed to point out one or two dark little secrets—explained to him that she wasn't Native American like he initially thought, but Irish American on her father's side. That somewhere in her ancestral line was gypsy blood bronzing her skin. Victor seemed intrigued, but Amber felt awkward talking about her clan and instantly wanted to know about his. His parents were from Mexico and he had one brother, and when he spoke about the rest, she was ***enthralled***. She learned that he came from this huge Mexican family of nearly three hundred or more relatives, all-living close by, or in California, and on certain holidays, usually the big ones like Christmas, they would all gather together and have a huge party—like a fiesta! Amber was in heaven. The more she learned about Victor Sanchez and his marvelous family, the more she was interested in him. If it weren't for him popping into the dark room unexpectedly, she would have never given Victor Sanchez a second glance. He wasn't her usual one-night stand boyfriend either; he was a jock, which was totally abnormal for her and she sometimes had to pinch herself that someone that good wanted to spend time with her.

After graduation, they dated awhile going to the movies,

meeting at the arcade and taking walks in the parks with their dogs. Talking, talking, talking, they communicated about anything and everything. It was all very innocent, casual and smooth. Nothing was complicated about Victor. He was always there when she called on him. Always available when she needed a shoulder to cry on, especially on the days her father never showed. He was there with open arms and restful comfortable hugs. The further she hung around him, the more she wanted to be with him.

* * * * *

Victor parked his car in the driveway and shut off the ignition. "Now Amber, let me tell you something about Mama." He looked deep into her eyes and searched for a nice way, a cautious way to tell her. "Mama is, well, she's your typical Latina mother."

Amber was about to meet his parents for the first time. Amber was apprehensive herself, having never been introduced to any of her boyfriend's parents before. She was constantly shocked with Victor's sense of honor. Amber was willing to sleep with him months ago, but Victor refused. Told her that he would know when the timing was right. When the timing was right? Good Lord, she never came across a male with so much integrity! Definitely a keeper, definitely not a Smelly Ape. "Oh Victor—relax, I think I can hold my own with your mother, ***Latina*** or not. My Mom is ***very*** opinionated, and I think I hold my own with her."

Victor let go a hoot. "OK—whatever."

Amber fanned out her hand and combed her locks with it; bit down on her lower lip (an unconscious act she always seemed to do, by the way). "Will you stop?"

Victor watched Amber surveying her face in the passenger vanity mirror. "Thanks for wearing that skirt. Mama still thinks all girls should be wearing dresses, cried the day she saw a girl wearing pants."

"Oh my," Amber let go, fanning her fingers through her hair a second time. "I borrowed this from my mother actually; we're the same size, thank God. I just folded over the waist a couple of times to make the skirt look like a mini, so you like it, huh?"

Victor gazed down at her legs, so smooth, so tan. "Awesome. I hope Mama approves."

"Oh Victor, you're so nervous. Don't be! There's nothing to be nervous about! I'm going to make such an impression on your ***Mama*** and your ***Papa*** that you won't ever have to worry."

"I know, but this is sort of a special day. My brother just graduated law school, everyone will be there. My aunts, my uncles, all my cousins—"

"Good Lord Victor, ***relax!*** What could be so bad?"

Amber didn't know what she was walking into, but when Victor opened up that door—all one hundred Sanchez' that day alone—she knew exactly what he meant! She had never been so panicky. Amber's family only consisted of her sister and mother, and that was it. Her grandparents both died ten years prior in a train accident and her father's parents were virtually strangers to her.

The Sanchez home was both elegant and comfortable simultaneously, with warm Spanish colors of terra cotta, brown and green, simple sofas, La-Z-boy chairs and hand-painted oil paintings of Jesus. Countless pictures of family members—some so old—were faded and ripped. A display of tropical palms filled several corners of the space as smells of fresh oregano finished every crevice of the living room. Outside, a piñata hung from a large tree and directly underneath the standing timber, a hefty Bar-B-Que with a massive piece of Tri-tip sizzled in the center of the grill. Streamers trimmed the rafters, while screaming kids filled the swimming pool. Each person was laughing and enjoying him or herself; it was like walking into a wondrous circus.

Amber was in awe of every little thing; grassy play area away from the pool, several enormous fruit trees midpoint and an endless amount of folding chairs lined up against the walls for relatives to sit on. Victor told her once about every activity—he and his brother along with dozens of other cousins—played during the summer in this great backyard. Fabrizio (Victor's father) learned welding at a very early age, became so successful at it; he was able to purchase the four-bedroom/three bath home in the San Fernando Valley with half an acre early on. Now the home was paid for and the Sanchez family lived relaxed and celebrated often.

Victor guided Amber around and introduced her to every relative that he came across. Tiá Lorena, a red-haired beauty, her husband Lamberto, equally just as handsome. Heavy-set Tiá Sonya, skinny Tiá Gemma and her husband Simone, just as thin. So many aunts and uncles, she couldn't keep track. Cousins: five Javier's, two Justino's, ten Maria's, Connie, Hector, Priscilla, Monica, Jorge, Sylvia, Magdelena, the list went on forever and ever. And everyone (oh, and Amber couldn't believe it when it happened) greeted you with a hug or a kiss on the cheek! She didn't know ***any*** of those people, and they all welcomed her with such a personal gesture. It was all so amazing and uplifting she actually felt like she was walking on air.

Walking around with a stupid smile pasted to her face, Victor was suddenly taken away when it happened. It was so swift, such a surprise; she actually felt her heart jump. A man on the other side—across the backyard laughing with a woman—tempted Amber's intrigue. She didn't recall being introduced to him and tried to figure out who he was. The man was ***very*** handsome and assuredly nodded to every affected lady that walked by. He certainly was put together very nicely. Tall in height, several inches taller than Amber, she assumed; broad shoulders with a slim waist, tawny skin, groomed chestnut hair. She actually felt compelled to converse with him, which was really odd and felt her feet moving towards his vicinity. Where the heck was she going? Amber turned away from him instantly, the fellow made her feel sensations she ***never felt her entire life!*** Frightened of the temptation, she marched around in the opposite direction bumping into bodies looking for Victor. Bumping, knocking, bashing into the crowd until Victor spun her around to face him—he'd been following her this entire time!

"You OK?" Victor asked visibly noticing Amber's uncertainty.

Amber blinked the man out of her system. "Um—oh, Victor,

I was looking for you, where'd you go? Don't leave me all alone to fend for myself again, you brat," she squealed, pinching his shoulder.

"Ouch...sorry, but my cousin Javier wanted to show me the present he got for my brother." Victor then put his arm around Amber's shoulders and hugged her near.

Amber gave him a small peck on the cheek. "Where is your brother? I haven't met him yet."

Victor squeezed her tight, "First things first. Ready to meet my parents?"

Amber sucked in her stomach, "I think so. For sure."

He led her back into the house and towards the vast kitchen domain where other family gathered. Victor then walked over to this large lofty woman and tapped her on her shoulder. "Mama—Mama, can you turn around for a moment?"

Rosalba Sanchez rotated around with a spatula in the air. "Qué? What's so important to take me away from my sopá?"

Victor swallowed hard. "Mama, this is Amber. You know, the girl I told you about? Amber?"

Rosalba's eyes grew wide. "Oh sí, yes...Amber, your hair, usted es alto...***so tall*** like me, boñita, you're so ***pret-tie!"*** Rosalba grabbed Amber and gave her a meaningful hug. Full-size arms around her body (and to be complimented on being pretty) what a marvelous feeling! Slightly taller than Amber, Rosalba was a comely woman, with gray streaked brown hair, a strong nose and sherry eyes. Here was a mother who loved her relatives, Amber recognized, treasured everyone around her and showered them with her affection, her grace and cooking.

Amber was then twirled around to greet Victor's father.

"Papa, this is Amber."

Amber was startled once more with a huge fond greeting and a smack. Fabrizio was slightly taller than Amber, with a thick parrot chest stretched over bulky muscles, a man in good shape for his age. Fabrizio was also good looking; Amber couldn't help but blush. "Nice to meet you Mr. Sanchez."

"Ella es hijo encantadora, usted está seguro que ella es su

amiga?" Fabrizio guffawed, joking with his son. Amber was a lovely girl and Fabrizio teased Victor and asked if she ***really was*** his girlfriend.

Victor punched his father fondly, "Don't Papa, and yes she's my girlfriend."

Amber looked at Victor questionably. "What? What did he say?"

Victor's smile dropped. "It's good, don't worry, it's ***very*** good."

Amber was astonished that day. Meeting aunts and uncles, first, second and third cousins, relatives she never believed existed but in books. There were so many names to keep track of, different faces, looks and personalities, she knew she would never be able to comprehend them all, and then finally, making his debut fresh from Harvard Law School, Eduardo Sanchez. Victor called him ***'The pride and trophy of The Family'***. All the hard work, the overtime Fabrizio and his uncles worked just so Eduardo could go to Harvard. Oh how everyone, including the relatives that didn't contribute financially took credit in Eduardo's accomplishment.

Amber was guided over by Victor's arm around her shoulders to his brother. Eduardo had his back turned towards them. Amber immediately recognized the man's external appearance the moment they approached him privately. Her heart dropped, it was ***him!***

"Eduardo, I want you to meet someone," Victor asked moderately tapping his brother on the collar. Victor wasn't hesitant introducing this girlfriend to his brother. He felt confident not only in Amber's facade, but with her admiration for him not to fall for Eduardo's charms. Although Victor loved his brother immensely, Eduardo was brutal competition when it came to exclusive female attention. Girls Victor dated always seemed to plunge head over heels in love with his brother.

Eduardo circled around and gazed at Victor first—his smile however weakened when his eyes straight away crashed into Amber's.

"This is my girlfriend Amber Fitzgerald," Victor stated, proudly hugging her shoulders.

"Nice to meet you Amber."

Boy, Victor's brother's presence was compelling; Amber couldn't help but substitute stares. Amber was entranced by the sheer innuendo in his eyes. His smile so sensual—the reaction dropped straight to her toes. Eduardo Sanchez was ***so*** different from Victor Sanchez. Several inches taller than his little brother, Eduardo stood erect and swollen with pride. Nut-brown hair neatly combed behind his ears. Olive tone silk shirt opened slightly to show shades of darkened chest hair, a gold chain around his neck. Black slacks creased to flawlessness, Italian leather loafers. Are those green eyes below those dark eyelashes? Oh yes, he was a pole apart from Victor; lovable inoffensive Victor, her boyfriend. Amber looked away from his controlling brother and back at Victor. ***My boyfriend.*** Victor was harmless, never could hurt a fly kinda guy. Dodger Blue T-Shirt, faded jeans, white Converse tennis shoes.

Amber hugged Victor thoughtfully. He was the only fella she ever thought about lately. He was caring, loving, and welcoming, always doting on her, always asking her if she was happy, hungry, thirsty, warm, hot or tired. He had her heart at the moment, and—as she hugged the life out of Victor one more time—examined Eduardo Sanchez strolling away.

"I think I love you Victor and your phenomenal family." She gave to him happily.

"Yah? Well, you know I love you Amber Fitzgerald."

They kissed lightly. Her eyes closed and she felt the softness of his lips, the affection in his emotion, and the worship in his words. ***Well, you know I love you Amber***....she thought over and over. And she ***did*** know it. He said it almost daily to her, it wasn't forced and it flowed often; she could almost count on it.

That night, as she disrobed for Victor (the first night they slept together) she felt the adoration he held for her. It was slow and effortless, almost like a leisurely dance, coming together with little or no struggle and very, very sweet.

Victor proposed to Amber the moment they finished climaxing. Would Amber accept? Oh hell yes! You see, although Amber very much wanted to be part of the great big Sanchez family, she also wanted to get out of her suffocating household. Her mother was on another one of her matrimonial pursuits and Amber was so tired of greeting yet another Father Figure. She wanted out, and out now.

At eighteen, you had too few choices. Legally you were considered an adult, but under the same roof as your parent, you still heeded their responsibility. She didn't want to be anyone's responsibility; she wanted to live her own dream. Her job was just that, a job. It wasn't a career, she'd never been ambitious or had the desire to attend college, so she took her skills as a typist and went to work as a receptionist in a law firm. She wasn't making much money at first, or enough to rent her own apartment in LA, so she had to find better employment, a second job, or at least, find something else that could aid her out of that tomb. Enter Victor Sanchez, he proposed to her, outstanding! This was her chance to escape. He was working, had a budding post with the City of LA and with two incomes coming in, she could well afford to get an apartment and obtain her freedom! ***Viola!*** What a great idea! Her train of thought flabbergasted her sometimes. She was acting like her mother and brushed aside the fact that she might be following in her same path, marrying to meet financial means.

She did love Victor though, who didn't? He wasn't a Smelly Ape that's for sure. He was pleasing, obedient to his parents and a jovial sort of character, who shared his affection daily, always helped his mother, sat down with his father to watch soccer, cuddled his nieces and nephews, and even petted stray dogs. He was an excellent choice.

After Victor left her room that night, Amber laid in bed awake just thinking about ***it***. Marriage. Her and him, in a lifetime of wedded bliss. Her future was suddenly mapped out for her and plans for decorating an apartment, buying groceries for her and her husband along with not having to answer to anyone's rules packed her dreams come true. Oh what a meaningful feeling; dreamt through rose-colored glasses, never foreseeing practicalities like utilities, laundry, unemployment and the possibility of never having children.

Damn that decision…At sixteen, Amber wanted Teddy Turner's (a senior who wore really cool corduroys and wallaby's) attention so much she gave her virginity to him on his very first visit to her house. She wanted to show him her MVP trophy, but ended up showing him her underwear instead. The following day at school he ignored her, subsequently, making her feel like dirt. A couple of weeks later, she was pregnant and scared to death to get an abortion. On her way to the free clinic, she experienced unpleasant discomfort in her lower abdomen. Once there, the doctor informed Amber of her ectopic pregnancy and had to remove one of her Fallopian tubes. The comprehension had no dismal affect on a sixteen year-old that mainly wanted the situation just to end! During surgery, the doctor also found a mild case of ***endometriosis***—scarring in her uterus as well—and informed Amber when she awoke that she would never be able to conceive normally again without the support of hormones or possibly through the aid of test tubes. Test tubes? Good Lord that was too much news for a sixteen year-old to fathom. She wasn't going to get married anytime in the near future, so why concentrate so much on her physical impairment? Now it's ***all*** she can think about. Not being able to give Victor any children that would devastate him! Victor loved kids and the thought of her being barren made her cry. Amber squeezed her eyes shut, tried to focus on apartment hunting instead and was immediately interrupted by a sudden burst of Victor's brother. Now why on earth would ***he*** enter her fantasy? Amber shook her head, buried her face under her pillow, felt her breathing go from calm to acceleration. She felt like a nitwit tonight practically ogling his body when they were introduced. She got so tongue-tied, she even forgot to say hello!

It simply wasn't fair. No human being should be allowed to possess that much magnetism. He reminded her of some GQ model; one of those gorgeous men you never thought existed. Tan and exotic looking, he had a masculine jaw line but with smooth feminine skin tones, such a contrast, she doesn't know how else to describe him other than "basically beautiful". She'd never seen a man so devilishly handsome! It was those eyes that threw her off, those hypnotic heavy lidded grass green eyes. The elegance of his facial features sent her to a mystic abstraction, so romantic and gracefully interpreted and she felt like she was swimming through fog for the rest of the night. She shouldn't have shown him so much concentration either, trying to imagine what he'd look like minus his silk shirt. Lips pressed against hers, hands underneath her bra. ***Good Lord!*** The image wouldn't go away. She rolled over to the other side of the bed and dug her head underneath several more pillows.

Eduardo Sanchez Go Away!

He was Victor's older brother, so what. So what...so what...so what...oh my...was she ***in love*** with Victor? Amber suddenly hurled all the pillows away from her face like a cushiony volcano. If she ***were*** in love with him, then why was she suddenly having a sexual fantasy about his brother? Good Lord, she should be in love with him she's going to marry him!

Rolling over in her bed, Amber became frightened all of a sudden—panicky and insecure. She was damaged goods and wasn't too sure about her outlook for her new fiancé. Could Victor love her enough for the both of them? She was already enamored with his family; would passion come for him later?

Eduardo

Persistence breeds determination, and determination creates boldness. So when a man owns his assertiveness, perceived as being accomplished with his intellect, then its deliberate self-assurance, arrogance and occasionally, conceit.

And what does this mean? It means power to me. I've always known I encompassed potential. I like to win. I feel accomplished when I prevail. I like to know that when I walk into a room I command attention, that my presence of authority is immediate. I thrive on prestige. I was born to be successful. There is only way I'm determined to go, and that is up. Excel at school, exceed at my profession, and succeed at becoming abnormally wealthy by the developed age of thirty.

No one is going to stand in my way, no one. And if someone gets offended along the way, then they should have never tried to ride my coattails to prosperity. I welcome complication. OK, I accept that I'm considered selfish in my need to fulfill my aspirations, but I have to. Call me vain, call me one dimensional, call me a master at domination, but whatever you call me, do it with envy. And I appreciate the smile I just gave you. That was my intention. Like I said, I always get what I want, I'm inflexible and oh so fortunate.

As I stare at myself in my bathroom mirror, shades of confusion tickle my intellect. A weak laugh escapes my throat as I shake my head in utter disgust. It was a drive by; I must be catching a cold. I lost my composure tonight, my focus; she practically suffocated me with intrigue. Yah, ***she***. It was a woman...

Amber Fitzgerald.

Turning on the water faucet, I lean down and rest my arms alongside the vanity. I continue to look at myself and shake my head. Splash cold water onto my face, it's cold, it's startling, but it's temporary.

My brother threw me for a loop tonight. Meeting his girlfriend had been a mixed blessing. Amber was unique, no doubt about that. The hesitation that I did feel was the mental preoccupation of what it felt like to kiss her. ***That*** unbelievable motivation engrossed me the entire evening and I can't fathom why.

Along with my mental power, I've been favored with a good-looking face. I hate that word—***handsome***. I like to say that I embody advantage. I like to be taken seriously; I'm a double threat, both in business and in my personal life. So when speaking to an associate, who happens to be female, the conversation always seems to detour into flirtation. Sometimes I'd like to shake her senseless and ask her to stop staring. Favored men can never be friends with a female; the notion of coition always seems to get in the way. I'd rather concentrate on improving my intellect.

I've had girlfriends before, but on my terms. I never allow myself to care for someone beyond the physical. Love is for the lamebrain. I don't have time to fall in love. I'm never alone; I'm constantly being approached. I'm a magnet for the opposite sex and I'm comfortable with the price tag. ***I decide*** when we're together. ***I decide*** if I want to spend time with her. I hold all the control, not the female. Too many times have I witnessed men crawl on their knees through humiliation to accommodate their girlfriends or wives. I've learned my lesson at a very young age, and yes, I did demean myself by handing over my heart, while she accepted it, squashed it, only to ask for it once again. I swore I'd never allow another female to try and take my vulnerability again and I've been living by that rule.

As I continue to stare at myself in the mirror I notice the tiny blemish on the right side of my jaw; a mark, a flaw where I once shaved my face too close and caused a scratch on the bottom of my cheek. I took my father's dull razor and decided I was "man" enough to start shaving. Stubborn at fourteen, I thought I knew what I was doing. My father showed me once, and I grabbed the razor out of his hand.

Step One: Spread the shaving foam onto your face; Step Two: Take the razor and position it at an angle; Step Three: Gently take the razor and glide it across your cheek in one continuous motion.

One continuous motion? What do you do when you forget to flex your jaw to accommodate the razor's flat edge? Hope to God that the girls never stare hard enough to notice the two-centimeter disfigurement at the rim of my chin.

I knew at the age of ten that I was engaging to the opposite sex. The phone rang off the hook. Girls used to chase me around the block. Little notes in my math book. Annoying persistent giggling when I happened to glance their way, subtle hints at the harsh reality. Junior High was a learning process, trying to master the skills at seduction. In high school, I was a stud: Most Popular; Most Likely to Succeed; Most Desirable; Best Body; Homecoming King. But I didn't care. It was all so meaningless, trivial. Not much effort to obtain such trophies. School was all that mattered. Class President, now that's the title I was most proud of back then. Straight A's, those were my aspirations. But boy did those hormonal girls make it fatiguing for me to concentrate when the phone kept buzzing. The highest mark in Political Science would be tough to achieve if I had to stop studying to answer the phone with a hysterical female on the other end…

"Why don't you like me?"

"When am I ever going to see you?"

"Why don't you come over?"

"What are you thinking?"

Constant nagging and pulling for my attention when all I

really wanted from girls' back then was sex. I had bigger and better things to triumph over. My associate's degree at a community college, my bachelor's at UCLA, then onto Harvard; Harvard Law School to be exact. Harvard Law School offered a legal curriculum unparalleled in legal education. It was a dream I aspired to, a determination I felt to pursue.

Once there, the professors felt it necessary to single me out. My race, my skin color—their predetermination that I'd fail. A Latino didn't belong there, but I knew differently. I was bright, I was relentless and I was strong-minded to pass each course. But then those insistent females were still all around me. Tempting me with their hair, their lips—their curvy bodies. Meeting them on the steps of the historic Austin Hall; Langdell Hall for class, pretty temptresses following me to my seat. College girls are no different than high school girls. Oh hell yes, they'd all fight to the death and exclaim that they were at Harvard for their education, women's rights or whatever the girl was into but I proved otherwise. They were all identical once the blouse was subtracted from the body. Blonde, brunette, redhead and smart, brainy, extremely intelligent—they all wanted a piece of me. And oh how comical and obvious it was! I can always sense when a woman is attracted to my carnal charm; the way they curl their hair around their finger, their obvious nervousness in the way their voice cracks, their hands go every which way but calm and the apparent giddiness at some idiotic remark I happen to give out. I know all the signs; study their body posture, suggestive nuances. But they're just females, an end to a means, and they fulfill the need of the moment. And who am I to complain? There were unquestionably many, ***many*** moments...

For now, I'm renting a one-bedroom/ one bath bachelor pad on La Cienega Boulevard. After I pass the BAR, I'm going to purchase a town home somewhere along the beach: Malibu, Santa Monica or Pacific Palisades. I love the sea air, the wide expanse of the deep blue ocean. As I look out my window on top of the 15th floor, I notice the hustle and bustle of the streets down below. I'm part of that turmoil, and I love it. I love it! What a life I lead. My dictation of it thus far has been straightforward, all my goals have been met; I'm in charge. At least I was in charge, because now I feel like I'm spinning out of control.

Running my hands through my hair, I find my bed finally and lie down. Hands folded behind my head, Amber Fitzgerald pops into my reflections of the day. I roll over slightly and try to get comfortable, I can't? That girl invades my mind again. Another chuckle escapes my throat. Sounds silly, but I can envision myself holding her...***oh hell***...that really was pointless. Almost feels like...one day...I will? Good God, that was truly insane...I must be getting sick, coming down with something, catching a cold, a fever, something.

I roll over to the other side of bed. Again, she pops into my head.

I roll back over to the other side.

I want to steal her, I've concluded, but I keep brushing the thought out of my rationale. I have to keep reminding myself that Amber was Victor's ***girlfriend.*** She's his girlfriend, Eduardo. Girlfriend...darling...sweetheart. Remember sensing the attachment in your brother's eyes? You would never act on betraying him again. Never. Or would you? I could never exploit my attraction to her, never. I can't, I won't. Well...maybe. No, think of Victor. Your little brother...No can do.

The thought of it runs rampant throughout my brain. My heartbeat is accelerating now. I wish Amber were lying here next to me. Good God, this was getting hallucinatory!

Get it under control Eduardo!

But what was that feeling I felt when I was beside her tonight? A connection? What the hell was that all about? I have never experienced sensitivity like that before with a woman. The moment I leaned over to welcome her company, I noticed her lips parting from my presence. Instantaneously, I felt amazing magnetism, a mind-boggling urge to stay near ***her?*** Fascination washed over me, my heart pounded uncontrollably. I wanted to grab her in my arms and kiss those parted lips. I was sexually attracted to her; I knew that straight away. Walking away from my brother however, I knew I'd have a dilemma and recognized instantly that I was in ***big trouble***. I was around that girl for no more than thirty seconds, but yet, I felt dispirited for drawing away? I could either steal her away for the evening, or give my little brother a gift. I love my little brother...I don't like to see him hurt.

I try and close my eyes, but Amber's dark tresses assault my sleep. She was definitely different. Diverse from the other girls I usually favor. ***Blondes***. Any blonde. Women with caress worthy light-colored hair. Dirty blonde, light blonde, platinum blonde, flaxen whatever, I settle for nothing less. Baffles my mind how I'm suddenly attracted to this girl, with her tantalizing raven splendor. Amber is no raving beauty; in fact, she's even sort of plain. Most of my dates wear make-up; she appeared to bear none. She had a pert modest nose, supple complexion; nothing stunning to say the least...it was ***her eyes***. Those eyes, not from any one color, but...hers looking through mine; like she was handing over a mystery, a key to her very soul and this is what is so baffling to me.

Why is she so damn fascinating anyway? I'm trying to find the answer, but it escapes me. Maybe it'll arrive in the morning, I must get some sleep. But I'm one determined fool. I always find the explanation, that's my perseverance. Once I set my mind to something, I always achieve my goal. But what objective could this bring about?

With much effort, my eyes finally feel heavy. I'm still not asleep, but I'm tired enough for my lids to remain shut. Again, Amber pops into my head. Damn that sexual attraction! There are two types of women who gain my full attention. The first was a woman who could build up my salacious nature—my physical attraction. There had to be a minimum of three visible attributes I like about a woman, whether it's her hair (blonde), her eyes (usually blue or green, never brown) or her body. The females that usually turn my head are the ones with evident contours, slender waists, and tone bottoms with curvaceous breasts. Did I mention breasts? Good God, checking out the rest of Amber tonight definitely was my doom. Her height wasn't even a factor because her body was so amazing.

Hourglass shape with round shapely hips, long tone tan legs and a bra size I could only imagine could contain the most desirable pair of breasts. My perverted nature sends images of my mouth gliding across her pink, projected nipples. The consistent semblance stirs an arousing response in my better part.

Good God Amber Fitzgerald, get the hell out of my head!

When I'm sexually attracted to a woman then heaven help her. The female ***will*** be in my bed and she'd be leaving totally satisfied a few days later. I can only think of two women in my past that I've been harshly sexually captivated by. Back in high school Stacey Somers (the girl who broke my heart by the way) was a devote Christian and holding off for marriage. Good God, I tried everything to get her to sleep with me. If I was determined back then to get into her into pants, she was just as stubborn fending my body away. The second girl was at UCLA. Tarin Howard, was a highly sought after cheerleader and my pursuit of her was unmerciful. We dated and slept with one another for several months continuously until Tarin was offered to pose nude in Playboy. Well Hell, that got me disinterested in her real fast. She'd rather display her breasts for the whole God damn world than to me privately? We broke up, Tarin posed nude and I concentrated on education and graduated Magna Cum Laude.

As I roll over in bed for the umpteenth time, I'm positive I want Amber Fitzgerald. Good God, her appeal was going to destroy my better judgment! All my life I've never lacked for anything. I have the personality, the mentality and the funds to obtain anything (including women) that my heart so desired.

Inaccessible...

Unreachable...The challenge and the intricate pursuit...

Good God...as I feel myself drifting away in dreams of her...Amber Fitzgerald is going to destroy me...

Victor

My birthday is next month. I'll be twenty-one. Never thought I'd be married by this age, never thought I'd be lucky enough to find someone to love and cherish as much as I love and cherish Amber.

She's everything I ever wanted in a girlfriend; why not make her my bride? The way she makes me feel when I'm around her, she makes me smile all the time. She's got this cocky sense of humor, I mean, it's almost like a dudes. Direct and straightforward, she tells you like it is, and I respect her opinions. We never argue, and I think that's a good thing. I've had girlfriends in the past who've nitpicked everything I ever did and it was always so laborious trying to make them happy or smile.

Why don't girls realize that when we guys play sports we can't always give them our undivided attention? I mean, I'm out in center field and she's like ***"notice me—I'm here—whoo hoo—notice me".*** I'm not one to date or sleep around. I mean, don't get me wrong, I'm no virgin, I just don't see the point of sleeping with girls I can't have a conversation with. Not like my brother, ***bastardo*** that he is. That guy doesn't realize the power he has over women. If I had just a tiny bit of his bravado I'd be invincible. The man is a dating legend; I don't know how he does it. Gets girls phone numbers and then has them for dinner—literally. Doesn't he ever want to know what they're thinking rather than knowing what they look like naked? Can you tell I'm just a little bit envious of the dude? Don't get me wrong, I ***love*** my brother. Without him, I wouldn't be half the man I am today. He taught me how to come out of my shell (or rather how ***not*** to be shy) around other dudes my age and how to approach chicks. Without Eduardo, I'd be in some jail cell or maniacally pushing the buttons on some video game. And smart, damn, my bro is smart. I mean, intellectually stupid smart. I don't know how many times I've gone to him for help with Algebra, Science, History, English—all those hard subjects. He's helped me bring my C's to B's and support me on the Varsity Baseball Team. Hell, without him, I wouldn't have lettered in Baseball, Basketball or even Football for that matter. My C's would have been D's, and I would have never been able to excel in sports. Yah, I was a jock. But I wasn't one of those exemplary jocks with the conceited attitudes, like my ***shit*** don't stink. I hated those dudes. I guess you could say I was unpopular socially, I hated those damn phony-ass lipstick chicks, I'd rather hang around other team members or girls I knew from class. I remembered seeing Amber in my Photography class, but she was always so shy. I often wondered what her face looked like if she pulled her hair away from her face. But, I'm ahead of myself; let's leave her for last (the best for last).

I've always hung around white dudes. I hate speaking Spanish outside my home (I am of Mexican decent and I've always wondered why ***Mexican*** wasn't considered the language of Mexicans—but Spanish—or Español) whatever. I hate being asked to translate to other Mexicans who happen to have just crossed the border. I mean, I was ***born*** here, in the San Fernando Valley. I've never stepped foot in Mexico. How can I be thrown in and automatically associated with a group of Mexicans that I don't even know? I hate that too! Just because you're Hispanic instinctively means you're supposed to speak Spanish? Whatever. Mama and Papa insist I speak Spanish the moment I'm at home though. Insist I speak Spanish to my elders. OK. I can live with that, but around my white friends? Forget it. And I think my bro has had it the hardest really. ***He*** was born in Mexico. He had to learn English in elementary, when teachers looked down on foreigners' back in the 60's. He hardly had any friends, kids used to tease him because of his accent and the color of his skin. Damn but it was hard to grow up in a white-ass neighborhood! Kids were always picking on us. Good thing I could kick a ball, or swing a bat, otherwise, we'd be homebodies! At the age of seven, my bro would lock himself in his bedroom and study for hours, trying to perfect English and pronounce the language without a hint of accent. Damn that boy was determined. Told ya I wasn't bright like Eduardo, but hey, I can hit a 75-MPH fastball into center field! Eduardo can't even hit a pitch if it was lobbed to him underhand two-feet away (laughing out loud)! But I love the dude; I admire him for going to school for so many years and getting his goddamn Bachelor's Degree and then to top it off going to Harvard? What kind of brainy psycho goes to Harvard? Eduardo Sanchez, that's who, can you tell I look up to the dude?

Amber and I, we like to kid around and joke with one another. If we do happen to have an argument (which is almost never), I'm usually the one who apologizes. I don't know what it is, but I don't want her mad or upset with me. I guess what it really boils down to is I never want her to ***leave me.*** All my girlfriends have broken up with me; I've never been bold enough to dump them first. Oh, not for the lack of wanting to, I've had some really unhealthy relationships, especially when my bro was involved. He can be a little annoying at times, especially in the female department. Damn if he hasn't already taken two of my steady girlfriends. I don't blame them really, although at the time, I was really, I mean, ***really*** upset with him, like my whole world shattered. But hey, the girls weren't into me, I figured they were just into my bro, and used me to get to him. Skanks. No biggy, life went on, I found other chicks that dug me.

Carla Pinkton (my first real girlfriend), man I thought I loved that girl. She looked like Jodie Foster, with dirty blonde hair and bright blue eyes. She was awesome. We could make-out for hours. I tried to get to second base with her, but she kept pushing me away. I figured, no biggy, eventually she'd let me rub her eventually. We were going out for three months straight and during the summer, she would come over to my house and go swimming. ***Bad idea.*** Summer meant my bro was on vacation too and spent most of his time at home. Carla and I barely stepped foot outside and I noticed that she was entranced by the pool. I turned to look where she was staring and there he was. His goddamn arms crossed above his shoulders lying in his underwear on a lounge chair. He was trying to get a tan, and didn't bother to put on a bathing suit. It was his house too, but fuckin' Eduardo, couldn't he just be a little bit more bashful? I remember I went over to him and kicked his shin. His limbs lazily reclined off the sides of the plastic, exposing not only the thickness of his ***huevos***, but his hairy ass legs. Eduardo opened up his eyes immediately and was about to return the jolt. Damn but Carla didn't nearly expire at the sight of my bro standing there practically naked, bronzed from the sun. I yanked her away from his cocky attitude and pushed her body into the pool on purpose to cool her down. It didn't matter; she ended up trying to get me jealous by throwing herself at several of my teammates as well. Whatever.

Dawn Johnson (yah, that was her real name), was the girl I thought I might marry one day. Dawn was also a blonde and tall and slender. We met at a baseball game; her twin brother was our Varsity's third baseman. Damn that dude was awesome. I think he got a scholarship to Arizona State. Lucky him. Seems college scouts look for height along with talent. I had the talent but didn't have the height. I mean, I had the constant STATS; can you imagine having a .540 batting average and still not be good enough to play pro ball? Damn I admire those dudes; pro baseball players are the elite of athletic perfection. But that's OK, more to life than baseball, I'm learning now. I wanted to be a professional baseball player all my life, but my life took another road. I'm lucky to even have a job. I'm working with the City of LA. City jobs are hard to get into and I guess it pays off having so many cousins, because my cousin Dante got me the job.

Back to my girlfriend...Dawn let me get to second base, third and even score a homerun! God Bless Her. Yah, she was my first. She took my virginity and vice versa. We were reckless in our relationship. We didn't care where we got it on. The car, the park, school gym, baseball diamond, wherever. She was awesome too; her demur attitude tied in with her ability to sexually please me made her my ideal woman. Damn, we went together for nearly nine months straight, she even met my brother a few times and she never fainted at the sight of him. I thought I was in heaven until one day she confessed to me at the beach (the day I was going to give her an engagement ring) that she had slept with Eduardo. Slept? You mean ***had sex***? Are you fuckin' kidding me? Why would Eduardo do that to me? He ***knew*** we were going together. He ***knew*** I was sleeping with her as well. Why would he force himself on her? Oh shit, I was so upset! I vowed never to speak to the dude ever again. Took me a long time to get over Dawn; I was five months into being single when I bumped into a dark-haired angel.

So what if Amber's a little taller than me, she's got an awesome body! Her bra size, damn that girl is fine. Her tiny little waist and shapely ass, I can't get enough of simply looking at her! The way she kisses, it's like she over powers you with her zest for life. Giving, definitely a generous girl, my Amber; such an accommodating person, pleasing and loving. We can talk for hours, we have similar interests. She loves to try and make me laugh and I love springing the latest jokes on her, and we get a kick out of the silliness and bowl over laughing. Damn, I want to give her everything. When we're married, I want to try and save for a house. Somewhere close to my parents home so we can visit often. A three-bedroom/ two-bath somewhere in the west valley, which would be nice, with a huge ass backyard like my parents for all my kids to run around in. I know I won't be able to afford a pool, but my parents have one, so we'll go swimming over there. Damn, I can't wait to get married and make Amber legally mine. Sometimes I like to watch her from afar and wonder what she's thinking. Sitting by herself in a corner of my parent's home, with my family all around, she looks so buried in thought; is she thinking about us? About our future? About all our kids? I want at least five; I wonder if she's ready for that. I know she loves my family, and I know she's also wanted a big family of her own; we have that in common too. I know she's had a rough time growing up with all her mother's boyfriends; I want to give her a stable life, a family of her own and a marriage that she can be proud of. God, I love Amber so much! I hope she's as happy as I am!

CHAPTER**THREE**

Love Me, Love My Family

The happiest day of her life had to be her wedding day. Amber stood in front of the floor length mirror and admired her reflection; her long tresses were twisted tightly above her head, ringlets fell about her face and her extended sheer organza veil cut down along the curves of her body making her appear like another woman overall. It wasn't so much her wedding day that she was excited about, but all about entering into a family she never had. Always wanting that stable family unit with lots and lots of kids with lots and lots of relatives; something she never had or felt while growing up. Damn the man who created her. The emptiness her father produced. That ache, that need for a family. The husband, the wife, the kids, all together and never apart. And Victor was the perfect man for the job. He came equipped with the perfect candidates. The Sanchez Family.

Amber's hair was professionally done, thanks to her sister's vocation. Molly Fitzgerald was a make-up artist working for a major movie studio. Right out of high school she knew what she wanted to do, become a movie star. And when that didn't happen (or not quick enough) she worked on them. "Close enough to spit on'em", Molly always said.

"Oh my goodness, that dress is absolutely ***mag***!" Molly spurted out, wanting to touch the dress, but doesn't. Molly was nearly as tall as her sister—the two girls getting all of their height from their father; Molly's hair was slightly lighter and shorter than Amber's though, but just as straight. Although

Amber took Sam's hazel eyes, Molly's were noticeably chocolate just like their mother's.

"Isn't it though?" Amber stated, admiring the dress again. "Do I look all right? The buttons in the back all straight?"

"Let me see, turn around," Molly instructed, viewing the pearls running down her sister's backside. "And your hair; The Mane Shop really did a great job, huh? I told you they were the best!"

"They did, I love it, if only I could look this good every day."

Molly brushed aside her sister's curls. "You do Amber, gawd I'm so jealous of you sometimes—you always look so ***mag***!"

"Will you stop saying that?" Amber scolded. "Say magnificent if that's what you're really saying."

"For sure," Molly simply let out.

Sheila Thomas, Amber's mother, entered the bridal suite at that moment. Compared to the girls, Sheila was about half a person shorter than her daughters! She was a striking petite with processed treated blonde hair piled high on top of her delicate head. Dressed in her shiniest glitter, Sheila outshined her daughters by far in her over-indulgence.

Sheila halted and took in Amber's loveliness. "Oh baby, you look breathtaking. Now don't be nervous, are you nervous?"

"No, why should I be?" Amber expressed.

"I don't know I always seem to get nervous on my wedding days..." Sheila laughed. Amber and Molly both laugh too. The three girls laugh so hard they start to howl.

Sheila Thomas was married six times, yes ***six times!*** Amber was only three when Sam Fitzgerald broke Sheila's heart and asked for a divorce. Sheila soon searched for the next husband, someone she didn't love, but a man, her supporter, who could provide for her and the girls. Take care of them all. Never mind about love. Who said anything about love? It was an act Sheila was willing to do for herself and her children. Sleep with a man she was only fond of just so that he could pay the bills and keep a roof over their heads. What a grateful gesture Amber often thought. What an enormous act to follow! Sheila had been some woman. Amber could never do that, or was she doing that now?

But Amber loved her Mom. Loved her mother for making such an unselfish decision over and over just so that she and Molly could have clean clothes, a house in an excellent school area, breakfast, lunch and dinner, a dog and cat, bikes, toys, and eventually cars for both of them. What an astonishing considerate achievement her mother had unfolded. And the girls treated their mother with respect. Respect foremost and always. Sheila had been their mother and ***their father*** actually. In between Father Figures, Sheila had to be the disciplinarian, the chauffeur, the coach, the nursemaid, the cook, the maid, Mother Theresa all rolled into one. Chores had to be enforced. Restrictions had to be followed through. She was a frightful powerhouse when Amber was growing up. Diminutive Sheila, her amazing mother. In another's eyes, what her mother did and the reasons behind why she married so many times would raise an eyebrow or two, but Amber never really saw it that way. She loved her mother for all the emotional sacrifices she must have endured, and always wished she could tell her how eternally grateful she was and always would be. But how do you express that?

And talk about Father Figures. Amber was growing up with all ***these men.*** And which one would she latch onto as her Father Figure? The quiet sheet metal worker, the angry cop, the doting hospital administrator, the shy attorney, or the arrogant bartender? And in what of those Father Figures would she find in her own husband? A combination of all of them? Or should she bet on finding someone more like her own father. The absent Sam Fitzgerald?

What Amber needed in a husband was someone to treat her right, someone who would be there for her and ***always*** there like a comforting blanket that would fulfill the need of the cold moment. Like the warm sun, the twinkling stars, the white moon. That was basically why she felt so at ease with Victor in the first place, he took care of her. He gave her the attention that she craved. He was a devoted Father Figure, taking care of her and her economic insufficiency.

* * * * *

The bridal party was ready. Four bridesmaids, four groomsmen: each on their respectable sides of entering. Amber was at the end of the girls waiting for her father to walk her down the aisle. Waiting, waiting, she was always in anticipation of her father! She wasn't a bit nervous though. She was calm, collected and anxious even. She was about to walk through the church doors and into a remarkable family; a household she always wanted and wanted to get the show on the road.

Amber and the bridesmaids were standing just outside the entrance to the church when the girls began to giggle and hollered "you're in the wrong place mister" and "what the heck are you doing?" To her surprise, Eduardo appeared out of nowhere and walked past the procession, admiring all the girls in their long flowing gowns.

"You all look terrific, ***fantastic***, you're gonna 'cause a commotion for sure, not a dry eye in the place," Eduardo said, parading himself down the line towards Amber. The girls all laughed silly and whispered enthusiastic exchanges amongst themselves. When he reached Amber at the end of the line, he stopped cold.

Amber held onto her bouquet uneasy now. Eduardo's glare took her very breath away. For a limited moment, Amber felt unstable about her decision to marry Victor. Having that man directly in front of her, giving her the most amazing arousing response jumbled her commitment.

Eduardo slowly brought his eyes away from her distracting wedding dress. Amber's unexpected close attention had rendered him speechless. It took every inch of will power he possessed not to draw her over his shoulder and kidnap her. He allowed too much time pass. He wanted to give those lustful feelings some time to pacify. To his astonishment—they didn't subside—they only grew! Good God, what was happening to him? He purposely stayed away from his mother's house while the family prepared for the wedding. He passed the California State BAR, threw his mind into law, sending out resumes and going out on interviews. He even purposely avoided going to the rehearsals! Even though he had woken up restless from dreaming about her for the past several months, it tortured him inside to know what he'd be doing to his little brother.

Eduardo stood back, held his hand over his heart and mouthed the word ***"wow."***

He really shouldn't be affecting her heart so much the way that he did, but Eduardo couldn't have expressed anything more special to Amber at that moment. He really was quite amazing, her new brother-in-law. Amber beamed.

Eduardo gazed down at the floor, clearly doubted his decision and stepped away. The bridesmaids all looked into his direction and examined Eduardo as he sauntered back into the church.

The events of the day were almost perfect. Everything went according to plan. Sam ***did*** show up on time to walk her down the aisle, and she was finally going to have that wonderful wedding a little girl always dreamt about. With gorgeous bouquets of flowers, candles lit eternally and a church filled with family and friends, it was ideal. It was mostly the Sanchez Family and their kin, but she didn't mind, she was becoming one of them. That cherished group, with such rich heritage. And when she saw Victor, and he saw her, tears formed in both of their eyes. In fact, there wasn't a dry eye in the place just like Eduardo predicted. Everything was unspoiled, absolutely beautiful, when something happened that Amber didn't anticipate during the middle of the ceremony; faultless Eduardo forgot her ring?

Amber noticed Eduardo fidgeting in the corner of her eye, she couldn't help ***but*** see him directly behind Victor; he was his Best Man. He was tilting back and forth like he had to use the restroom. Then, when the minister pronounced, "If there was anyone who felt that these two should not be married" she actually saw him close his eyes? Like painfully close them! Was she imagining it? She was still reasoning how her brother-in-law was acting when she heard the minister proclaim through her study: "Do you have the rings?"

Amber took Victor's ring from Molly (her Maid-Of-Honor) and then turned around to find Eduardo whispering to Victor. Eduardo forgot the ring, her ring. Wonderful. Great. ***Thanks Eduardo for ruining my perfect wedding!***

Eduardo removed himself from the line of groomsmen and rushed to one of the back rooms of the church. Five minutes later, he rushed back with the ring in his hand. "It's here," he stated, brushing a chestnut wave back into place.

Amber sighed with relief; Victor smiled, in fact, the whole congregation beamed. What relaxation, and then they were married. A simple kiss finalized her entrance and she was finally a Sanchez. After eleven months of courtship, five months of being engaged, she was finally married into a big amazing family.

The reception was nearly a blur. They rented out an American Legion banquet hall and the facility was filled to capacity. She'd never seen so many people in one place nor introduced to so many relatives, more so than on Eduardo's welcome home Bar-B-Que. And there were (and she's not kidding) around five hundred guests in attendance. Could they really afford this wedding? No fretting, Victor kept reassuring her, his parents were paying for everything and that made Amber more relaxed. There were homemade appetizers—Mexican food, of course—and an endless amount of alcohol. Booze everywhere and in everyone's hands. Children freely occupied the dance floor, his or her chance of grabbing everyone's attention. It was cute, fun, then the respected elderly entered the dance floor and the room was hushed as they twirled around and did the samba to cheers and whistles galore.

The cake, the food, was absolutely impeccable. Sam stayed for the whole event, and Amber was grateful for it. Amber hadn't seen her father in over a year and he didn't disappoint her in her time of triumph. Amber loved the attention the guests all gave to her that evening, she felt like royalty, receiving glowing compliments of how lovely she looked. She felt extra special that night and floated on air, until...

"Amber...walk me over to your brother-in-law," Molly expressed, grabbing her sister. "I don't want to make a fool of myself going up to him alone."

Amber held back, "Oh Mol, he's not your type."

"He's a babe, that's my type," Molly giggled, pulling her

sister towards him again.

Amber's heart began to beat faster. She didn't want to talk to her brother-in-law right then and there. She was still upset at him for blemishing her perfect wedding day. Disturbed by him period. "Oh Mol, I don't want to talk to him right now."

"Oh com'on, please, I'd do it for you," Molly complained, pulling her sister's arm practically out of its socket.

"Wait—wait, don't rush me. Let me pick up my dress for crying out loud," Amber pleaded, feeling her shoes beginning to yank at the extensive fabric.

Amber had been the one to coordinate the eveningwear for the nuptials. Victor, bless his heart, wanted nothing to do with such intricate decisions as picking out bridesmaid dresses or groomsmen tuxedos. Amber (who was never into dressing up herself) had the girls wear long taffeta blushing pink gowns, with matching shoes and a corsage of the pinkest roses on their wrists, while the boys wore baby blue jackets, matching polyester slacks with frosted patent leather shoes. ***Cobalt and rose***, Amber wanted immediately, ***the vision of country flowers across a meadow, how romantic.*** And hell, it was the 80's...

Although the wedding party looked either too gaunt in their skirts or bulging at the waistline in their tuxedos, Eduardo had been "Tony Manero" come to life and wore his like a clone to John Travolta in ***Saturday Night Fever***. Holding up the wall, his jacket was removed exposing only his vest; his legs, casually crossed out in front of him watched the girls approach as they progressively reached his locale. He stopped sipping his Budweiser for the moment and first glared at Amber. Their eyes lock and hold.

Oh Amber couldn't believe it! On all the days, he made her ***blush***, cheeks so hot; she swore that everyone could see the redness on her face. "Eduardo," she managed to get out, "Since you didn't come to the rehearsals, I wanted to introduce my older sister Molly, Molly this is my brother-in-law, Eduardo Sanchez."

Eduardo greeted Molly and shook her hand and held it. "We've met already."

"When?" Molly asked breathless, staring into his green eyes.

"Before the ceremony, remember?" Eduardo pronounced,

toying with her.

"I-I," Molly retorted, trying to recall last speaking with him.

"You know, when I told you how nice you looked."

Molly's round eyes caught Amber by surprise. "Oh stop it," she regrouped, slapping Eduardo playfully on the shoulder. "That comment was for all the girls, not just for me."

Amber rolled her eyes at that obvious display of flirtation.

Eduardo gave Molly one of his penetrating smiles. The one he reserved for his female prospects. That half-smirk tossed in with a quick lift of the jaw that always seemed to make girls fancy him.

Amber and Molly noted it—the enticement worked. Molly unquestionably wanted him while Amber was uncertain; she was downright enthralled by him. No, it wasn't all of a sudden; it was something she's always known, but ran away from. She was intensely fascinated by him and couldn't understand why. Amber lifted up her dress and strolled away. She just got married to his brother for crissakes! What the hell was she doing being fascinated-drawn-enchanted by that man!

"Amber," Eduardo called her back.

Amber quickly turned around. "What?" She asked, dropping her dress to the floor. She noticed her sister still in awe of him. He ignored Molly—she was acting like a stupid little schoolgirl twirling her hair.

He paced away from Molly for the moment and concentrated on Amber. "I want to apologize for misplacing the ring during the ceremony," Eduardo quietly mouthed. What the hell was he feeling now? His heart was beginning to pound—felt his throat close up. Good God, he forgot what he was going to say next?

"It's over, let's just forget about it," Amber managed to assert.

"My brother has good taste," Eduardo expressed, disgusted with himself for presenting that double-edge entendre. He elevated the beer bottle up to his mouth, took a long sip. Good God he could use another beer.

Now why does he make drinking look so erotic as well? Amber's expression goes clean. "What?"

Good God Eduardo get it under control! He quickly noted her questionable manner. He related, "Your ring."

Amber remained intently looking at him. ***Who does he think he is flirting with me on this day? What an asshole! God, he's so conceited! He can have every fricken' girl here if he wanted, including my sister, but he still wants to see if he can get the bride? Yah, right!***

Molly stood back and watched her sister with her new brother-in-law. She couldn't help but notice the tension between the two. She thought it was extremely odd how both of their bodies seem to gravitate back and forth towards one another while they spoke. It was strange. But she would never admit to that, she had too much pride in her own appearance to think that Eduardo would be interested in her little sister. "It is a nice ring Amber." She chimed in joining the circle.

Amber broke away from Eduardo's gaze for a moment and tried to focus on her sister. "Yah Victor wanted diamonds, but I said no." She cackled, "What girl doesn't want diamonds?"

Molly laughed along with her. Amber's smile collapsed with settling on her brother-in-law's face. His expression was grave. ***Good Lord, what's wrong with this guy?*** Amber noticed he looked pissed off now...What the hell was wrong with him?!

Eduardo drank the last swig of his beer and focused on his mother approaching wanting to dance. Good God, thank you for the rescue!

"Eduardo—mehió, come dance with your Mama," Rosalba asked, grabbing his arm.

Amber was suddenly left with a perplexing question. She didn't quite know what the ***doubt*** was, but she felt something went terribly wrong. She looked at her sister. Molly seemed to notice it too. Amber's eyes filled with water instantly.

"Amber?"

Amber hiked up her dress and ran away from her sister at that moment, down the hallway and towards the ladies room. She was cornered by one of Victor's Aunts, Tiá Lorena.

"Oh mehiá, you look absolutely beautiful, like a princess! Victor must be so proud! Rosalba and Fabrizio couldn't be happier!"

Amber stared at Tiá Lorena for a moment. With her lavender polyester chiffon dress, high heels and Jackie O hair-do, she was a sight. "Thank you," she managed to say. But Amber was still in a daze.

"I'm gonna go find that husband of yours, swing him around on the dance floor for awhile, do you mind?" Tiá Lorena asked jovial.

Amber smiled, spun back into consciousness. "Mind? Will you? I've been dancing with him all night; my feet are beginning to hurt," she laughed, jiggling her feet around in her shoes.

Tiá Lorena kissed Amber's cheek and off she went. Amber watched her as she melted in through the crowd of other dancers. On the horizon, she spotted Eduardo gyrating to the dance beat. He was dancing with Molly, hugging her near and moving her around skillfully. Her older sister was a big flirt. A little too accommodating sometimes, but Amber knew Molly would make a good match for her brother-in-law. They had a lot in common. Molly used to be a song leader, she was very popular; Eduardo and Molly were used to grabbing all the attention. But the more she watched them dance, the more Amber became covetous. The panorama made her freeze, envious for some reason. She was resentful...***why? He's nothing, nobody, just my new brother-in-law. I hope he gets together with my sister; they'd make a good pair. They would...Really...Then they could get married, we could do things together, all four of us. That would be fun...It would be wonderful, great...Fantastic...yep...the four of us...together... the four of us...Dammit! Then why does that make me so God damn jealous?***

CHAPTER**FOUR**

Why Do Birds Suddenly Appear?

Anniversaries can be wonderful and romantic, but when you're practical and handy oriented like The Family, Rosalba and Fabrizio decided that for their 26th wedding anniversary they'd like their immediate family to go away, for the brothers to get together and spend some quality time.

Fabrizio loved to fish and suggested Cachuma Lake in the Redwood Mountains just above Santa Barbara, California. Several hundred campsites quietly located within forest territory, Cachuma Lake was surrounded by captivating mountains, blue skies, and fresh air and encompassed campgrounds that accommodated recreational vehicles and boats. The grounds even had barbecue pits and picnic tables. Amber loved all the amenities too: hot showers, general store, coin laundry, swimming pool and miniature golf area. It was a wide-open territory full of activity. The Family chose a cliff side campsite overlooking the lake; it was magnificent there with a serene ridge and plush forest setting as its backdrop, it was the perfect spot for The Family among woodpeckers galore.

Victor set up their tent first. Amber helped as much as she could in between feedings because ***Adrian Andrew Sanchez*** was born six months prior and Amber was already hesitant about bringing him outdoors.

Eduardo arrived late and Victor offered to help his brother set up his tent. Eduardo looked desperately lost hammering stakes into the ground trying to put his tent together. Amber couldn't help but chuckle at the sight of him banging his thumb over and over.

Amber was glad she had Adrian to keep her preoccupied for once. The hours she used to spend thinking about her brother-in-law were now spent on Adrian's immediate needs. She loved being a mother, never realized how much she wanted ***to be*** a parent. Amber was surprised with the urgency she felt to start a family. She always felt something was missing between her and Victor. Their short two-year marriage was monotonous to say the least and Amber felt misplaced and occasionally unloved. Victor settled into the husband role immediately, providing for the couples' financial needs but Amber always-wanted more. Victor worked late hours in order to pay for their expenses and Amber oftentimes felt lonely and forgotten. Amber was beginning to believe that marriage wasn't for her and contemplated divorce but just didn't want to hurt The Family, and she definitely didn't want to be reminded that she could be cut from the same cloth as her mother. No, she definitely did not want to be like Sheila. Maybe a family, a child would change things, spark up their romance? Purchasing every known ovulating device known to mankind, Amber was on a mission. Seducing Victor the moment he walked in through the door, springing up on him in the shower, after breakfast, in the middle of the night, she wanted so much to have that family. She wanted everything all at once and wasn't happy until she got the complete package. After month after month of disappointment and heartache, she was finally pregnant. In utter disbelief she couldn't believe it and ended up staring at the damn blue line on the pregnancy test for nearly two hours. Amber finally got what she wanted, but was it enough? She had to take hormones, just as the doctor suggested. Her pregnancy was anything but effortless: acute morning sickness, Progesterone suppositories, and temperature monitoring and bed rest. But the end result was magic. And oh how she loved her little boy! So much responsibility held in such a tiny little package. Amber cherished every moment she had alone looking at him, smelling his intoxicating baby essence, so much love showered over her sweet little present.

* * * * *

The following morning Amber left at dawn to take a shower before the baby woke up. When she returned, Victor was waiting for her with his fishing gear in his hands. "Papa wants us to meet him by the lake, feel like going?"

Amber took Adrian from Victor's arm and placed him on her hip. Adrian whined a little and started to whimper. "No, I'll just stay here and put him down for an hour. How long will you be?"

"I don't know, two hours maybe three. You sure you'll be OK?" Victor leaned over and kissed the top of his son's head.

"Yah sure, I brought a book. I'll just sit down by that tree over there and wait for you guys to come back."

Victor gave Amber a peck on her cheek, "Sounds good. See ya later."

He left quite anxiously, Amber realized watching her husband scoot off in a hurry. Victor had been fishing since the age of five and couldn't wait to cast his lure in the water. Fabrizio used to take the boys fishing when they were little, getting up early on the weekends and driving out to the nearest fishing spot. Victor was hooked, whereas her brother-in-law was caught in another pond.

Amber turned around and went back to her tent. What to do now? Adrian was still fussy, a definite sign of him tiring. Amber sat down on her air mattress and gently tried rocking Adrian to sleep. If her little boy wouldn't take a nap soon he would be unbearable later that afternoon. He was just one of those babies who needed at least three naps a day. Thirty minutes later of alternating positions, singing lullabies and humming to him, Adrian was finally asleep.

Amber peeked through the mesh one last time before she decided to step away from the tent. She walked over to the side of the cliff and took in a breath of fresh air. There was a light breeze collecting off the lake and shooting up the campsite and Amber felt tranquil. It was stunning that day—a good day to go fishing—***and*** read a book, she decided. She dragged her camping chair over to the nearest tree and positioned herself underneath it. She stretched out her legs, opened up her book when she heard a growl. Her head whipped around and realized that her brother-in-law's tent was occupied. Someone was unzipping the tent from the inside? But she thought she was alone here with Adrian! Didn't ***everyone*** go fishing? Oh damn, she should have never taken that shower!

Amber perceived the thin ply opening up—out popped defined masculine legs. Rolling her eyes, Amber sharply turned around and gazed out at the blue water beyond. How was she going to handle being alone here with Eduardo?

"I hate camping."

Amber swallowed hard and then rolled her eyes again. Figures. She turned to face him. "Why didn't you go fishing." It was meant to be a question but it came out like an interrogation.

"I wanted to take a nap, but I'm unable to," Eduardo complained, dusting off his shorts and shirt. "Tossing and turning, I have the most uncomfortable air mattress known to mankind." He grumbled further, continuing to dust off his attire. Apparently there was more grime in his tent than on the ground. "How the hell did so much dirt get into my tent?" He asked peeking through the opening one more time.

Amber giggled, "You're supposed to sweep it out every night."

Eduardo let go one of his sensual smiles as he glared back at her laughing at him.

"Oh stop being such a baby," Amber continued, "It's camping; you're supposed to be uncomfortable, supposed to get dirty."

"I'd rather stay at a five star hotel," Eduardo quipped, continuing to dust off his shirt and shorts.

"Well, your parents wanted us to come here, it's their anniversary, and we all agreed, even you mister." Amber complied, gazing away from him and out at the water. He was making her heart flutter again and she tried to calm herself down.

Eduardo dragged his camping chair over by where she was sitting.

"This is nice," he let out, taking in the gust flying up from the water.

Amber gazed down at the lake. Wasn't she just thinking the very same thing? "Yes it is." But then he made her tense. There was so much more to her brother-in-law that she wanted to know! She didn't know how to approach him—Good Lord he was making her disoriented! She knew how to act around other males; she was practically one of them, but with Eduardo, he suggested difference.

"What're you reading?" Eduardo asked noticing her tight clinched book within her hands.

Amber surveyed her paperback. "Oh—some stupid romantic novel I picked up at the supermarket."

"I'll trade you." He asked, pulling out his thick hardcover from behind his back.

Amber took one good look at it. "No thank you," she mocked, making a sour face. "That book is all yours."

Amber watched Eduardo clean off his suede-hiking boots again, then pull out a leaf from within his dirty sock. "Now I'll need to take another shower."

Amber started to chuckle again; he was being such a pansy! But he was adorable nonetheless. He sure knew how to dress, even for the outdoors. Expensive Ralph Loren wool blends, beige khaki shorts and leather boots. And dammit, why was he so gosh darn cute with his hair all mussed up? Amber blushed, turned away and opened up her book. She couldn't get passed the first few sentences!

Eduardo opened up his book, skimmed through the first few pages. Did he really want to read this law book for the fifth time?

Silence fell upon them. The trees bristled in the brisk wind that flew off the lake and up the canyon. Hawks soared over them searching for mice. Kids in the nearby campsite started to argue over seashells they found down by the lakeside. Amber couldn't take it anymore.

"How tall are you?" She blurted out.

Eduardo grinned, glad she spoke first; it was a safe subject. "Six—four, why? How tall are you?"

"Five foot eleven, rather tall for a girl."

"Not for a guy like me," Eduardo teased, rolling his eyes

only to close them. Why on earth did he just flirt with her?

"I'm two inches taller than Victor."

Good, she didn't notice. Eduardo began chuckling, "Yah, my little brother didn't get the height gene like I did. Took after my mother's side of the family—all broad and lanky."

"I've always been shy about my height, how about you?"

"On the contrary, I rather like towering over people."

Amber laughed. Eduardo held his breath; Amber's eyes fairly sparkled when she did that.

"I bet," she strained to believe otherwise.

"You played baseball?"

Amber smiled inwardly; her emotions were beginning to swirl with glee. How else would he have known ***that*** if he hadn't already asked questions about her? "Softball, big difference."

"What—soft ball, baseball, no difference really."

"Of course ***you'd*** say that."

Eduardo turned away from her for a moment. She's irritated, why?

"Victor told me you'll be twenty-seven next month?"

Another harmless query and he answered swiftly, "Yep, big birthday next month."

"So you're six years older than Victor?"

"Almost seven, why? How far apart are you and Molly?"

"Barely a year. My parents couldn't keep their hands off each other," she snickered, disbelieving the serenity in her own voice.

Eduardo once more held his breath. "That must have been hard to grow up with divorced parents."

Amber gulped, Good Lord, she wanted to change the subject now. "Yah, consider yourself lucky to be brought up by parents who still love each other."

"I appreciate them every day."

Amber gazed out at the waves in the lake. "You live in Malibu now?"

So ***many*** questions. "Yah, just bought a town home near the beach a couple months ago, I'm working at a Westside law firm, why?"

"Just wondering..."

Eduardo was stumped with all the sudden inquiries—and then it hit him. Even though Amber was now his sister-in-law, she was still a ***female,*** and he was used to females attempting to acquaint themselves.

Silence again. The wind began to blow more frequently, leaves and fine sand swished on every side of them. Eduardo reopened his book, smiled internally. Amber started to read again, her heart beat so fast; she still couldn't get past the first paragraph!

"Why aren't you married yet?" Amber asked sticking her foot in her mouth. "Why hasn't some girl gotten her hooks in you?" Good Lord, did she just come out and ask that? Well, the silence was unbearable. She'd rather have Adrian crying in her ear than sit by her brother-in-law a moment longer wondering what the hell he was thinking!

Eduardo began to laugh quietly. He sat up and repositioned his lazy body in the fabric chair. "Why I am not married...Good question," he let go, crossing his legs out in front of him. This was going to take awhile. "Who the hell would have me?" He replied allowing her a peek at his soul.

Amber felt more feminine around her brother-in-law than she ever did with Victor. ***But why?*** She swiftly became further relaxed with him with each breath she drew. She ached to know more and more about him. "Who the hell my ass," she joked back with him. "The entire female population that's who! And don't go shaking your head at me mister, you know you're good looking."

Now that she got ***that*** off her chest Amber could loosen up even more. There—she said it. She unequivocally came out and told him that she thought he was attractive. Did he even doubt it with all the blushing that she did?

Eduardo was taken-back. Amber was blatantly flirting with him now. Only this time his coy rejoinder wasn't so eager. This was Amber ***Sanchez.*** He was nevertheless still sexually attracted to her, but he wasn't about to just spill his guts to her—so what if she was family. "I'm very selective Amber."

Amber didn't know why but that word ***selective*** stuck in her throat. Eduardo was an egocentric (she could only assume by his appearance alone) women came ***onto*** him. He probably had a Little Black Book filled with over ten thousand names! "I'm not surprised with so many choices. You're a spoiled man Eduardo Sanchez."

Eduardo couldn't believe his luck. Here he was extremely fascinated with this girl and she was coming onto him very strong. She not only enchanted him, but her sudden openness sparked continued interest. He had to keep reminding himself that she was ***married***—and to his ***brother*** no less! But his lascivious temperament won the battle within and Eduardo wanted to find out how far he could interest her.

"Do you see me complaining? ***I love women.*** I appreciate the difference in our bodies and the way they smell. Heck, I'll even listen to a stunning female I'm interested in talk about her cat all night long if it was guaranteed she'd sleep with me."

Amber stared at him agape. ***Good Lord!*** Why was his admission suddenly making her all hot and bothered? Because this was Eduardo Sanchez, that's why! God's gift to women. Of course he'd be a snake behind those expensive wool blends. He could afford too when there was no struggle involved. "You don't have to be so crude about it," Amber retorted, feeling her heart about to jump out of her chest.

Eduardo was puffed up pleased with himself. Amber went on the defensive, noticed her cheeks flush red as she turned away from him. But then he felt contrite. Should he apologize for having just made her covet him?

"You know what Eduardo? I believe you," Amber sharply returned. "You should be selective. You need to find someone who will love your faults more than they treasure your looks. In fact, that's the very reason why I fell in love with your brother. I looked beyond the exterior and found a wonderful human being."

Eduardo noted her coldness and gazed away from her for a moment. What the hell was she doing? Helping him find a girlfriend now? This was a first. He knew he got to her. Amber suddenly attacked him with waiving her devotion to his brother in front of his face. But, wait a minute, what did she just say..."What faults?"

Amber seethed. "Oh please Eduardo you're ***not*** perfect."

"Who said I was?"

Amber closed her mouth. Yikes! She just better shut up now. Was that Adrian crying? No, darn it! "Well, I'm only assuming you think you are. But I see differently."

Amber thought he was flawed—unreal. Never in his pretentious life had he come across a woman who thought he was ***lacking.*** It further intrigued him. "OK Amber, define your findings then. Why do I appear imperfect to you?"

Amber gulped. Damn his Harvard Law School dialect! She really did it this time. Her flirting with him got out of hand and now she's irritated him. Good Lord did he look magnificent annoyed! "OK ***sorry—***you're perfect then."

"No—no, you can't just toss accusations around like that and decide to alter your judgment."

Amber sat up straight in her chair. "You're high maintenance."

Eduardo guffawed. "I am? And what else?"

What else? Good Lord, did she really start this embarrassing conversation? How the hell does she get out of this? "...And you'll never be able to find a partner who will meet your expectations."

"My expectations? And what do those appear to be?"

What would those be? ***Good Lord! What the hell was she doing?*** "...Well, now don't get mad when I say this—and don't go telling Victor I told you so—I really don't want to hear his words later."

"It'll be our little secret."

Amber's mouth went very dry. "You do realize that you're unattainable."

"Now, why would I be so unattainable?"

"Oh gee Eduardo, do I really need to spell this out for you? You know already, I can tell by that stupid smirk on your face."

Eduardo's grin diminished instantly. "OK—I'll be serious, I truly want to hear your conclusion."

Amber drew in a long breath. With his legs spread apart, Eduardo had one limb casually up on his thigh. She brought her eyes up from his physique and gulped when she noted his expression changed from annoyance to sensual. And then she knew but immediately denied it, the warmth from his eyes alone spiraled through her core. "Have you ever been in love?"

Eduardo's heart sunk, it was a direct hit through the inner layers of his psyche. "Does it matter?"

"Yes."

She seemed serious. "No...But I've been in lust though," he taunted her.

Amber's grin decreased. Having Eduardo confessing that he's never been in love affected Amber in such an extrusive way. All of sudden his affection was all that mattered. And, why, oh why, did she want him to fall in love with her? Good Lord, what an awful question bouncing around in her head. She had Victor; she finally had her baby boy salvation so why did she ***now*** want her brother-in-law? "Not the same Eduardo, you've got a lot of self-examination to muddle though."

Eduardo looked at her quizzically. Self-examination? "How so?"

Amber noted that his usual intoxicated expression mellowed to a stern blank pout. "I think you need to lower your standards when looking for a mate." She spat out, surprised how easy it was to insult him. "I think you're used to drawing in all the attention...and that each date has to be better than the next. You don't seem to settle for someone who's merely adequate, but seek excellence...and I don't think you're going to find that perfect girl."

Eduardo, for once, was silenced by her sudden analysis of his partiality. How did she know? How in the world could she read him so easily? He gazed away for a second and then back at her. Amber met his eyes and held his stare. "Maybe I've already met her."

Amber choked back. Oh heavens, why did that admission ache? Having another woman hold all of Eduardo's attention suddenly caused Amber to flame with jealousy and envy. "And you let her get away?"

Eduardo smiled inwardly. Boy was that the truth. "No, I've concluded that she let ***me*** get away..."

Amber hooted. "You are so bad." And good, oh, very, very clever how he reeled in her conflicting emotions, Amber was suddenly feeling sorry for him. Maybe he was a better fisherman than she first realized.

"I know I'm confident," he claimed, gazing out at the water beyond. "I have to be in my line of work. I'm up against the best legal minds in court; I have to be self-assured in my presentation. So if that makes me conceited then so be it. As for my lady friends, I don't look for perfection...that's overrated. The female has to be unique though." Eduardo stopped right there and looked back at Amber. The wind blew in her hair causing strands to rise and float above her shoulders.

Why was she suddenly hearing ***"Close To You"*** by the Carpenters? ***Why do birds suddenly appear/Every time/You are near?/Just like me/They long to be/Close to you...***Amber realized she was enthralled by Eduardo's concession and had been intently looking at him the whole time trying to figure out which part of his face she liked the most. She blushed, turned away.

Eduardo noted his effect on her physically. Amber's weight shifted in her chair creating distance between them. She began rubbing her neck and was edgy for some reason. Why was she so interested in his personal preference anyway? What could she benefit from all this?

Amber was over-stimulated by just conversing with him. She wanted to sit on his lap now, run her fingers through his hair and rest her head on that wool jacket of his. Damn that song! Damn Eduardo Sanchez! The further away from him the better—and she'd better change the subject and fast. "I think Adrian's crying."

"How can you tell? I don't hear anything."

"Mother's intuition," Amber cracked, leaving her chair and escaping towards her tent. She unzipped the porch and threw herself in. Good Lord what an idiot she was, peering into his personal life! Why on earth was she ***that*** interested? She had Victor. Victor cherished her, brought her up on a pedestal. Eduardo was...well, honestly Eduardo was just someone she would have ***never*** been able to access. Being Eduardo's sister-in-law suddenly gave Amber opportunity to get to know a man as handsome as he was. Being comely with money, he could have any ***unique*** woman he desired.

They long to be/Close to you...Damn that song! Damn him! Why were visions of him with other women threatening her very reason? All those gorgeous selective women, and why, oh why couldn't she fight the urge of exiting the tent and running back to tackle him? Eduardo shouldn't be idolized—he's the devil incarnate with dreamy green eyes.

Amber had to fight her way back to sanity; had to slam that door shut before fantasies of him would begin to take over. Her sexual impulses towards him were frightening and she didn't know how to deal with them. She had to remain calm, remain in control. Time to wake up Adrian, who cares about the three naps a day.

CHAPTER**FIVE**

Let's Be Friends

"Victor told me that you were hired by Aldridge & Watson? They're a highly reputable Century City firm. How did you ever manage that?"

It was amusement now, a game. She would say something funny, a joke with a double meaning and he'd end up with some cute comeback and over the years they toyed with each other continuing borderline flirtation. Amber always teased her brother-in-law when she went over her in-laws. He was always there visiting, dropping by unexpectedly, bringing a cake or pie, or simply waiting to get fed.

"They liked my smile," Eduardo presented her. He liked verbally jousting with her as well.

"Yah—right, and then they asked you to take your clothes off and model bathing suits." Amber quipped, gazing at her son Adrian (who was barely three) spilling the entire contents of his juice cup into the planter. "Adrian!" Amber snapped, pulling his little body away from the plant. "Don't do that. How many times do I have to tell you not to open up that cup?" She scolded, noticing that her son had tears in his eyes.

"Sorree Mommy..." Adrian gave to her.

The gape had broken her heart, but Amber felt she had to be tough with her son. She didn't want to look weak in front of The Family. There were even extra relations there to celebrate Rosalba's birthday, cousins Amber had never met before, along with some childhood friends from Guanajuato, the town where Rosalba grew up.

Eduardo knelt down to Adrian's eye level. "Look mehió,

Mommy is a little tense right now, why don't you just give her some slack?" Adrian nodded his little head and Eduardo eyed Amber laugh at the prospect of her son actually understanding what ***slack*** meant. He watched her caress Adrian's nut-brown hair. "Now, go see if Nana has any more of those cookies she's been hiding, and if she denies it, tell her to come to see Tió Eduardo," he stated, standing back up.

Adrian darted off immediately to find his grandmother even as Amber stood there bewildered. She never took Eduardo as the sort to be interested in kids, never mind being a father someday. Victor told her once that Eduardo wasn't the marrying type—he was a confirmed bachelor. And after going camping with him a couple of years back, she understood why. "Thank you," she expressed to him.

"Just thought I'd help you out," Eduardo grinned at her. Instantly, their smiles drop to lips parting slightly. Their eyes lock and hold and strong sexual tension are obvious. They turn away from each other's gaze and look among other relatives passing by them.

"Eduardo!" Rosalba is heard yelling at him from within the kitchen area. ***"Eduardo, venga aquí ahora!***

Amber snickered, "You are **so** busted."

Eduardo pats down his chest, "I know exactly how to handle her, just you watch."

Amber couldn't watch Eduardo work his wonders on his mother at that moment because Adrian decided that he'd rather dip his chocolate chip cookies in the dirt outside. "Adrian!" Amber yelled at him from within the living room. She immediately rushed outside to scold him.

Out on the lawn there was a live mariachi band, presents galore and tons of food that night. Carne asada, arroz con pollo, chile rellanos, corn on the cob, big pots of beans and Spanish rice, fruit, sodas, and a beautiful gigantic cake. Amber snuck a taste of the Tres Leche multi-fruit cake as she walked by and then grabbed Adrian's hand to lead him over to his father. Victor had been playing dominoes with his father and two of his uncles and Amber brought over a chair to sit by them. Peeking at Victor's dominoes, he strategically placed them against the others. He was a better player than his father and that made Amber proud. When you are naturally athletic like Victor, competiveness can span across any form of sport.

It was an unusual summer day in the valley, pushing nearly a 100°. There were dark clouds in the sky, causing the sun to play peek-a-boo with the atmosphere. Amber spent most of her time underneath the shady trees or beneath the patio awning when the sun did decide to shine bright. Victor and his uncles set up a folding table away from the crowds near the poolside under a huge oak tree in their backyard, and Amber spent almost an hour by her husband's side, watching him play dominoes. She was just about to scoot away when she spotted Eduardo pull his shirt over his head to go swimming.

It was harmless to look at him through the group of men playing diligently; it was risk-free, right? Amber observed her brother-in-law as he released himself of his yellow cotton shirt, beige Docker shorts and brown loafers. He was super lean and tan right down to his toes with muscular legs, the body of a swimmer. He was so rightly proportioned, not an ounce of fat on that incredible male. No wonder he was always so confident, he knew he was in a class all by himself. Eduardo raised his arms over his head and dived into the deep end of the pool. Amber was in astonishment, shook her head. Could that man get any sexier? His physique was unquestionably different than her husband's. Victor was shorter, same color skin, but in no way muscular like his brother's. Victor had hair on his chest too, but just barely in the center, while Eduardo's chest hair was on all the right places, body hair that seemed to thin out downward and escape underneath the safe-guarded lining of his Lycra bathing suit. Amber waited for him to sprout from the water, but didn't see him. She stood up, brushed down her skirt and pretended to look for something by the pool. Eduardo had not come up for air. Was he still at the bottom of the pool? Good Lord he could hold his breath! Amber instantly got concerned for him and walked over by the deep end. Adrian came running over to her and Amber just barely managed to grab her son before he fell in. She swung his body around and was grateful for the temporary diversion. Adrian enjoyed his little merry-go-round with Mommy and continued to spin with her around and around. They both got dizzy after that and fell to the ground cackling.

Laughing with Adrian still in her arms, she eyed in the distance, Eduardo exiting out of the pool. He was like a Greek God departing the sea, inconceivable, wet and slippery. Amber couldn't help but notice the bulge beneath his taut drown bathing suit. Eduardo reached for a towel and began drying himself off. Suddenly, he caught Amber staring at him. Amber gasped and looked sharply away. She tried to disguise her blushed facial appearance by grabbing Adrian and fixing up his messed hair. What was she doing checking out her brother-in-law anyways? Shame on her! But then she couldn't help herself and searched for Eduardo again, but he seemed to have left the pools side. She tried looking for him through the crowd of relatives, but he practically vanished. Amber shook it off and guided her son back to the other nieces and nephews.

Her in-laws rented a giant blown up dinosaur for the kids to jump in and Adrian took off running. Amber started laughing and heard a man chuckle behind her. She turned around, it was Eduardo. He was back in his shorts and yellow shirt. In the sunlight, the golden shade made his face look tanner, his eyes grassy, he looked sexier and more sensual to her than ever before if that was possible. Amber couldn't help but stare at that gold chain around his neck, something was hanging from the links and she wanted to reach out to see what it was.

"They sure do like to jump, don't they?" Eduardo assumed.

"They sure do," Amber agreed turning away from him.

"They didn't have those when we were growing up, huh?"

"I know," she expressed, thinking that the conversation was stupid for some reason. Small talk. Nothing else better to say. "Nice Speedo," Amber joked, trying to reason away her gawking at him before.

Eduardo started laughing. "Yah—well, someone had to liven up this party!"

Amber turned and faced him, crossed her arms across her chest. "Yes, we girls applaud you for the show." She teased, gazing around at all the various ladies now staring at her brother-in-law. Amber let go one of her bright smiles, unconsciously licked her lips.

Eduardo brought his eyes down to her mouth, glanced away cautiously. "What else did you hear about Aldridge & Watson?" He coughed, changing the subject.

"Well," Amber checked back at the jumper, Adrian was having the time of his jumping life. "I know they don't handle personal injury, but one my attorneys said that they had this huge case about a girl who got run over by a tractor on the beach and ended up settling it for quite a substantial amount."

Eduardo focused on Amber as she purposely looked away. "Oh yah, I think I heard about that," he agreed, surveying her attire from the tip of her head down to her espadrilles. Amber was still watching Adrian jump while he grabbed the small opportunity to study her up close. Her raven hair was pulled back into a pony-tail with a blue scrungy, bright blue crystal earrings dangled every time she moved her head and mesmerized him. A baby blue tank top extenuated her bosoms, her legs, so faultless and smooth, were exposed through a half-jean half-cotton skirt—Good God—his inspection of her consumed him in seconds and there was no hope for him after that; he was completely smitten.

Amber continued to stare at Adrian bouncing in the balloon, could sense Eduardo's eyes fixated on her form. Her cheeks flushed hot, Eduardo noted his effect on her, turned away, cleared his own throat.

Did my heart just skip a beat? What the hell was going on? Why do we keep looking at each other this way? Not good Amber, not good. Amber pretended to forget the conversation and walked around the jumper. Adrian was laughing and giggling with the other kids as Amber eyed Eduardo melt away across the transparent mesh of the blown up dinosaur.

Eduardo made himself disappear. It was happening to him again, those uncensored feelings. He thought they'd settle, should have subsided by now—but nope—no departure in sight. He was not only sexually attracted to Amber, he required being in the same proximity with her, which left him totally in doubt. He was hunting her companionship now? That was really mind-blowing! He never wanted friendship from a woman before. He didn't want a relationship, dashed away from them every chance he got. No, Amber still held his interest and he had to disengage before it truly rendered him to pieces.

For the rest of the evening, in between the meals and the cake, Amber tried to avoid Eduardo at all costs. He was scaring her now and she didn't know what to make of it. Here was her brother-in-law, he was someone to have fun with during the family functions, kid around with, have a legal conversation with and now she couldn't stop thinking about him. The feeling was totally surprising, but at the same time, quenching. Eduardo kept staring at her in the way her low-life boyfriends used to do. Only this time, this particular fellow wasn't so repulsive. He was beyond her reach, a man she thought she could never get. The more time she spent with Eduardo the further his magnetism drew her in. What the heck was going on? She had a wonderful husband. A husband, who adored his child, worshiped ***her***. Victor was her knight in shining armor, taking her away into his castle and harboring her from fear. And currently—without warning—she was being tugged by this dragon, the desirable, enchanting, mysterious, mythical beast that was Eduardo Sanchez, Attorney-at-Law.

CHAPTER**SIX**
Longing for Passion

Amber was in the middle of drinking some coffee, when she had to blink twice. Eduardo was in a corner of the living room with some blonde. Who was ***she?*** Where did ***she*** come from? ***Selective,*** Amber thought. ***So this is what he likes...blonde, slender and strikingly beautiful? How very fortunate for him, how very fortunate for her, grabbing all the attention from the most handsome man at the party! Damn her!***

Instantly, Amber stood up, went to find Victor. Once she found him—talking to one of his cousins—she interrupted their conversation and blurted out, "Who's that girl with Eduardo? She's cute."

Victor and his cousin, Hector, turned and glanced at Eduardo. Having been incarcerated for nearly two years, Hector was your typical careless juvenile offender.

Hector spoke first, "I don't know, but she's ***fine,***" he presented with street gang slang.

"Oh, I think she came with one of my cousins," Victor suddenly expressed.

"Who?" Hector wanted to know.

"I dunno, I think she came with Monica," Victor voiced, turning away from his brother.

"Think I might go introduce myself, get me some ac-***tion,***" Hector mouthed choppy.

"Yah-right, look who you're competing with ***estúpido***, she's not going to notice anyone else tonight," Victor voiced, patting his cousin on the back; "You're going home alone my friend."

Amber continued to stare at Eduardo and his acquisition. Victor noted her concentration. "Go over there Amber, introduce yourself, maybe you'll hit if off since you're so attracted to her," he snorted.

Hector guffawed too and the two humorous guys give each other high five's. Amber gave her husband a sneer. "Funny."

The sun set early that afternoon and Rosalba and Fabrizio turned on the Christmas lights they left up throughout the year and illuminated the backyard like an outdoor concert. Amber continued to sip her coffee and studied Eduardo and his conquest from afar.

Amber couldn't stop staring at them. The female was drop dead gorgeous, tall and slim, also wore a tank top with very tight (Amber assumed) size zero jeans. Her hair, blonde, was shorter than Amber's, but just as straight. The female complemented Eduardo in looks, they formed a stunning pair. She was titillating at her brother-in-law's witty remarks (Amber could only presume) as she watched with a sense of torture in her heart. They got close; he whispered something in her ear. Her eyes spread outward; she playfully slapped his shoulder, threw back her hair and almost spilled her drink in her hand. He went in for the kill, bodies gently rubbing up against one another; Eduardo grinned and eyed her breasts as she continued to throw her head back in seduction. Amber was breathless now and no longer drinking coffee; she was so envious of that stupid girl. Whoever she was, Amber suddenly envisioned herself in her place, flaxen hair melting into ink. ***Amber throwing her head back, feeling the length of her hair drape to her waist, his hand on the small of her back, Eduardo caressing and playing with her hair as she spoke to him tenderly.***

Amber blinked out of her fantasy and gulped when Eduardo stole a kiss from her. A girl he barely met and he actually moved in and brushed her lips? Gee, was he really that good? ***Of course he is stupid! He's the devil incarnate with dreamy green eyes.*** Good Lord, Amber couldn't stand it anymore, she had to glance away, she was utterly exhausted from screening his performance and deliriously covetous of that stupid blonde.

Later that evening, it began to rain. A light mist turned into a thunder and windswept shower. They were asleep, at home, when Amber was suddenly woken up by a thunderclap. Victor was snoring and was unaffected by the sound, God bless him. Amber got up from bed, and wandered into her son's room, checked in on him sleeping peacefully. He too slept through the loud sound, God bless them both.

You wouldn't have known by the rain coming down in sheets that it still had been summer. It was hot in the house, too hot. Adrian's room was in the front of the dwelling and faced the street as Amber walked over to the windowsill to make sure the screen was still open to let in some fresh air. While continuing to gaze out at the falling rain, Amber ran her hand underneath her pajama top to rub her own nipple that began to protrude. It was an aching feeling she felt inside, one she felt was missing; to feel desirable, consumed with longing. Sleeping with several boys before her husband, she searched for conclusion, that impatient craving to be returned.

Victor was a pleasant lover but Amber was never completely satisfied. She couldn't quite put her finger on it after making love with him, a touch of emptiness, a pinch of disappointment, a mood gone astray. Amber was the one who always initiated sex with her husband; she controlled their lovemaking, why hadn't he ever taken charge? Why was Victor so passive all the time? Why didn't he ever take control? Amber was invariably burdened with bringing herself to climax, creating several different positions for them to try. Why was ***she*** the one who always thought of such intimacy? She didn't want to admit it, not realizing the mistake of getting married too soon, but Amber still sought passion. Wherever and whenever, it was an emotion she never really captured.

The rain was relentless now and the street was beginning to flood; you could barely see the glow of the street lamps in the distance, outside it was so gray, so foggy, but yet...***Good Lord***, could it be? Amber narrowed her eyes once more; maybe her mind was playing tricks on her. No, could it be? Was that her brother-in-law's ***car?*** Was it really Eduardo's Porsche? Amber stood back from the window for the moment. Impossible. She peeked back behind the curtains. It was the same shape, even the same color as his. Why would it be Eduardo? Why would he be ***here?***

The mixed emotions she felt stirred her senses. Why was he here? What does he want? Her mouth became very dry, the thought of him being outside in the middle of the night brought upon curiosity and wonder about him. She felt heat between her legs now. Did he see her touching her breasts a moment ago? ***Good Lord!*** If he had, she would never be able to look him in the eye again. But why was the thought of him watching her suddenly burning her with such gratifying pleasure? Because it's the devil incarnate, that's why! Every time Amber was next to him she became intoxicated with wantonness. It must be hard for him really, to grow up knowing he exuded so much sexuality. Amber would withdraw from the world! She wouldn't know what to do with so much attention...or would she? That little modest realization made her giggle as she peeked through the curtains again. The Porsche was still there. Maybe it was one of her neighbors' friends or something. She'd make a mental note to ask in the morning.

Amber's eyes grew wide when she spotted the driver exiting the vehicle and scurry into the pouring rain. The man was striding towards her front yard? Amber then realized it ***was*** Eduardo. She'd recognize him anywhere. She leaned back and away from the window. She didn't want him noticing that she'd been watching his approach. She waited for a knock on the door, there wasn't one? What the hell was he doing here!

Amber sprinted towards the front door and waited on the other side. Her heart pounded stubbornly. He hadn't knocked yet? Good Lord what was he doing? Amber gazed through the peephole. Eduardo was kneeling down placing something on her front porch. He was about to scamper back into the rain, when Amber flicked the porch light on, unlocked the door and flung the entry open.

Eduardo was unprepared—kicked in the teeth was more like it. Amber filling his brother's doorway unequivocally captured his very breath. Her long dark hair went wild and draped off the sides of her shoulders; her pink camisole barely covered two impeccable curvy breasts. Raised nipples visibly inviting, her exposed toes dangled in front of him stimulating his reason. Having been spellbound by her scandalous arrival, he cleared his throat, turned away for a second to regain his composure.

"Eduardo?" Amber asked astonished he was there, in her doorway, in spite of being drenched, inescapably handsome.

"God Amber, I didn't mean to wake you," he let go, brushing dripping hair away from his eyes.

Amber watched Eduardo continue to stand his distance in the persistent drizzle, "Good Lord Eduardo, get out of the rain before you get sick." She motioned for him to come in closer, away from the rigid downpour and under the porch awning.

Eduardo slowly approached and brought his eyes down to her feet and up her body again. The insinuation in his eyes caused Amber's heart to sink. She had forgotten that she was in her meager camisole and hadn't put on a robe.

An arm length apart from her, Eduardo had no other choice but to dig his hands deep into his jacket pockets. He wanted to apprehend her; his lustful nature inundated him. "Guess you're wondering what I'm doing here," he jibed, offering a purely erotic grin.

Amber was cold the moment she stepped outside, but now, an invigorating heat passed through her body from his smile alone. She let go a sniggle, "Well, kind of."

"I was dropping off my date," Eduardo explained, gazing away from Amber's bareness.

"The blonde?"

"Yah, she—," Eduardo stopped having been caught off guard. How did she know? The blonde was too tempting by far. She had an open invitation written all over her precious little physique. They made out for the longest time on her couch but he still couldn't bring himself to have sex with her. The female even stripped for him, but all Eduardo could think about was getting over to his brother's house and dropping off that God damn tape! Amber consumed him, overpowered his sexual drive, why the hell couldn't he get her off his mind? The thought of Amber's keen perception stumped the hell out of him. He even forgot what he was going to say. "She...the girl, she lives a couple of blocks from here actually, near Wisteria, down the road, if you make a left, and then another left, that's her house." Eduardo then shut his eyes, he was blabbering again, couldn't keep his mind straight. Amber had wrapped her arms underneath her chest and practically pushed her bosoms out the top of her camisole.

Amber noticed that Eduardo changed from shorts to pants, but he was still wearing that saffron shirt. That gold chain of his shimmered from the porch light, it captivated her. Amber snickered, "But that still doesn't explain why you're here."

Cornered? Trapped? Why couldn't he remain calm? Why did her allure approach so swiftly? He wondered what the hell she was looking at, his shirt, his chest, his jacket. "Where's Victor?"

Amber looked at him quizzically, "Asleep, why?"

Eduardo finally governed his emotions. "You're up—he isn't, just curious that's all."

"I was—"

"Amber," he chimed in, cutting her off, "Mama wanted to make sure that Adrian didn't wake up tomorrow morning and not have his favorite video to watch. That's why I'm here, figured I could drop it off, leave the video on your front porch and leave a message on your machine that I left it there."

Amber turned around, eyed the Disney VHS tape on the floor and knelt down to retrieve it. "Oh—thanks, you didn't have to do that," she voiced, surveying the video.

Eduardo took a step backwards, exposing his backside to the rain.

Amber chuckled again, "Eduardo isn't your jacket suede?"

"Used to be."

Amber tore her eyes away from his flushed gaze. On the verge of different smile, she felt her flesh turn to mush. "Well...thanks again."

"You're very welcome."

Their eyes lock and hold. Spirits diminish and fixation washes over them. With the backdrop of raindrops pounding on both the awning and Eduardo's jacket, in a matter of moments, camaraderie altered and their impatient friendship turned into genuine yearning. Eduardo wanted to trail his mouth across her perky chest; Amber wanted to wrap her legs around his hips and feel him within. Simultaneously, both of them turn away, apart from each other's hypnotic trance.

"Well," Amber sighed heavily, "Goodnight then."

Eduardo took another step backwards and permitted the raindrops to pounce sporadically on his coat. "...Goodnight."

Even though she knew he couldn't see her waiving at him walking away, Amber did it anyway. She waited to go inside until she knew her brother-in-law was safely in his car.

Eduardo shut his car door then banged his head purposely on the steering wheel. He had to stop torturing himself. Being absorbed by Amber's irrepressible appeal was making him crazy. Why did ***she*** have to be so Goddamn unattainable?

Her brother-in-law's sudden examination of her body caused sentimentality to swell up in her eyes. The suggestion placed Amber in subterranean uncertainty. She did the same thing to him, right? Appraised his physique for her own personal pleasure, why wasn't he allowed to inspect her? Because Amber was already in lust with Eduardo Sanchez, and having him desire her as well would quite dampen her marriage for months to come.

Eduardo fired up the engine, put his vehicle's gear in reverse and gazed over at the doorway one last time. Amber was still there, watching his exit. Good God—he didn't want to leave too?

In all honesty, Amber felt as if a part of her soul was retreating and driving away in the rain. Amber glared back at the Porsche and watched it as it came to a standstill at the stoplight, hesitate, and then slowly disappear around the corner.

Amber ran back into the house, locked her front door and turned the porch light off. She stood silent for a moment, wondered at the VHS and then started to grieve for the quantity of passion her brother-in-law exposed through his green eyes.

LETICIA

I guess you could say I've lived a sheltered life. Mama and Papa hovered over me constantly and watched my every move. They never allowed me to go to parties or out with my friends in fear a boy might "touch me" inappropriately.

I'm a virgin.

I've never been kissed further on my body other than my neck. I'm not a prude, I'm just obedient and I love my parents and obey them. I love my faith in Catholicism. Going to church with my parents every Sunday and twice a month on Wednesdays. That's never bothered me really. I just wished when I was younger I could have spent some time out with my girlfriends, going to the mall, movies or to school dances. Sometimes I feel I'm about to explode, I want to do everything I've always dreamt of doing and one way or the other, I ***will*** get everything I've always dreamed of.

In two more months I'll be twenty-three. After getting my AA at Glendale College, I enrolled into real estate school to get my license. I love looking at houses. Dreaming of what could be, with lots of kids running around in the yards, envisioning different painted walls and furnishings. I want to share that dream with other folks, so I decided to pursue real estate. I'm working for a small real estate firm in San Fernando right now, I pay commission to them when I sell a house and they let me use all their resources: faxes, Multi-Listing-Service, computers, printers, telephones, advertising, they're great. I love my job.

I finally got the courage to move out of my parents' home after being under their roof and guidance for so long. It's a good thing too, because I don't know how much longer I could have kept trying to hide my romance with Gregory Rodriguez. I miss him really. And he was so bad for me. I would sneak out late at night through my bedroom window and meet him down the street. That's so immature, but I had no other choice! I love kissing Greg too! But silly me, immaculate Leticia, I still push his roaming hands away when he tries to unhook my bra. I do have small breasts. I've always wished my breasts were larger, oftentimes ogling other women who've had breast implants. I could never do that.

How do I describe my ex-boyfriend? Greg was not quite perfect for me. Always a bit on the edge, with a temper, I don't know why I attract those kinds of men with a dominating presence. They always seem to think that I'm this docile woman. Or maybe I am, being intimidated so easily.

I guess I should have given him what he wanted. All men seem to think I've already done ***it.*** Can't believe I'm still a virgin at my age, not many women out there like me besides. Greg tried to get me in bed, tried often, but all I kept thinking was my parents and how they would be upset with me if I didn't get married first. And, there was something else about Greg, he made me feel uncomfortable. He was sneaky; I could see it in his dark black eyes. Since I wasn't giving him what he wanted, he was out getting it somewhere else. He was a cheater, and I could sense it. And maybe I should have been stronger emotionally, should have kicked his butt to the curb long ago; but seeing we had been dating for nearly two years, I thought maybe, just maybe there was a proposal just around the corner. But oh well. Greg wasn't the one for me. And when he dumped me, I wasn't surprised. But given his lame excuse that we were getting ***too serious***, I knew there had been another woman.

I know my soul mate is out there for me. And my man is so vivid, I've dreamt of him so many times. When I was a little girl, I would pray at night and ask God to send me a man who would be kind and nice to me. He had to be arrogant and proud of whom he was: Hispanic, intelligent, almost noble in his tall, slim, broad body. His solid shoulders, light brown hair...and if it was ***really*** meant to be...green eyes, the same color like mine. I know my dream man is out there somewhere, lurking around, looking for me. I just know he is.

CHAPTER**SEVEN**
A Costly Mistake

Eduardo had bought his silvery Porsche just a few months prior and decided to drive his new baby to The Beverly Center to do some shopping. Damn but it was expensive to be employed by a Century City law firm! Costly leather shoes, fashionable shirts and ties, suits with famous designer labels on the lapel. Damn but he didn't need another tie to go with his new navy blue suit he bought just a week ago. ***Damn, damn, damn!*** Shopping was demoralizing, it just wasn't for him, he'd rather be reading, his nose in a book. He should look into getting one of those personal shoppers. Did those exist? He'd make a mental note to ask his Assistant when he returned to work on Monday.

Eduardo glanced around at all the various designs—concentrated mainly on the ties inside a glass case. Spotted, striped, plain, argyle, he didn't know which one to start with, initiated laughter at a display of nearby cartoon character ties: Bugs Bunny, Porky Pig, and Road Runner. Now ***those*** would go over well with the partners in the firm.

"That tie would look good on you," he heard the female say.

Eduardo turned to peek at her. She was mediocre, slender, ***and brunette.*** He was disappointed for the moment, then examined her further and noticed ***her green eyes***. "You think the guys at the office would give me any grief?" He played along with her, bestowing one of his fabulous smiles.

A modest chuckle left her mouth. "Now there's a vision."

Eduardo eyed her walking away and then observed her as

she pretended to search for something in the undergarment section of the men's department. He would have never approached her if she didn't approach him first. He wasn't remotely interested in her and left her on her way.

Eduardo then asked the clerk to see two ties from the glass case: the navy polka-dotted Kenneth Cole and the jade silk Perry Ellis. He was at the mirror switching ties around when he heard the woman say, "I like the dark green one, it brings out your eyes."

Eduardo looked back at her. She was the same girl. What a shock. "You think so? I like the navy one as well, I'll get both," he proclaimed to the clerk. In turn, the clerk took both ties from his hands and began ringing up the charge on the register.

"I think that's a wise choice, they both make you look distinguished." She smiled at him flipping her hair away from her shoulders.

He didn't dare give her anymore of his interest or even his name. No crystal ball needed here, she would to start to follow him around the mall; he could almost perceive it. He turned away with his purchase and began searching for shirts to accentuate his new ties.

A few minutes later, he heard…

"Could you help me out with something?"

Eduardo turned to look at her again. He knew it was the same girl; it was like trying to pull gum from a shoe.

"My father's about your height and I need to see if this shirt would fit across your shoulders." Her expression was sweet.

He relented, "Sure, go ahead." He mistakenly presented her with another marvelous smile.

She blushed, turned her head away. Eduardo spread out his arms. The female stood behind him, draped the shirt across his shoulders and spread her fingers across the fabric, freely touching every hard muscle on his back.

Her touch was slow, easy. He rolled his eyes realizing that she was trying to seduce him. "So what's the verdict?" He required—his arms spread out like ***Christ the Redeemer***.

"Attorney eh?" She asked, folding his arms down.

"What gave me away?"

"Verdict, the fancy ties," she smiled, glowing at his sensuality.

"Yah...well are we the same size?" He asked, getting bored.

"Definitely, I think my father's going to like his new shirt," she said, suddenly sprinting away from him.

He knew she'd simply be a leisurely activity, but he couldn't help himself. She was nice-looking in her own way. Latin too, diverse to what he usually dated. Her hair reminded him of Amber's ebony tresses. Her eyes were identically compared to his, so what could it hurt? "Hey, you can't expect me to live down the fact that you had me perform a perfect impression of an airplane now do ya?"

That got her to turn around. "Want to get a cup of coffee?"

Her name was Leticia Mendez, had lived in Sun Valley, California for most of her life after moving from Brawley when she was a baby. Brawley? Now ***that*** got him interested. His parents were from Brawley. Instantly they had something in common and talked about it for hours.

Leticia couldn't believe her fate. The man sitting across from her without a doubt was the most handsome man she had ever seen. Having just recently split with a long-term boyfriend, she decided to go shopping and take her mind off her woes. She spotted him at the counter initially. His handsomeness combined with the fact that he was Latino caused her to freeze in her tracks. He was her Perfect Man and the husband she dreamt about when she was a child. Women in the same department each gave him second glances but he didn't seem to notice or care. He was extremely confident. Leticia loved self-assuredness in a man, and this particular man exuded charm in addition to poise. He was so enticing; she couldn't help but fall in love with him at first sight. She had to keep him interested, no matter what.

Eduardo dated her on and off and had no intentions of the relationship to go any further—none whatsoever. He had no physical urges towards her and never once tried to steal a kiss. She was merely binding his time to the next and helped fill the void of wanting someone else.

Leticia invited Eduardo over for dinner one night. She wanted to show him how much she loved to cook. Rather display her capabilities, he thought. Was it a ploy? He knew so at the time. He wasn't marriage material—even mentioned it to her on their second date. She shrugged it off, informing him that she was only interested in him as a friend. Yah right, then why cook him dinner? It was a losing mind game, but he'd just come from visiting his parents an hour earlier and Amber and Victor had been at the house. Amber walked around wearing a very tight, exceptionally curvy sundress that he just couldn't seem to get his mind off of. Amber bewildered him again, attracted his every sense. He entered Leticia's residence that night already feeling quite aroused from Amber's womanly curves.

Come to think of it, it was quite stupid of him to allow Amber to smolder him like that, but when Leticia was in the process of serving him a second piece of chicken; Eduardo grabbed her waist from behind and ran his hands up her body towards her breasts. Leticia dropped the platter on the floor and immediately turned around to receive him and his touch. Leticia moaned with pleasure—wrapped her arms around his neck, diving in for a kiss—she had never felt desire so strong before.

Eduardo knew Leticia wouldn't pass that little advance up, ***no woman did.*** It was his passion for Amber that sent him into another direction. He didn't want Leticia; she was merely a substitute, her body simply available to satisfy who he craved. She was warm, pleasing, her kisses steadfast, neat. He tried every attempt at unhinging her bra, but she kept pushing his roving hands away.

"What's wrong?"

"I want to, but..."

He reversed for an instant, but soon grabbed her body back. "...But what?"

Leticia wasn't going to give up without a fight. It was Eduardo's erotic gaze that weakened her knees. Eduardo knew instantly his consequence on the poor girl, she didn't have a chance, and he brought her body back into his and held the back of her head, keeping her lips under his control.

Leticia couldn't send him away even if she was thinking visibly—and she definitely ***wasn't*** thinking clearly! She wanted to be with him; after all, he ***was*** going to be her husband one-day, she felt so in her heart. She never favored another man like she did Eduardo Sanchez. Never allowed her body to be rubbed the way she allowed him to touch her.

Leticia gave in without further ado. They made their way towards the bedroom and threw their bodies on her bed. Eduardo closed his eyes. A terrible thing to do! Straight away he envisioned the only female on his mind. On top of Amber: sensually kissing her neck, inside her ear, her breasts. Amber was so beautiful to him, her body answering to his every question.

His kisses got deeper and deeper as he pulled down her bra, feeling her gasp for air. Leticia ran her hands underneath his shirt, pulled at his back, tried to draw down his pants, inviting him inside. She didn't quite know what she wanted, but she wanted it now and the heat between her legs ached to feel all of him, pressing her, dousing the fire ignited within.

Eduardo unbuckled his belt, unzipped his zipper and obliged. He was untamed visualizing Amber beneath him quivering to his contact. He didn't want to stop the mental picture and pushed his manhood into her, thrusting again and again. Her sheath was constricted, tighter and dryer than expected. Suffered her body go limp; he heard her small cry and whimper. The sensation was ***not*** what he projected nor experienced in quite awhile. She closed her legs in tenderness. He reopened his eyes.

Good God, she's a virgin!

Leticia threw her head back in pain. She didn't expect it to hurt so much and tears began to fall from the corners of her eyes.

Eduardo looked down at her as she began to cry. He stopped—felt his bulk unwilling to retreat. Oh hell he forgot his condom too! He pulled out immediately and tried to control his urge, tried to relax and clumsily laid down beside her on the bed.

Not even moving in the slightest, Leticia laid still. She

wanted her first time to be wonderful, passionate, but not like this. Leticia felt short-changed. The deed unfulfilled. She closed her legs immediately and tried to forget the pain and embarrassment.

"You OK?" Eduardo apologized, scooting away from her body like she turned blue. "I didn't know...honestly, I had ***no*** idea."

Leticia reached over for the blanket, shyly covered up her midriff and breasts. "I know, I'm sorry too, I should have told you, but you were...I mean, I should have told you."

Eduardo sat up; spread the comforter over his torso as well, "I feel like such a jerk."

"Eddie...it's ***OK***, don't worry, I'm all right. I'm glad it was you," Leticia expressed, leaning over to caress his strong worried face.

"Are you sure?"

She blushed, her green eyes widening with emotion. "I couldn't help myself...I felt like I needed to be with you. You have such a strong energy on women, but I bet you already knew that, didn't you?"

Now she made ***him*** blush. He turned away, laid back down, ran his hand up and down his bare chest.

Leticia watched him attentively while he did this. Eduardo was so incredibly sexy, his nakedness screamed ***come touch me***. Suddenly feeling the urge, Leticia rolled over and started kissing his neck.

What was it about him that women just seemed to want an auxiliary sexual encounter? That his dates wanted to make love through the entire night and he just rather leave?

Eduardo was feeling a bit uneasy now; knowing full well that he'd just spoiled her virginity. Leticia was the type of woman who held out for marriage and he wasn't a marrying man. He was also quite upset with himself for not thinking clearly. He should have put the condom on prior to his sudden burst of rhapsody. It made him ill how he could have been so senseless. It was Amber—***Goddamn her!*** Why did he have to fantasize about making love to her? He's ***never*** done that before, never needed to. He was always physically attracted to the women he bedded. He really had no desire to be with this female, and to top it off; he's just committed the pinnacle of mistakes by not protecting himself. He didn't want to have sex with this woman again.

Eduardo pulled away from Leticia's wandering mouth. He rolled out of bed, glanced over at her lying there—noticed the considerable amount of blood on the blanket.

CHAPTER**EIGHT**
Competition

O*r maybe,* Amber thought one night; ***my Father Figure was my mother***. And why not? Sheila had to be somewhat of a father to her as well. Amber never really had a true father, or at least one step-father that stuck around long enough that she could really get to know. The only parent that really stuck around was Sheila—that forceful, strong-willed, stubborn mother of hers. Opinionated yes, caring yes, a little bit of both really. And in this strange time of playful exchange with her brother-in-law did she realize why she was so attracted to him in the first place. He introduced her to that presence of unyielding strength, the force that her mother encompassed. It was what drew her to him.

Eduardo was a man who knew what he wanted, and knew how to get it. He encompassed primeval testosterone with a can-do attitude. He was intelligent, unrehearsed, and dressed like no other with passionate eyes that could look deep into your soul. And confidence! She'd never seen someone with so much self-assurance; it practically oozed out of his body. A strut and saunter that was a habit. Saunter, yes, definitely saunter. What was it about men who sauntered? Did they practice it? Was it acquired when you were attractive? To enter a room in such a way as to control it? All eyes on him and nothing else, and when the physical attraction was not achieved, the walk would definitely clinch the arena? Why do females instantly look in the direction of the male who saunters? Was it instant magnetism? Awe of assurance and conceit? Whatever it was, Eduardo possessed it. Men like

Eduardo were never interested in Amber. They might look at her body yes, but never wanted to date her. Men like Eduardo wanted a celebrity, a super model or at least a centerfold. Amber was none of those; she was a tomboy through and through. Played softball, skinned her knees, challenged the boys at burping.

Everything was comfy, cozy for Amber until Leticia walked through that Sanchez front door. Amber and Victor had just finished telling The Family that she was pregnant for the second time, and everyone was sharing their best wishes when Leticia appeared. There she was. There ***they*** were; both of them with their arms around each other's waist, obviously in love, stealing every bit of Amber's joy.

Amber was feeling more than content lately that she had the love and comfort of Victor and now after years of effort, Eduardo's attention. It ***was*** his attention, his utmost consideration that she constantly tried to achieve. It was fun, exciting, in the ways that she won. Her innocent flirtation evolved into intrigue. It felt special to know that a man like Eduardo was interested in a tomboy like herself even if they were just friends. At first, she really didn't want all his concentration, but after playing with his curiosity, it became almost necessary to her. Call it a game; call it entertainment or sport, but Amber was feeling worthy now; she was a woman who had the power to entice. The capability of snapping her fingers and then suddenly, Eduardo would appear. She would walk across the room, go into the kitchen, he would follow. She would walk outside; sit down near the pool, he would materialize. At the dinner table, choosing a chair, Eduardo would sit next to her. They'd laugh, tell each other a joke, poke fun at one another, talk about their same interests; it was all very safe, protected still by the ***Sister-in-law*** slash ***Brother-in-law*** Act. That accepted action between a man and a woman who were wed into the same family.

And then ***she*** came into the house. With her long lean figure, ebony hair, made-up face and incredible green eyes. The moment Eduardo stepped into the house with Leticia; Amber knew all her merriment would vanish. Amber was no longer in control of Eduardo and his wonderment. He was going to be totally consumed by the exquisite Leticia, his new claim, his fresh prize. And she should have been a bitch, she should have been stuck up, wretched, but she wasn't.

And oh how the Sanchez's cheered at her existence! Raising their hands up in the air as if they were praising the Lord at church on Sunday's. Never have they seen a maiden as ***"cuando bastante as Leticia"*** and oh how her eyes ***"were greener than Eduardo's"*** or the ***"leaves on the flowers around the house"*** they continually repeated as if singing an acclamation. The Family flocked to her like she was some sort of movie star entering their humble habitat. She was exalted instantly, the zenith of Latin perfection. She came from a Catholic background, unlike Amber who never attended church, Leticia and her family went twice a week. She was a virgin—Amber could only assume darn her— loved children, could cook, and had a career, car, apartment, many things Amber never achieved at her age.

Amber was jealous immediately. The way Eduardo smiled effortlessly when they exchanged special glances, veiled looks and confidence in one another. ***But it doesn't matter***, she kept telling herself, ***I have Victor***.

"Amber, this is Leticia."

Just the way he said her name with that ethnic accent, sent Amber raving into another dimension. You see she thought it was pronounced "Luh-tish-sha", but when Eduardo said her name, it was "Le-tee-see-uh." ***Whatever***, Amber thought.

"Glad to meet you Leticia." Amber extended out her hand; Leticia grabbed it, gave her a kiss on her cheek and held Amber's hand within hers for a moment.

"Oh, I'm so glad to meet you finally. Eddie's told me so much about you, and Victor and the family, I feel like I know you already, I hope we become great friends." Leticia let out honestly, sweetly.

Amber was shocked at how nice she was. Darn it! ***Eddie?*** She thought. ***When did he shorten his name? They had given each other pet names? This is sick, nauseating and why am I so goddamn jealous? Darn it! Damn him! Why wasn't I ever***

allowed to call him that?

"Eduardo, congratulate us, we're having another baby!" Victor announced coming up behind his wife and wrapping his arms around her waist.

Eduardo's expression goes clean. Amber was getting further and farther away from his reach. Was she ever even available? Good God, another baby? He closed his eyes slightly, grabbed Leticia's hand and squeezed it tight. Hopefully the temptation of kissing his sister-in-law would fade now that she was going to have another child with his brother. Just proved to Eduardo extensively how devoted she was to him. The thought of the dedication made him smile. "Congratulations," Eduardo happily gave to the couple.

Amber watched Eduardo escort his ladylove to the backyard. She observed them through the sheer curtains, nuzzle up to each other and kiss delicately. Then Eduardo closed his eyes, looked sadly down at the ground.

"He said he wants to marry her," Rosalba whispered into Amber's ear. Both women gazed at Eduardo as he hovered over Leticia like she was some porcelain china doll. "You like her, no?"

Amber turned to look at her mother-in-law, "Yes, I do actually, she seems nice."

"Her family has been going to St. Ferdinand for two generations. Eduardo was very lucky to find such a rare flower." Rosalba patted her daughter-in-law on her back. "Sí, yes, this is a great day daughter, come with me to start the dinner, no?"

Amber broke away from the happy couple and looked straight into Rosalba's eyes. ***Yes, she was her daughter,*** she thought. ***One of The Family, this special, wonderful, loving family.*** Rosalba was such a gracious person. So gentle, so loving to all her family members and that most definitely included her. Amber was already accepted into The Family years ago. The Family was just excited, elated that's all and Leticia was still just a guest until Eduardo made it final.

When Victor and Amber got home later that night, Victor couldn't stop talking about her holiness. How his mother and father just opened up their arms and treated her like she was already a member of The Family.

"Did you see how Mama kept holding her hand like Leticia was going to fly away or something?"

Amber was in the other room surveying the empty crib. She whispered back to him, "Yes, and did you notice how your father kept stuttering?"

Victor escorted a sleepy Adrian to his own room. "Untie your shoes mehió before you take them off."

A sluggish Adrian slowly began untying his shoes. Victor pulled out his son's pajamas and began undressing him. "What did you think about her eyes?" Victor inquired as Amber walked into Adrian's room.

"I don't see what the big deal is, so they're green, whatever," Amber gave out, trying to play them down.

Victor slipped the pajama top over his son's head. "Yah—I know, but they're so green, Eduardo's are green, but ***hers***—I've never seen eyes like that before."

Amber was already upset about the evening and the momentous Leticia introduction. "They remind me of cat's eyes."

Amber helped Victor lay Adrian down in his bed. She covered up her son with a comforter and Adrian closed his eyes immediately, dreaming about cats.

Amber and Victor closed their son's door and tipped toed down the hallway to their own bedroom. Victor began taking off his watch, his belt, and his shoes.

Amber just stood there, drained. "Eduardo's gonna marry her, huh?" She let out, surprised of the words that came out of her mouth. She didn't intend on it sounding so suspicious, but Victor was oblivious. As far as he was concerned, Amber was his faithful wife, in body and mind.

"Eduardo is a lifetime bachelor. I'm surprised he did bring her home."

Amber was amazed. ***I've known Victor for how long now? Over ten years? And how many girlfriends has Eduardo brought home to meet his parents? None, if I can recall correctly. So why on earth did he bring her home? He must have asked her to marry him, he must have...Darn that Le-tee-see-uh! Where on earth did she come from? Stealing all my***

thunder! How come she just couldn't stay glued to a pew in her church and become a nun?

Victor turned on the TV as he lay down in bed. Amber turned her back to him, disrobed and pulled her shirt over her head, messing up her hair. She unhooked her bra, pulled one of her husband's old T-shirts over her head and turned around to face Victor and his weird grin. "What?"

"Why do you always change your clothes with your back towards me?" Victor asked incredulous. He was still mesmerized by Amber's beauty. Her waist petite, her chest perfect and her hips so sensuous, he always liked staring at her.

Amber had to think fast. Why ***did*** she disrobe with her back always towards him? Why did she always feel shy around him? He's seen her naked obviously, procreated, had intercourse. It was a strange thought; she never really gave much credence to. "I don't want you to see my big belly," she let out convincingly enough.

Victor opened up his arms for her. "Amber my love, come lay down with me. You must be tired."

Like a little girl being called by her father, Amber crawled into bed next to Victor and into his unrestricted arms. He squeezed her tightly with all the love he had to give.

"My poor baby," he cajoled, kissing her forehead, "You're tired aren't you?"

Amber closed her eyes, "Yes, I am," she confessed. "Was all day, in fact. It was a long day."

"I know. And my brother coming with his fiancée didn't help things much."

Amber straightened up. "What...Fiancée? When did this happen? Didn't we just meet her today?"

Victor laughed and enclosed Amber's body. Arms still wrapped around her shoulders, he let out, "Yah—I know, but later on, after everyone stopped drooling all over her, Eduardo told Papa, and Papa told me. Eduardo asked me to be his Best Man, I said yes."

Amber tried to free herself away from Victor's clutch. "Unreal. Here it took me five months in order for your family to warm up to me and all she had to do was bat her cat eyes and she's a Sanchez."

Victor continued to beam. "Amber, are you jealous of Leticia? Mama loves you, you know that."

"Yah, she loves me, she has to; I've been married to her little boy for ten years now, she's obligated to love me." Amber didn't quite know where her little tantrum came from, but there it was, out in the open.

Victor nodded his head. "Amber, my family loves you. Don't you ever think differently."

Amber wasn't quite sure anymore. After that horrible display of worship, she now believed that Leticia had been chosen for sainthood. ***"Uggh***...I'm tired—I'm going to sleep!" She exasperated, rolling her body over to her side of the bed.

Victor followed her lead, curled up next to her and playfully laid his face down between Amber's face and neck. "Wanna make love?"

CHAPTER**NINE**

You Can Count on Me

Two weeks later, things began to get quite hectic. Rosalba and all the Aunts were busy planning the wedding of the century. Leticia's parents would pay for the wedding, but Eduardo insisted to pay for the reception. Eduardo was doing well at the law firm and wanted to shower his family in sophistication. Eduardo and Leticia decided to rush the event for the following month. ***I guess she can't wait till the wedding night,*** Amber thought jokingly.

Amber, Leticia, Rosalba, Tiá's Gemma, Sonya and Lorena all gathered around the bulky dining room table. Forming an assembly line, the women put little almonds into lace sacks tied up at the top with a white ribbon. ***The perfect little party favor for the perfect little wedding.***

"Qué significa usted?" Asked Tiá Gemma to Leticia.

"What do I mean?" Leticia answered in English so that Amber could be involved in the conversation. "Father Rodriguez is taking a vacation the week of the wedding; he won't be able to do the ceremony."

"Las vacaciones? Un santo varón lejos de Dios? What kind of priest takes a vacation from God?"

Amber just caught the end of that conversation, having been totally immersed in her production and began to laugh along with the other ladies at the table.

"What will be served at the reception Leticia, have you made your selections yet?" Tiá Lorena asked, plopping in almonds without even looking.

Leticia smiled, hesitated for a long moment, then looked at

Tiá Lorena and said, "Veal."

"Qué veal?" Tiá Lorena asked Tiá Sonya.

"Vaca de bebé."

"Aaah, pobrecito," Tiá Lorena said suddenly feeling sorry for the baby calves.

Amber knew some words in Spanish by now (being around the relatives for ten years) and felt badly herself about the baby calves too and decided she wasn't going to eat the veal at the reception and will opt towards the fish.

"Have you seen Leticia?"

Rosalba let go her attention from the almonds and looked up at Eduardo. Looking around the table she said, "She was just here mehió, maybe she went outside to get more ribbon from the car?"

"Maybe," Eduardo said, looking around the room. "Amber, can I talk to you for a moment?"

Amber looked up at him scared. All of a sudden she was pinpointed from the others. Delivered. Her head on a silver platter and sacrificed for idle gossip within the female group. "Um," she let go, looking around at the other's. They all look her way; stopped, halted abruptly from their production line. "Um—OK, just a second." Amber placed down her ribbons and got up from the table and gazed back at everyone one last time. They don't pay any attention to the two of them now and she walked away.

Eduardo guided Amber outside and into a corner, but not completely away from viewing distance of his father, brother and uncles playing horseshoes. "Amber, I want to tell you something you can't tell my mother or my aunts, OK?"

Amber was taken-back. He was going to ask her to keep a secret? ***Oh God, what was she doing! Here he is, probably completely utterly in love with Leticia, and here I am some fool of a girl with a stupid little high school crush on his ass! Shake out of it Amber! Erase him from your head!*** "OK."

"Leticia's pregnant and I want you to see how she is. I think she's locked herself in the bathroom. She's been throwing up since last week. Can you go see if she's OK?" Eduardo was clearly upset, open honest eyes staring straight into Amber's.

Amber was astonished. How high was that pedestal

again? "And you want me to keep this a secret?" She quipped. "From Victor even?" She bit down on her lower lip for no apparent reason.

Eduardo looked down at her lips—lost for a moment in thought. "Yes. I know it sounds silly, but she doesn't want my parents knowing just yet."

Amber grabbed his arm. "Don't worry Eduardo I'll keep your little secret," she exchanged, walking away.

Eduardo grabbed her back—an impromptu hand holding sent chills up both their spines. He tried hastily to shake off the goose bumps. "Thanks Amber, I knew I could count on you."

Amber let out a deep breath as she walked away from him. ***Good Lord!*** Why did he grab her back? Gosh darn Eduardo, why does he make her body react that way? Amber walked past the women still making the party favors and straight toward the bathroom down the hall.

Amber knocked on the door softly. Quietly, she asked, "Leticia? Leticia it's Amber—you OK?" A few moments pass and there was no sound coming from behind the door. Amber goes to see if the door was unlocked, it wasn't. "Leticia?" Suddenly, an awful gagging sound was heard from behind the door. Amber knew that sound; either Leticia had a bad eating disorder or she was definitely pregnant. Amber voted for the eating disorder, but no such luck. "Leticia, can you let me in?"

The door slowly unlocked. Amber looked behind her, doesn't see anyone paying any attention to her way in and goes into the bathroom.

Inside, Leticia was crotched down over the toilet bowl sacrificing a gift to the porcelain Gods. ***Oh my,*** Amber thought, ***oh how the mighty have fallen…if Rosalba could see you now.***

"You OK?" Amber knelt down to her and rubbed her back. Amber knew it wouldn't help her stomach feel any better, but it would help Leticia's inner strength.

"Oh Amber, please don't tell anyone, please don't tell anyone." Leticia was terrified. She stood up, hugged Amber tightly. "I'm going to have a baby, and I have to get married before I show. Oh God," she cried, letting go of Amber now.

"What have I done?"

Amber noticed the mascara running down her cheeks, she resembled a morbid clown. She goes for a tissue and freely wiped Leticia's face as if it were her own. "Don't cry Leticia, I'm not going to say anything, we're friends, right? Friends don't rat on other friends."

Leticia smiled, grabbed Amber again. "Oh Amber, you truly are an angel. Eddie always praises you."

HE DOES? "Oh Leticia, you don't have to go that far, I know Eduardo only tolerates me," Amber expressed, fishing for some more compliments; she wanted to pry into their little shrouded world.

Leticia shook her head in contrast. "Oh no, Eddie say's you're the best, the best thing that ever happened to Victor and the family."

HUH? Amber couldn't believe it. The best thing? She thought Leticia had been the best thing. "I wouldn't go that far," she laughed.

Leticia looked at herself in the mirror. "All my life I was brought up with certain morals, certain standards that I had to live by. I was supposed to be a virgin, remain a virgin until I got married. But it's so hard, so difficult to be involved with someone like Eddie and remain true to the church."

Amber was enthralled. She wouldn't have believed it if she would have written it herself. The confession Leticia was about to unfold, a nasty little confidence.

"I'm twenty-three Amber. Twenty-three and expected to be a virgin," Leticia continued with a short laugh. She pulled out a paper cup from the dispenser on the wall and filled it with water. Opened up one of the drawers, spotted the tube of toothpaste, grabbed it, opened up the cap, squished some paste onto her finger and applied the gel to her teeth.

"I was sixteen," Amber offered freely, trying to make Leticia feel better, but making herself feel worse.

"Yes, so were all my friends. They all lost their virginities to their boyfriends in high school, and me, well; I was hanging on for the prince on the white horse." Leticia laughed again, still rubbing her teeth with toothpaste.

And she thought Eduardo was a prince? Amber laughed at the thought of it. "Yah, well, we all have needs. And, well, sometimes we can't wait." Amber didn't know what the heck she was saying, but it sounded good.

"Eddie loves me," Leticia lied. "Loves me so much, he said he couldn't wait till our wedding night."

Amber's eyes bugged out. Unbelievable. ***Couldn't wait, my ass...He was just horny as hell. What's wrong with that guy? Spoiling her virginity. Taking away something so precious to her, something she probably denied to boyfriends, probably fighting them off with her bare hands, one by one. Oh God, there's a weird thought...*** "Victor said he does, very much." She ended up saying.

"I know he does," Leticia tried to persuade herself, letting go a weak smile; "I just wished we would have waited."

Amber stroked her hair, "Some men are very passionate," she voiced thinking of Eduardo as she said it. Her brother-in-law with his sensuous eyes—electrifying contact—she could only imagine how he was in bed.

"He's...really dynamic." Leticia expressed. "Not like demanding or anything like that, but very passionate."

Amber's jaw almost dropped. ***Yep, she knew it!*** This was just too much...just too much to absorb. Here was Leticia, offering free tid-bits on their private moments together, clandestine lovemaking, sex with each other. "Really?" She asked frankly intrigued.

They both sat down on the edge of the tub. Leticia suddenly brought her hand up to her mouth, intensified for an instant trying to hold back barf. Amber rubbed her back again. "He's quite, ***large***, so to say. I mean, I have nothing to compare it to, but he made me bleed so much our first night together."

Amber bit her lower lip. Large? Did she just say ***LARGE***? Unreal, the thoughts she had towards him lately, dreaming of him, thinking of him, and now knowing that he was ***large***. "Everyone bleeds their first time."

"No, I don't think so, not this much. I had to go to the hospital afterwards," Leticia expressed, covering her mouth up again. "They had to sew me up."

HUH? Amber was now absolutely, positively dumbfounded.

"Wow that must have been really painful."

"We've only done it once after that; I'm scared to, actually," Leticia uttered, her eyes locking with Amber's. Woman to woman, female to female, hazel eyes looking into green.

Amber just shook her head. "Scared?"

"Yah, if it wasn't for the baby, I don't think Eddie would want to be with me." Tears swelled up in her eyes straight away and Leticia began to cry.

Amber suddenly felt incredibly bad about herself, about her selfishness, her self-seeking attitude towards this woman who was going to be her sister-in-law soon. She pulled Leticia's body close to hers and hugged her gently. "I know he loves you Leticia. I know he's probably ecstatic about the baby, I've seen Eduardo with Adrian and he's really quite gentle with kids; he's probably just nervous, all men get nervous about becoming a dad for the very first time. This is so exciting; we're going to have babies together."

Leticia wiped away her tears with her tissue. "After you put it that way, it does make it kind of exciting. Thank you Amber, you can't imagine how frightened I've been these past few weeks, not being able to confide in anyone. I know deep down in my heart that the things that you've said are true, sometimes a woman just feels like she has to have them validated."

"You're very welcome," Amber awarded her, thinking about the last time she heard that same phrase directed at her.

CHAPTER**TEN**
Planting the Seeds

Well, it was after all, the wedding of the century. Better than hers, she had to admit.

Leticia's dress was impeccable. A halter gown made of white satin it exposed her lovely slim shoulders and long arms, a tight form-fitting bodice covered in shimmering crystals enhanced her midriff while a stunning organza floor-length headpiece embraced her head. She even wore lengthy white gloves to give herself a more regal appearance. No one could tell by the dress and no one would ever know she was with child. Amber would keep their pregnancy concealed, for Eduardo, for bestowing his trust in her, and to Leticia, her new sister-in-law. Leticia, who would have thought? Here was her competition. The girl she wanted to hate. The girl she must hate in order to continue on with her delusions of Eduardo.

Two hundred guests crammed into the elegant dining room of The Verandah Room at The Peninsula in Beverly Hills. The room was showered in gold, elegant draperies, lavished table settings with an abundant array of pink flowers everywhere. Fancy linens and cutlery, china, stemware, heck, even the food was first class: salmon steaks and veal cutlets, Cristal Champagne and chocolate mousse tarts for desert. The Sanchez family were treated like royalty that evening, and gazed upon Eduardo's generosity as a catalyst for envy.

Amber grabbed Victor and forced him out onto the dance floor. "Dance with me!" She coerced. "I want to dance," she let go happily.

Victor was obliging; he thought Amber looked absolutely amazing in her long flowing chiffon bridesmaid dress. "Are you having a good time?" He asked, spinning her body around. The dress spread out with the motion, a picturesque pink sphere.

Amber pulled into Victor close. "I'm having a wonderful time. I'm having the best time!" She let out, bumping into other guests as she said it.

Victor smiled, "Whoa Amber, calm down. I don't want you to hurt the baby." But she didn't. She wanted to let loose and unfasten her inhibitions, her inner Ginger Rodgers with her feet dancing away. Victor continued to chuckle and enjoyed every moment Amber went senseless. The fast song melted into a slow one and Victor pulled his wife into him. "Oh thank God for slow songs."

They continued dancing slow, moving awkwardly together in activity when Amber concluded that Victor had no rhythm. Amber then wrapped her arms around her husband's neck as Victor draped his arms around her waist. They danced together through two songs, rocking softly to the slow beat.

Victor eyed Leticia walking alone by herself in the distance and decided he wanted to dance with his new sister-in-law. "Leticia's free, I'm gonna ask her to dance."

Amber looked over at the Bride, she looked a little gloomy. "OK," she agreed, walking backwards, bumping into a body.

When she turned around the Groom took her breath away. Confident black tuxedo, ashen shirt—unbuttoned for some reason—his tie unraveled, dangling around his neck. He came across utterly sexy in his attire. Good Lord, was he even aware of the gapes he was getting while merely standing there?

"Wanna dance?"

Amber smelled the alcohol on his breath, but didn't care. She didn't hesitate; she wanted to grab the opportunity to be in his arms. She placed her hand in his. It was warm to the touch, masculine, more so than Victor's. He placed his hand on her lower back, swayed her body to the music. And their bodies ***did sway***, and migrated correctly. So much in fact, they had the same pulse, tempo and identical pace.

Eduardo was caught off guard once again. Being a former tomboy, Amber had more rhythm than any of his past lady friends. He held her near, got a whiff of her invigorating aroma and Heaven help him, there was no hope for him after that. Visions of her ending up in his bed consumed his every thought.

"Eduardo."

Eduardo blinked back to consciousness. "What?"

"The wedding went ahead without a hitch," Amber conveyed, still moving in time with his direction.

He nodded graciously as other guests stared at them dancing together. They made an ominous pair. He let go a sigh, "Yah, I know."

Amber could tell by his guise that he was dejected. ***But why?*** This should be the happiest day of his life! "What's the matter?"

Eduardo gazed into Amber's eyes. He was drunk but still had his wits about him. He wanted to devour her. Having her within his arms—Good God—so close to his arousal, intoxicated or not, his salacious nature was going to destroy him. "Nothing...it's nothing."

Amber was aware of two things all at once: how easy it was to read his mind, and how wonderfully at ease he was encircling her. "I've never been to Beverly Hills; everything here is so…luxurious."

"Appearances can be deceiving."

"Well, your wedding was beautiful—"

"Enough about the wedding Amber," he snapped. "I don't want to talk about anymore."

Amber closed her mouth. Good Lord! Even inebriated he still harbored a ruling presence. "You don't have to be so snippy about it."

"Sorry...Good God, I'm sorry."

At least he apologized—she didn't think he would. The lights suddenly were dimmed and Amber closed her eyes again. He was in her arms for just a dance and the music was nearly over. She didn't want to upset him any further and decided not to say anything else. Damn but it was thrilling, exhilarating—to be in his arms! All Amber could think of ***next*** were reasons for him not to take his arm away from her waist. She relished in the fact that she found a partner that could actually ***lead*** for once. ***"Careless Whisper"*** being played by a saxophone was quite romantic, Amber realized and pressed her chest against his once more. It was an idealistic feeling, her body against his...and then she felt it. Eduardo had placed his hand on the small of her back and gently pressed her body against the obvious swell in his pants. It was done with such finesse if she wasn't totally aware of his hands already she might have never felt his stimulation. She wondered what it would be like to be in bed with him. His arms holding her close through climax...his electrifying contact on her skin...George Michael music playing in the background.

Eduardo brought her body in closer and glared down at her. Amber's eyes were still shut. Her purple eye shadow glimmered in the twinkling chandeliers up above them. Her hair done up in a French twist, her lipstick matched her dress, that pink, subtle shade that enhanced her beauty. She was quite striking in iridescent lighting—and with the alcohol damning his reason, his resistance came undone instant-taneously and his prurient nature took control. "What's it like to kiss you?" Eduardo whispered into her ear.

Amber immediately opened up her eyes, broke apart from him and pushed his body away. It was bizarre, an abnormal scene in the middle of leisurely dancing couples. She glared into his eyes; his look was pure but impassioned. She was at a loss for words. ***He just got married for crying out loud! What the hell was he doing flirting with me like that? He's drunk Amber, probably doesn't even know what the hell he just said. Good Lord, why doesn't he just take that coat off already? His tie is practically falling off! Isn't he sweaty in this hot crowded space? Good Lord, where's Victor? Where the hell is Victor!***

Amber searched around her, no husband in sight. She walked slowly backwards searching for her husband. Her constant fantasizing about Eduardo was doing her in, wishing that her life were different, had taken another path, another road—towards Eduardo. They had both chosen law to pursue: him, an attorney, her, a Legal Assistant. They both had a lot in common and they constantly talked about the law and the cases that they were involved in. Oh how did it get so fanatical?

Amber found her husband finally. Victor with his Tió Lamberto. The extreme one, who, at sixty-two still smoked weed.

"Can we go home now?"

CHAPTER**ELEVEN**
Awakening

Amber was preoccupied that Easter, absentminded and worried. Two things crammed her brain that holiday, the situation at work and her brother-in-law's troubled question.

Should she sue?

What's it like to kiss her?

One of the attorney's at her firm was upsetting her. The pressure so great, Amber was even contemplating on quitting. But she couldn't, they needed two incomes in order to survive, pay the mortgage and the car payments, Adrian's tuition, health insurance, utilities, the list went on forever. Money was tight in the firm and since Amber was the last one hired, she was oftentimes unpaid for months at a time, only to receive a portion of what's owed to her. She knew she had a potential lawsuit, but how could she afford an attorney when she hadn't any capital? And then there's the likelihood of getting fired. Oh, it was an endless mind battle within. If it weren't for Victor and his unsteady position with the city utilities department (consistent government budget cuts), she would have no reservations about suing.

And then there's that ridiculous seed her brother-in-law planted inside her head. What's it like to kiss her? Why on earth would he ask such a question? Boy, he must have been really drunk to be so bold. Or was he normally that forward? ***Of course he was,*** Amber realized, remembering that day when he leaned in towards that blonde and stole a kiss. She had to stop thinking about him so much. Every time she was near him, she wished his lips were pressed against hers too.

Unenthusiastically, Amber walked around aimlessly watching the children search for Easter eggs. Adrian, who was five that year, was amongst the youngsters on the annual Family egg hunt. Amber was nearly five months pregnant, but barely showing. Her figure, still curvy, just her breasts enlarged. Just what she needed, to bring ***more*** attention to her already large bosom?

The children all carried their baskets and searched high and low for all the colored eggs. Victor and some of his cousins were in charge of hiding all the eggs and made sure they were hard to recover. How awful of them. How's a two year-old supposed to find an Easter egg on top of the roof?

Feeling even more listless than before, Amber couldn't help but look for her brother-in-law, he was somewhere in the backyard, but seemed to disappear. Leticia was laughing with Tiá Jemma in the corner, but she didn't see Eduardo anywhere. Then all of a sudden, Amber felt her heart begin to pound. She didn't even have to turn around; she knew that he was in close proximity. Trying not to make it look so obvious, Amber languidly turned her head and was astonished to find her brother-in-law secretly showing her son locations of nearby buried Easter eggs.

"Eduardo!"

He stiffened up, he was caught. "What?"

"That's cheating...what are you doing? He's supposed to look for those himself."

"Yah, but my brother's skillful at hiding eggs, the poor kid only found one, thought I'd help him out."

Amber tsked at him, "You are so bad."

"I know," Eduardo agreed, winking and bringing his finger up to his lips and shushing Amber to secrecy.

Amber's heart began to flutter again. It was so hard to deny what she felt for him. She tried to disguise her enthrallment though and walked away from him, not even turning her head in the slightest and tried to calm herself down. She gazed directly in front of her and headed towards the kitchen.

Amber found Rosalba and her sister-in-law, Tiá Sonya

washing dishes in the kitchen.

"I can help," Amber suddenly pronounced, hoping for the preoccupation.

Rosalba looked over at her daughter-in-law. Such a sweetheart. Así que dulce una chica. "Si—yes, my sister wants to show me something in the bedroom, can you take over for a few minutes?"

Amber's eyes grow wide, "Of course Mama, you don't even have to ask."

After the two sisters left, Amber grabbed the dish scrubber and began to rinse the food off the plates. She was left alone now and welcomed the solitude. Washing dishes wasn't a chore at the moment, it was a blessing and she started thinking about the little girl she was about to give birth to. Last week she and Victor found out the baby's sex through an ultra-sound. They were hoping for a girl, and their wishes came true. Needless to say, Victor was elated, and drove the family to the paint store to buy pink paint and now bedroom number three looks like a Pepto-Bismol nightmare. Later that night, while skimming through a list of girl's names, Amber felt Victor's possessiveness for the very first time. Arguing about names for crying out loud! He wanted to take control over his daughter's name? Amber liked ***"Valentine"***, while Victor chose ***"Kristina."*** After a long drawn out discussion, and the possibility of Sanchez war, they came to an understanding; ***"Valentina Marie"*** would be their daughter's name.

Brush, brush, brush...rinse, rinse, rinse...oh no...***He*** was in the space. Amber's heart began to pound once again. She gazed up from her focusing and centered on him entering through the open doorway.

"Ah…they got you doing KP?"

Amber turned away as Eduardo conveniently passed behind her back and went to look at something in the refrigerator. She smiled, "No, I volunteered, I had to keep my mind busy."

Eduardo glanced up from the freezer. "Why? What's wrong?"

Amber's heart sunk. Like she would confess everything to him! "Oh, it's nothing."

"Oh," Eduardo voiced, pulling out an orange from the bottom of the frig. He threw the fruit up a few feet and then caught it with his other hand. "Oh well, see ya out there."

"Yah, see ya."

Amber continued washing the pots now. Big huge containers filled with what once looked like potato salad. A few more minutes pass and Amber began to wonder where her mother-in-law and her sister went. She grabbed a few glasses and dumped them into the soapy water. Just then Eduardo caught the corner of her eye again. What does he need ***now?***

"Where's my Mom?"

Amber stopped what she was doing. "She was just here, she said she was going to her bedroom, did you check there?"

Eduardo walked out of her view and Amber instantly went back to rinsing out the glasses. She nearly broke one on the center of the porcelain sink when her brother-in-law appeared around the corner again walking towards her.

"Need some help?"

Amber nodded her head no.

Eduardo could tell there was something deeply bothering Amber. Her usual rejoinders were not apparent. "Tell me what the problem is then."

How could he tell? Amber blushed, swallowed, and then turned away. She tried to finish the dishes but her heart was beating so darn hard. But yet...the more she thought about it, there was one thing she could have him help her out with. "Eduardo...how do you treat the females in your office?"

What an unusual question, Eduardo thought. "All the same, why?"

"What does that mean, all the same?"

"I treat all women with respect," he said matter-of-factly, "Co-workers, Assistants...***family."***

Amber gazed down at the ground. Although he probably didn't mean to do it, Eduardo's last comment melted her knees. His look was sweltering and she couldn't help but turn away from her own heat rising. "I wish all men thought the same as you do."

Eduardo came in closer to her, grabbed the glass out of her hand and began to wipe it dry with a dishcloth. "Why? What happened?"

Amber watched in awe as Eduardo placed the dried goblet back up into the cupboard. "Will you help me out with something?"

"Sure, anything."

Amber sighed. Thank goodness. Having a high profile defense attorney on her side would help out tremendously. "There's this attorney at my firm, he's actually the head, and he's not paying me. I need you to represent me, I won't be able to pay you right off, but as soon as I get my money, I can make payments—"

Eduardo hushed her mouth with the dishcloth. "There's no need Amber, you're my family, how much does he owe you?"

Amber batted the cloth away, "Two month's salary."

"What a bastard."

"You can say that again."

"No need to sue Amber. I just need to place the fear of God in him. I'll send him correspondence on Aldridge & Watson letterhead and enforce compensation."

"You think that will work?"

Eduardo guffawed at her comment, "Amber...we just won a celebrity malpractice suit, I was on the news last night, didn't you see it?"

Amber grabbed the wet dish out of his hand and started to hoot. "Yah—right, I'm pregnant remember? This body falls asleep at nine o'clock!"

Eduardo yanked the dish back, smiled and then his grin weakened when Amber licked her lips. "Too bad, I looked pretty good."

Amber rolled her eyes. Then again, he ***always*** looked good, darn him. "Did you tape it?"

"Of course."

"You're so bigheaded," Amber snickered, locking eyes with his.

"For the office archives silly girl."

Eduardo was enjoying himself too much all of a sudden. Helping Amber out with a simple household chore, he even forgot what he came into the kitchen for. Amber was standing too close for comfort—her hazel eyes looked deep into his soul.

Much too close, Amber realized. She simply must step away. The fragrance of him unnerved her. He smelled of soap, masculinity, cologne and vitality. She wanted to run her hands up his muscled chest, feel the power he so easily generated through his sexy pores. Without warning, Amber was caught in his web. His eyes, so green and narcotic caused her lips to part. Her mouth watered, her breasts ached to be touched...Good Lord, why does she think this way around him!

Eduardo's will power deserted him. His brain was sending messages down to his feet, but his desire absorbed his port and he remained level. Good God, Amber was radiant. The pregnancy caused her cheeks to fill with a pink hue and her already full luscious lips appeared swollen and begging to be kissed. Her gaze glittered and cheerfulness bounced around the browns of her eyes. Good God, if only he could just freely wrap his arms around her. Offensive thoughts beat down his groin. He wanted to know what it felt like to have her plump breasts up against his upper body. She was staring at his chest again...he wished to God he knew what she kept staring at.

Eduardo sighed heavily and did a double take when he eyed his mother and Tiá Sonya watching his exposure. He folded the dishcloth, placed it down on the counter and headed out the area without a further word.

Rosalba and Sonya blasted looks at one another. Eduardo ***never*** offered to do housework before. That was women's work to him. Both of them felt the level of Amber's and Eduardo's keen friendship. Was it familiarity? Or was it something else entirely?

CHAPTER**TWELVE**

Desire & Contractions

Amber was so glad that Adrian's birthday landed on a Saturday. Normally, her son's birthday would land in the middle of the week and she would have to scramble around and figure out if she would have it on the weekend ***before*** or the weekend ***after***. It was the little things that usually made her crazy. It was the big things she thought she could handle.

Eduardo asked her what it felt like to kiss her. ***What did it feel like to kiss him?*** She began to wonder. Her constant daydreaming of him was even clouding her normal routine. She was nearly nine months pregnant now and she oftentimes missed her appointments because she was spending too much time thinking about her brother-in-law. Her mind would wander off into a zone all its own, a private sector of her brain where she could envision her and him together.

Thank goodness for friends in high places! Eduardo's simple letter enforced her boss to indemnify her and was even treated with elevated esteem when the law firm realized that Amber was related to ***that Sanchez***. Boy, Eduardo sure was making a name for himself within the legal community.

But today was her son's day. Adrian's 6th birthday. Boys and girls from his kindergarten class would be there along with some of the kids around the neighborhood and most especially, the Sanchez Family; about thirty of them this time, mostly the relatives with kids Adrian's age or younger. No balloons for her son, no way. Adrian would have none of it. He wanted streamers only, ***'no baby stuff Mom'***, he insisted. And if she bought theme type paper plates and napkins, he said he would walk out of the party. Would she do that? Oh no, Adrian was just like his Tió Eduardo in a way, he knew what he wanted and wasn't shy about being direct.

She would obey her son's wishes and do the best she could decorating the backyard with streamers, tablecloths and colorful displays of The Power Rangers. No baby stuff, huh? Her son was head over heels in love with The White Ranger. Watched them every Saturday morning, had several figures of The White Ranger and the other Power Rangers as well: Red, Yellow, Pink, Blue, Green and Black. His favorite, The White Ranger was special. He was the most powerful Ranger. "Tommy" was the individual the other Rangers looked up to and needed when the other Rangers were getting beaten up by the monsters of the moment. He was the ***hero***, and Adrian wanted to be him. Amber decided long ago that she was going to surprise Adrian with a White Ranger impersonator. Having the White Ranger come by the birthday party to surprise her son would be the highlight of the day.

The house was set. Victor was outside turning on the propane to the Bar-B-Que grill when the first of the guests arrived. It was several kids from Adrian's class, a couple of boys and a few girls. They all ran outside towards the backyard. Adrian was so excited to see them at his house, he ran around from room to room showing all the kids furniture, TV's, his video games, where the bathrooms were then finally the patio.

Sanchez relatives began to pour in. Aunts and Uncles with cousins and more cousins came shuffling through the door. Amber was beginning to get slightly overwhelmed.

Her huge belly felt heavy as she bounced around from family member to family member. Leticia and Eduardo arrived soon after. Leticia was just as bulky as Amber, and she was appreciative of the fact that she didn't have to feel singled out and awkward in front of The Family. She had a partner, they were a pair of pregnant ladies and she was thankful for the non-comparatives. They were in the same boat; both pregnant within weeks of each other. It was odd in a way, if you really thought about it. How the hand of God stepped in.

Making sure Amber had an equal gift Leticia wouldn't be envious of and vice versa. The attention would be split evenly between the two. Their kids would grow up with one another; have the same interests, even the same devotion.

Amber eyed Eduardo walking over to Victor first. They shook hands, patted each other on the back and greeted each other with love, admiration. ***Good Lord! Eduardo looked good***. Light blue cotton shirt tucked in comfortable expensive white linen shorts. Amber turned the other way when she felt the first of two strong contractions. ***Oh my God, not now!***

She rubbed her tummy, let go a couple of breaths and sat herself down. She didn't mean to bring more attention to herself than she did, but somehow it didn't matter. She felt a little light-headed when Eduardo ran to her side.

"You OK?"

"I think I had a contraction," Amber let go, continuing to breathe through the second less intense muscle action.

"Leticia's been having them too," Eduardo expressed, chuckling at the thought of both of them feeling the same pain.

"Oh no, is she?" Amber asked, surveying his attire again.

Victor eyed his wife in apparent pain and hurriedly walked over to her side. "Eduardo? What's wrong?" He asked with the Bar-B-Que prongs still in his hand.

"She thinks she had a contraction," Eduardo stated.

Victor got excited. "Really? How fast they coming? Have you timed them? Do they feel like the ones you had with Adrian?"

Amber looked up at her husband. ***He looked good today too.*** Jean shorts, dragging black Oakland Raiders football jersey, Nike tennis shoes. "I think I'm OK now," she breathed, getting up to her feet.

Leticia spotted the three of them and quickly ran towards the excitement. "What's wrong? Everything OK?"

"She's having contractions," Eduardo stated again.

"Having?" Amber counter-stated. "I only had ***two."***

"Did they just start?" Leticia asked quizzically rubbing her own stomach.

"Yah, can you help me with the games?" Amber asked

Leticia wide-eyed.

"I will," Eduardo chimed in, looking into Leticia's eyes as he said it. He couldn't tolerate to see her in any more pain. If his brother wasn't going to give Amber special attention today, then he certainly was.

Leticia smiled back at him. "Awww, what a thoughtful husband I have," she let go rubbing his arm.

"Yah—yah, what do I do first?" Eduardo asked Amber, watching her wobble around gingerly.

"Adrian wants no kiddie games; imagine no games at a kid party."

Eduardo gazed around at all the guests. "That's my nephew! Everyone seems to be enjoying themselves thus far; I guess the little guy knows."

"Thank goodness. Wait till you see the surprise I have for Adrian, he's gonna love it!" She exclaimed, biting down on her lower lip as she said it.

Eduardo brought his eyes down to her lips—closed his own mouth and tried to escape being utterly captivated again. "Can't wait."

No kiddie games, Amber thought. What about a piñata? She remembered the conversation she had with her son just before the party. "Yah, we can have one of those...but no pin the tail on the donkey or stupid drawing games..." OK, so where does that leave her? The White Ranger surprise and a piñata filled with candy that would have to do.

Eduardo gathered up all the kids and began to put them in line according to height. Each kid would have a few swings at the bouncing papier-mâché Power Ranger, and cousin Hector, who was keeping himself out of trouble lately, would do the honors at making sure each kid missed the object before the last kid in line had their turn. Amber made sure each one of the little ones had a plastic goody bag to collect the flying candy and everything was all set. She was just about to wrap a bandanna around the first toddler when she felt another contraction. ***Oh no!*** She pulled away from the child and arched her back and waited until the feeling subsided. No other adult noticed her in discomfort but Eduardo who set eyes on Amber frequently. Amber made it look like she was just adjusting her outfit. Covering her belly again and pulling down her shorts. He was sure he'd be running to her side again, he studied her body movement relentlessly.

First kid, swing! Missed! Another swing! Missed again! Another, and another, swing, swing, swing! Miss, miss, miss. ***Gee, Hector is good,*** Amber thought. Two more kids, two more misses. Five more kids, five more misses. ***This is turning out to be good.*** Finally, after the twentieth child, it was Adrian's turn. The Birthday Boy. Amber tied the bandanna around his head to cover his eyes and got out of the way. Adrian was a good baseball player, and she knew he would have an accurate swing. One swing was all it took. The piñata burst open and the kids all ran towards the cascading candy falling from the sky.

Amber felt another contraction. ***Oh no, not again!*** She ambled back into the house and tried to disguise her pang as she pushed on into the den. She laid her head against the wall and closed her eyes and waited patiently for the tightening to recede. ***You can do this Amber, you can, you have to…It's for Adrian, it's his day…you can wait to have this baby until The White Ranger comes…you can wait…please wait baby, please wait…***

"You OK?"

Amber reopened her eyes—what a surprise. Her brother-in-law was worried about her and followed her into the den. How nice of him to be so concerned.

Eduardo went to reach for her but stopped short. He couldn't stand to see her in so much pain.

Inches apart, their eyes embrace. He didn't touch her; he didn't dare. What the hell was wrong with him anyway? What kind of carnal pervert was he? Even when she was about to give birth he was ***still*** sexually attracted to her?

"Yah—I," Amber tried to find the words, "Had another contraction."

"Maybe you should sit down. I'll go get Victor." Eduardo expressed turning the corner.

"Eduardo!" Amber yelled at him bringing him back into view.

"What?" Eduardo asked with baited breath.

Amber grabbed hold of the allusion in his eyes, mouthed out the words '***thank you'*** and Eduardo noted it, gave her one of his amazing half grins and sprinted back around the corner.

Amber tried to calm herself down. The mixed emotions were driving her crazy. Lust and strong muscle contractions ***do... not... mix!*** She practiced her breathing once more when she heard the earsplitting screaming of youngsters from the backyard. The next thing she heard was Adrian running around the house calling out her name.

"Mom!... Mom! ***MOM!*** Where are you?...MOM!"

"I'm in here!" Amber screamed back at him.

"Mom, Mom! The White Ranger is here Mom! The White Ranger! Thanks Mom thanks!" Adrian gave Amber a big hug and kisses and then ran back outside.

Amber closed her eyes again. ***There... it's done...My son is happy; I can have this baby now***. And just when she allowed herself to relax, her water broke.

Victor rushed in from behind the corner and spotted the water on the floor. "Now?" He asked anxiously.

"Now." ***Oh God, not now!***

CHAPTER**THIRTEEN**

Love Makes You Do Foolish Things

After Valentina was born, routines halted. Victor and Amber were much too busy to be driving over to The Family's house every Friday night. Eduardo and Leticia were busy too with their little girl, Kyra. The two girls were born weeks apart from one another and drawn out hours turned into days and weeks, and the weeks turned into months of predictable days of diapers, bottles, powder, and lotion, spit up, bibs, pacifiers, crying and restless evenings.

Amber dragged herself away from the crib. Up late one night, Valentina had been crying mercilessly with a stuffy nose. It was Amber's shift, Victor had already given the baby six hours of his attention and Amber told him to lie down already. He was a good father, just like she thought. Beyond the call of duty father, and just as he had been a doting husband, he was just as equally giving to the children. And oh how he loved his new chestnut-haired baby girl! Cooing at her, making her laugh, holding her constantly. If he wasn't Valentina's birth father, she would have to take him in for questioning.

Amber walked through the dark house, not switching on any lights. It was that kinda night. Nothing bright, ***please***. She sat herself down on the couch. She wanted to go to sleep, but couldn't. Her endometriosis was getting serious. Every three months she would miss menstruation. Her condition becoming so severe she suffered terrible stomach cramps. Her period was extreme that night, the pain bringing her to her knees. Now that she had her second child, her gynecologist suggested that she should seriously consider having a hysterectomy. But that important operation was not on her mind. Something else consumed her.

Amber sat on the couch and began to cry. Sobs so hard, she had to shove a pillow in her face to muffle away the sound. ***God I miss him...How could I have let this happen? I'm in love with him...I'm in love with Eduardo...What do I do? How can I stop this? Do I wanna stop this? Oh God I want to see him so bad...How do I see him without making it obvious? The Sanchez house...I would have to see him at family gatherings...Thank God for family events...I could see him out in the open and no one would ever know that I was in love with him...But how do I get myself over there? How do I invite myself over to the Sanchez house? Would he be there? How do I get him there? God, I think I'm gonna have to wait till another holiday, when's the next one? Fourth of July? Will he be there? He should be. Oh God, this is absolutely insane, INSANE! In love with your brother-in-law. This is terrible, taboo and unforgivable. No one would ever understand. And oh God, Victor's so good to me, so thoughtful all the time, so caring. It would devastate him if he ever found out. Trusting in me. Trust, what's that? Oh God, how could I have let this happen? This is so wrong. All I want to do is be with him. In the same room, same area, same anything...***

Amber suddenly had the stupidest idea. She was going to call their house. One o'clock in the morning, and she was going to ask for Leticia. Confide in her about the baby and how it was so strenuous to put her to sleep and if Leticia was having the same problem with Kyra...and if...and if he was there (she knew he would be) and maybe...maybe he would be the one to answer the phone, she could talk to him? Ask him sort of matter-of-factly if they were going to the house for the Fourth of July? That would be OK, wouldn't it? She could pull that off, couldn't she?

Amber walked over to the phone and stared at it for a long second. Lost in her tears, her drowsiness, she dialed their phone number. Wiping away her tears she cleared her nose with her handkerchief. One ring, she was getting nervous. Two rings, Eduardo answered.

"Hello?"

His voice was clear. He wasn't asleep. What was he doing up at one o'clock in the morning? Was Kyra up all night as well? Was he as delirious as she was? Amber hung up the phone. Started to cry again, anguish so deep, she slid to the floor with the phone in her lap. Suddenly, it rang on its own. She answered it immediately. "...Hello?"

"Amber?" Eduardo asked curiously, "Is that you?"

Amber was still on the floor. Good Lord, should she tell him? Should she confess her love for him? "Eduardo—I'm sorry...I wanted...I wanted to speak to Leticia, but I realize it's late, I'm sorry." She was about to hang up, but Eduardo kept talking.

"What's wrong Amber? You sound like you've been crying. Is it my brother? Did he hurt you?"

Why would he think Victor would hurt her? Victor couldn't hurt a fly! "No...I, no...I was just up all night with Valentina, she's had a cold."

"Yah, Kyra was sick last week, I think it's going around."

Then suddenly, she didn't care to talk to Leticia anymore. She just wanted to talk to Eduardo, continue to talk to him period. He is whom she wanted in the first place. Never mind about her sister-in-law!

"Amber, you still there?"

"Yes."

"Amber, get some sleep, it's late."

"Eduardo?"

"Yes?"

"Are you...are you going to your Mom's house for Fourth of July?"

Eduardo hesitated, "No, my firm is sending me out of town to settle a case, but Leticia and Kyra are going, why?"

Tears fell from Amber's eyes. That was not what she wanted to hear! But keep him on the phone Amber—don't let him get away! "What are you doing up so late? You don't sound like you've been sleeping."

Eduardo could still hear the moisture in her voice, "I haven't been sleeping at all lately."

The line goes quiet. A confession of some sorts—what was he trying to say?

"Me either." She confessed as well.

"My job is tough."

Figures. Why would he be sleepless because of her? "I bet."

"The media, the constant battle of trying to upscale our cases."

"I can imagine. I'm still having problems with my attorney. I can't do anything right by him. My work is never good enough."

"Well, we can get a little annoying at times," he laughed.

"You think?" She gives to him, chuckling as well.

"Why don't you find another job? You're constantly complaining about one or the other associates there; you don't get any respect Amber. You should look somewhere else."

"Yah, it's just that easy." Amber's smile suddenly dropped when she squinted in the darkness to see her husband filling the doorway. "I have to go now."

"OK...goodnight then, get some sleep."

Amber hung up the line. Walked over to Victor.

"Who were you talking to?" Victor asked questioning her acting peculiar.

It was the first time Amber ever felt guilty. All her flirting had been a game, a test of sorts to see how much she could get Eduardo's attention, and now she felt she had been caught in the act of sex. "Eduardo," she acknowledged.

"Why did Eduardo call?"

"Oh—he didn't—I did, at first, I was calling Leticia. She wasn't up; Eduardo answered the phone, so we started talking about work." Amber felt herself gasping for breath. She didn't want to hurt Victor, and this was truly the first time she felt like she had.

"Oh," he gave out, turning around and walking back to bed.

Oh? Amber thought, letting out a sigh of relief. ***Just oh?***

There's that acceptance thing again. That bizarre tolerance that walked hand-in-hand with The Title. ***Sister-in-law*** slash ***Brother-in-law*** upmost and always. That instantaneous fondness that supposed to be present the moment you put that wedding ring on your finger. That risk-free partiality that's there for every in-law, free of charge.

CHAPTER**FOURTEEN**
Torment Is All the Rage

duardo tapped his gold-tipped pen speedily on top of the binders he was working on.

Tap, tap, tap, tap, tap, tap!

The weightless eerie sound surrounded the barely lit room. It was nearing three o'clock in the morning and he had still been working. Not because he was forced with the drudgery, but simply couldn't sleep. His mind raced with thoughts of Amber again...How to be near her, how to get her to his parents home. She called the house? What for? She was still up late? Why? She said she wanted to talk to Leticia first, but then decided to talk to him. She asked if ***he*** was going to his parent's home for Fourth of July. Did she want to know about him exclusively, or was it collectively? Valentina was sick, was it true? He only offered that Kyra was sick because he simply wanted to keep her on the ***Goddamn*** phone! Good God this was getting bad. He really had to get it under control. Constantly worrying about her, wanting to be adjacent to her, the feeling was so tremendous, what could he do? Restrain himself and keep his distance, be preoccupied for once. Dive into work, achieve another goal. What goal? Find one ***dammit***, and find one fast.

He opened up a law book, read just a few words then gazed over at the phone again. Could he call her? Would she still be up? Why did she hang the phone up so quickly? Was Victor there? Victor was there, he realized, shutting his eyes. Good God what was he doing? Panting over his sister-in-law;

how truly egotistical of him and how utterly disgusting.

Fatigue was getting to him now, as he closed his eyes in heartache. Instantly feeling Amber's arms around his shoulders; small caresses inching their way down around his chest. It was a sensual feeling, it was exhilarating...it was ***real.***

It was Leticia.

Eduardo grabbed her hand, whipped his body around in the chair. Leticia looked at him cautiously at first and wondered what he was about to say. Eduardo began to mouth out the words ***stop*** but fell short of doing so. She reached over and took his face in her hands, gently kissed him on his lips. He didn't kiss her back. She instantly withdrew her hands from feeling unwelcome.

Eduardo stood up; she backed herself into the wall. He simply stared at her. What does she want now? What ***else*** does she want?

Leticia was breathless, eyed his body up and down. Eduardo was practically naked under his silk robe, wearing only his boxers and a frown. By the look in her eyes he knows what she wants. Is he prepared to give it to her? Knowing full well they could get pregnant again? Does he want another child with this woman, when he really couldn't stand the sight of her?

But Eduardo was prepared though, having been a bachelor most of his life and carried several packets of condoms in his desk no less. It had been almost a year since he had sex and he was loaded. He wanted to feel Amber so much; all he wanted to do ***now*** was clearly handle skin. He didn't dare kiss her on her lips, kissing on the lips was far too intimate for him, and all he wanted from Leticia now was intercourse. He began slowly breathing on her neck, softly at first, then sensually diving down to the tips of her breasts and nipples. She was more than willing this time he had her, it was what she wanted and hunted him out for. He pushed her body up against the wall, caressed and kneaded her small mounds in his mouth. She grabbed onto his hair and tried to pull his face up to her lips, but he didn't budge.

"Do you want to lie down?" He asked breathing heavily now.

"No, take me here," she purred, yanking off his robe, trying to pull at his underwear.

Eduardo lifted up her arms and clutched her buttocks as she naturally wrapped her legs around his waist, straddling his body close and solid against the wall. He still hadn't allowed himself to kiss her and guided her hips on top of his erect penis. In and out only once, Eduardo loosened her arms from around his shoulders and remembered the condom in his desk, allowing her body to release from his and slide back down as he searched through his desk.

"What the ***hell*** are you doing?"

"I'm looking...I'm looking for a...here, got one." He said, unwrapping the plastic and rolling it on.

Leticia looked at him mortified. "You can't be serious," she said with both hands on her forehead in disbelief. The sight of him and that ***thing*** over his penis placed a red flag in her brain.

He pressed against her firmly, only awkwardly this time. He tried lifting her up against the wall again, but her body suddenly felt like five hundred pound weights. Good God, this just isn't right! The mood had suddenly shifted from ***OK*** to ***see ya!*** He took a step backwards, unrolled the second skin and stepped back into the robe.

Leticia, still in doubt had been glued to the wall. "What's wrong Eddie? Why'd you stop?"

Eduardo looked over at her naked; her nipples were still erect and red from where he had been biting them. She was obviously in sexual agony. It was late, it was too late. He was tired now and wanted to sleep. "I'm going to bed."

"Eddie!" Leticia yelled at him strolling away. "I'll do it...I will. I want you so badly; I'll make love with you with the condom on. Please come back, please?"

Eduardo gazed at her begging. Begging? Now why did she have to go and do something as humiliating as that? Here was his supposed wife. A woman he was willing to marry and he couldn't provoke himself enough to make love to her? She was a virtual stranger to him now, he knew of no one else but Amber in his heart. He made love to strangers before and bedded more than a few girls with no names. How could it be that he was unwilling to have sex with this particular one? Was it because she was the doting sort? Continually asking him if he was fine, hot, tired, hungry, sad, and happy constantly with no end in sight? Pleading with him now to make love to her? Why doesn't she just get the hint already and just go away?

Eduardo suddenly found himself inside his Porsche, screeching down the calm neighborhood streets at sixty miles per hour. Find him a highway…any passageway…anywhere, where he can just ***go.*** Escape from reality into fantasy; his castle in the sky with Amber, even if it was just for a moment, just one little second. That's all he'd asked for. He'd do ***anything.*** Suffer any consequence imaginable. What he wouldn't give for just one little kiss. A simple kiss, what could it hurt? How could he steal it? Where could he take it? He charmed her; he knew so in his heart, could sense it when Amber gazed into his eyes. The chemistry that they shared—it brought approach so ridiculous—his boldness would be his doom. Would he be so daring? Would she slap him? Would she turn her head away?

Eduardo dimmed his headlights and rolled the car in neutral alongside his brother's front yard. It was a normal occurrence, his weekly routine. It was four o'clock in the morning now and everyone was asleep he could only assume. He laid his forehead down on the steering wheel.

"Good God...someone arrest me," he chuckled, realizing how utterly dim-witted he's become over her. "I've become Amber's stalker."

CHAPTER**FIFTEEN**

Fantasy Meet Reality

Amber didn't expect to see them that night. Eduardo and Leticia were supposed to be visiting someone sick in the hospital. But when they opened the door and announced that they were just stopping by for a quick visit, a sigh of alleviation passed through Amber. It was nearly six months since she'd seen him. Fourth of July had come and gone since the last time they spoke. Eduardo was constantly on her mind; when she was washing dishes, raking the leaves in the garden, doing the laundry, at her job typing away, in between the thoughts during her daily routine, and in between the thoughts about her children and Victor.

"Hey!" Fabrizio acknowledged. "Come—come, sit down, take your coats off and stay for dinner."

"No Papa, we're not here to eat, we just came by to say hello, that's all," Eduardo gave to him, hugging his father respectfully.

Fabrizio would have none of it. "Mehió, sit down, I know how hard you work, Leticia, tell your husband to sit down—dinner will be done in about twenty minutes." He walked away and into the kitchen where Rosalba was cooking. "Eduardo and Leticia are here, we have enough don't we?" Rosalba nodded her head and finished stirring around the potatoes and squash.

Fabrizio checked on the rice. "Oh, this is gonna be good Mama," he said to her as he kissed her on her cheek. Oh how he loved his wife. How lucky could one man be? Fabrizio was fine-looking in his younger days, and married Rosalba, a fine girl herself, when he was only sixteen. Rosalba and Fabrizio lived with her parents in the beginning of their marriage. Her family was poor, and with six kids to feed, they oftentimes found themselves starving. Fabrizio left to California first, which left Rosalba aching for him. She gave birth to Eduardo in a small country hospital just outside Guanajuato, Mexico. She hung onto letters that Fabrizio used to write to her from within the United States. He wrote to her about Brawley, California. It was a farming community and thriving in the 1960's. He wrote for her to come be with him, he missed her constantly, and knew they'd have a better life in the United States than in Guanajuato. He already made a couple hundred dollars and was anxiously pursuing Rosalba to come to the States to be with him. With a heavy heart, she took Eduardo in the middle of the night and kissed her family goodbye. Roaming around in the darkness like thieves, she reached the border with aid from her neighbors who oftentimes passed over the border in their trucks full of blankets and goods to sell. Rosalba and Eduardo sat in the back with the chickens and clay pots as they drove across and entered El Centro. Imagining that once she'd enter the United States that the streets would be paved with gold, but it wasn't. It wasn't so different than Mexico. It was still a desert, still humid and still desolate. Rosalba's crossing was easy, and unlike stories she's heard before where some Mexicans were forced to become slaves or died of thirst and starvation, hers was unhurried and unconstrained.

Valentina was finally asleep in the middle of the bed in Rosalba's room and Adrian was in the other room watching cartoons when Amber walked outside to the patio. Victor was busy watching the rest of the Tyson-Holyfield boxing match (the reason they'd come over there in the first place) when Amber felt the urge to go the courtyard.

"Hit'em! Sock'em!" Victor shouted, bouncing up and down on the couch.

Leticia sat down and joined him, placing Kyra's car seat next to him on the couch. "Who's fighting?" She asked, putting Kyra's pacifier back into her little mouth.

"Mike Tyson," Victor said not looking directly at her.

"Which one is he?"

Amber knew that her brother-in-law would follow her

outside. She perceived his attendance—which was why she left.

Amber turned her head around slightly, could smell his cologne as he quietly approached. That intoxicating musk that was all his consumed her and she felt weak in the knees, trying to calm her heart fluttering when he arrived alongside next to her.

"Amber, how are you?" Eduardo asked, gently brushing her shoulder.

She turned towards him, "I'm fine...how's that sick friend of yours?" Not really caring about that ***sick friend*** just solely concerned that he was there.

"He's fine. He wants to sue. That's why we were there." He explained guardedly. "Amber...I spoke to one of the partner's in my firm, and if you're interested, we'd like you to come work for us." Eduardo couldn't wait to tell her. That goal he needed to find? Well, he found it, he couldn't stand being away from Amber and came up with a plan to keep her within arm's length. He knew that his little brother wouldn't pass up a heavily anticipated boxing match and drove by his parents' home hoping that they'd be there.

What?! Amber could hardly believe her ears. Being by Eduardo's side daily? It was all she could hope for! Amber walked away from him. Removed from his side for a moment her heart was still racing. God help her, she had flirted with him constantly, and every time, he flirted back. Did he feel the same? ***Don't be ridiculous; he would never be interested in someone like me!*** Was he just being friendly? He did ask her what it felt like to kiss her. ***But he was drunk, probably doesn't even recall asking it.***

Amber walked towards the patio, fast, and hurried. To her surprise, he followed her. The game had suddenly gotten out of hand. When did the feeling change for her? That safe adoration she had for her brother-in-law, the expectations beyond the realness of it all. She suddenly jumped the safe harbor. Gone overboard, fell in love.

The patio was long and L-shaped. The area where Amber escaped to was guarded by solid, thick shrubs that needed to be restricted, but never attended to. No one could see them.

Not The Family, Victor, Leticia, the kids, no one. They were no longer saying ***hello*** or ***goodbye*** in front of the family, or talking safely behind a phone, they were alone, unaccompanied by relatives and spouses.

"Everything OK?" Eduardo asked, hopeful, anxious. Fervent appetite washes over him. It was an open opportunity. Just one little kiss...what could it hurt?

Amber turned around and gazed at his features. His facial expression was unusual, serious by far. He was deep in thought, she could tell that much. "Oh—I...it's nothing." Her face was on fire. Amber walked in further behind the shrubbery. She let out a deep breath, went to wipe away the sweat now forming on her forehead when Eduardo grabbed her. Swung her around and landed a kiss on her lips so solid—so full of passion, lust—he held the back of her head to keep her mouth under his control.

It was domination so spine tingling, Amber thought for a second she might be dreaming—dreaming a wonderful, passionate, uncontrollable, raging, delusion. He was A Perfect Ten. The absolute best kisser she ever came across and couldn't help but contribute her willingness.

Amber slowly opened her eyes and realized three things all at once: (1) when she reopened her eyes he opened his; (2) her hand somehow found his chest and his warmth radiated down to her toes; and (3) nowhere in her heart did she feel the contact was immoral.

Standing still, side by side, not moving, not breathing, Eduardo and Amber remained in awe of the brief intensity they seem to influence.

"I'm not going to apologize," Eduardo cooled down. "I've wanted to do that for such a long time." He placed his hand over hers that was still on his heart.

They stood intently looking at one another. Amber wanted to cry! Tears swarmed her eyes at once. She was so incredibly in love with this man and now to hear him tell her that he's wanted her? What she wanted now was to curl up in his arms and kiss him again.

Amber gently pulled her hand away from under his. "I won't mention this to anyone," she packed away, closing her eyes in torment.

Eduardo's intimacy level was spinning out of control. He reacted to kissing on a personal cavernous degree. If a female were fortunate enough to come in contact with his orifice, then she most assuredly would know his libido. Eduardo grabbed Amber's arm as she began trotting away. "Wait," he said, surveying her body in a matter of moments.

Amber's eyes locked with his. She knew now that his serious gaze was purely erotic. In his sea green eyes showed promise of what he could deliver, if only she would abandon her pledge to her husband. Good Lord why does she want to collide with him? She painstakingly wrapped her arms around his neck and pulled his body back to hers. His fervor, her heat, ignited a flame of greed. His tongue in her mouth—her stronghold embraces. It was ideal, everything Amber ever-imagined Eduardo would be like—the reality delivered. Victor had never taken her this way, never with such thirst, such longing, such supremacy. Victor was always so gentle, so thoughtful in the way he kissed her, entered her. Victor was tender ***period.*** Eduardo was dominant, forceful and flawless. He knew what he was doing. Knew how to kiss a woman and knew how to make Amber buckle to her knees.

Eduardo wanted to devour her. Her satin skin felt so amazing under his fingers. She kissed with the length of her body, her nipples hardened and he wanted to do more, explore longer, twirl his tongue around those raised beauties and hunt for further places to bring increased pleasure to her.

"OK, time to stop," Amber settled, pushing his body away from hers. "It's done...out of ***both*** our systems."

Eduardo stood defeated as he watched Amber walk backwards, her arms and hands waiving and pushing distance between them. He was stimulated beyond compare. Knowing full well that she wasn't immune to his inquisitiveness exhaustively undid him. "I take it that means ***yes,***" he cracked and then assumed, "You'll take the job?"

Good Lord! He was smug! But she loved it, she loved it! His conceit only fed her sensations. Eduardo gave her a triumphant smile, a rather devious exhilarating smile, she'd say.

Amber beamed. "Yes." ***And thanks for rescuing me...***

CHAPTER**SIXTEEN**

Desire Is All Relative

"Mr. Sanchez you're in contempt!" Judge Monroe exclaimed, pounding his mallet firmly on the mahogany counter.

Eduardo stared down the judge. Unreal. Does he know how comical he looks in that toupee? Maybe now is a good time to tell him. Eduardo threw a couple of files callously across the tabletop, making sure everyone in the courtroom knew exactly how much in ***contempt*** he really was. With smoke coming out of his ears, he stormed out of the courtroom after that unfavorable ruling.

"My God man, will you calm down!" Gordon Daggert exclaimed, trying to catch up to Eduardo who was hurriedly marching down the corridor towards the elevator. Gordon Daggert was Eduardo's equal sidekick who also graduated from Harvard. A fellow associate in Aldridge & Watson, Gordon generated his fair share of second glances. Gordon's followed Eduardo all through Harvard, he not only admired Eduardo's accomplishments—he idolized him.

"That fucking asshole doesn't belong on that bench," Eduardo shouted angry. "He knows it, the bailiff knows it—even the goddamn opposing counsel knows it. That's why they took the chance to suppress the new evidence and won!"

"I know—I know Eduardo, but you almost got sanctioned in there, you need to calm the hell down. This is only a minor setback, right? We'll come back tomorrow and hit'em with our dexterity. We always win, right?"

"I hate that fucking judge and the opposing counsel are all idiots! A first year law student could beat them senseless, what the hell's wrong with me?"

"What ***is*** wrong with you?" Gordon asked delicately, "You're usually cool as ice in the courtroom. Now you're just a ball of fire."

Gordon finally maneuvered Eduardo over to a nearby corner. He knew Eduardo was headed towards the parking garage and he wanted to remain with him.

"I've got a lot on my mind," Eduardo stated, still holding onto his briefcase with both hands. He was supposed to meet Amber for lunch that afternoon. After months of finding the opportunity to ask her out to lunch, Victor called out of the blue to let him know that he'd be down the street at noon and asked to meet. Eduardo had no other choice but to lie to his brother and said he was free. Needless to say, Eduardo had been on edge ever since the phone call. He looked forward to spending some time with Amber. The past few nights he could hardly sleep. Just couldn't get those never-ending questions out of his mind. ***She yielded.*** He felt her embrace him back. There was even a level of necessity behind her kiss. ***But why!?*** The awareness sent his thoughts packing. Did she desire him as well? Or was she just curious? He never knew a woman to simply be ***curious.*** It was all or nothing where he was concerned. Women were impatient not investigative. And now—Good God—was she just probing? Or did it go deeper than that? Did she think about him? Did she ***ever*** think about him? Good God, this could all be in his head. What a puffed up peacock he was! She probably didn't even consider that kiss anymore. ***Out of her system,*** she said. Out of her system? When was he ever ***in her*** to begin with?

"Personal shit?" Gordon asked openly.

Eduardo gazed around them. Other attorneys like themselves congregated and descended down the hallways of the downtown Los Angeles courthouse. "Something like that."

"Hey Eduardo, if you ever wanna talk I'm here for ya," Gordon voiced, patting Eduardo on his shoulder.

Eduardo wasn't about to confide in another complacent

bastard like himself. Talk, huh? Not where Amber was concerned. Piss off. "Maybe another time. I've gotta head out and meet my brother."

"OK...sure, then I'll see you back at the office then?"

Eduardo began walking away and didn't turn to face Gordon as he did. Eduardo waved his hand in the air to let Gordon know he'd see him later and disappeared through the revolving glass doors.

Fortunately, Victor was in the area and the two brothers decided to meet at a nearby restaurant. It was within walking distance and Eduardo welcomed any fresh air. It was springtime in California and the leaves on the sidewalk trees turned a spectacular orange and began to slowly fall off.

Eduardo was unruffled when he finally reached the dining establishment. So far the day's events were not favorable, and meeting Victor was no exception. He was suddenly nervous as hell and felt guilt running through his veins. Even though Amber returned his passion, Eduardo still felt to blame for initiating the contact and truly felt ill at the thought of betraying his brother's confidence.

A beautiful blonde waitress (obviously an out of work actress) approached Eduardo for his order. "Are you ready?" She asked, flashing him an ultra-pearly white smile.

Eduardo's salacious nature peeked; the girl was a prime piece to look at. Eduardo freely gave her one of his ardent grins. "I will be in a few moments."

The waitress took hold of the rouse and temporary interest from Eduardo. "If in fact you truly are," the waitress matter-of-factly expressed, jotting down information on the back of an order slip. "I'm off at five, here's my number."

Eduardo remained relaxed. He's used to the directness of women; their boldness for him was a natural occurrence. He took the piece of paper but didn't look at it. "Thanks for the offer."

Victor walked through the door a moment later and waved at Eduardo already seated. "Hey bro...How's it goin'? Day' am you look good."

Eduardo let go a laugh. Good God how he treasured his little brother. Growing up in Burbank (a little suburb in Los

Angeles) practically being the only Mexican kids on the block, they constantly got into fights over ignorance and stupidity. Eduardo was always in charge of Victor when they were younger and Victor was constantly getting picked on at school, the only thing that saved him was sports. Being able to play baseball and basketball helped with the neighborhood boys and they would oftentimes seek Victor out to complete their teams. Victor didn't mind, he was just a kid and simply wanted to be included. Eduardo would wait on the sidelines, or would offer to be the referee just so that he could keep watch over Victor. The one and only time Victor ever got beaten up was the one and only time Eduardo decided to throw caution to the wind to give his valuable time to a girl he was dating. She was constantly coming over and had been sent away, but on that terrible day Eduardo decided that it was more important to get to ***second base*** than to watch his little brother slide into second.

They were at the nearby Junior High school and a group of boys included Victor in their baseball game. Victor was really excited and Eduardo took the opportunity to go make out with Arleen Moreno in between the handball courts nearby.

"I'll be over there," Eduardo pointed out towards the large concrete area.

"OK," Victor expressed anxiously, "I hope I get to bat this time."

Eduardo escorted Arleen over to the large pillars and instantly dove in towards her mouth. Grabbing the girl fierce, Arleen surrendered and gave as well as she got. Eduardo shoved his tongue down her mouth and directed hers into motion. Dancing this wondrous ballet of sexual awareness, he had her up against the wall; her arms around his neck, holding tightly onto his back. Eduardo knew she'd drop her panties if he'd ask her to, but on the slight risk of getting caught by a roaming teacher—asked Arleen to unhook her bra instead. The girl was all too obliging being brought to a blistering temperature and Eduardo was in the midst of kneading her small breasts when he heard in the distance a small cry for help. Eduardo's arousal was instantly doused when he realized that the shriek for aid was a familiar voice. His hands pulled away from under Arleen's top and Eduardo ran around the structure. To his utter amazement, the team was surrounding Victor, taking turns kicking him in his abdomen, legs and sides.

Eduardo ran towards the brawling and yanked a couple of boys up off their feet and away from his brother. "Leave him alone!" He shouted off the top of his lungs. Eduardo threw a few more punches and managed to get two more boys away. "What the hell is going on here?"

"It's his fault!" The boys seemed to say in unison pointing at Victor still on the ground.

"It was an accident Eduardo, I swear." Victor pleaded, trying to get up to his feet. Eduardo leaned over to give him a hand and pulled his body up from the ground; Victor's groan of pain was apparent.

"You all right?"

"No," Victor cried, suddenly feeling a burning sensation in his lungs.

Eduardo pointed to one of the boys, "You!" Eduardo crooked his finger and demanded his attention. "Come here!"

The boy was suddenly panicked and scared.

Another boy came to his defense. "It wasn't him! It was the squirt's fault!"

"Shut up! Did I say you could talk?" Eduardo stared him down, the boy backed away. Eduardo was several inches taller than all the kids and his stance had been intimidating. "Now you tell me what happened. And so help me if you ***lie***, and I find out later that you did, I won't hesitate to break your skull." He wasn't really, but he was infuriated enough to at least make the kid believe so.

The boy believed him and was terrified. "I did it, I'm sorry, I did it and I blamed it on the squirt."

The boys all looked at the coward confessing, shook their heads in distaste.

"What'd you go and do that for, ***you moron!"***

"He didn't need to know nothin' ***you idiot!"***

Eduardo was exasperated now. "Who's going to tell me what happened now? Who's man enough to face the consequences?"

A boy, no taller than the others spoke up, "I am."

Eduardo shoved his chest into his. "A moron for a leader huh? Thought it funny to blame my little brother for something you're stupid friend did, huh?"

The boy didn't seem to be intimidated and Eduardo took note of it. "You don't scare me. The squirt cracked our bat, now we can't play!"

Eduardo fumed. Pushed the boy slightly, sending the wretched youngster downward on his ass. "Liar! That boy over there just confessed that it was ***his*** fault."

"Get'em guys!" The contemptible boy on the floor commanded. Simultaneously, the remaining group all jumped on Eduardo and tried to tackle him to the ground. Unsuccessful, boys flew off of Eduardo's tall frame one by one. Eduardo got in a few more punches here and there and the boys all cowered away.

Eduardo waited till the last boy was visible when he finally unclenched his fist. Eduardo wiped dirt and shoe prints away from his corduroys and eyed his girlfriend in the distance. "Catch' ya later Arleen—gotta take my little brother to the doctor." Eduardo then wrapped his arms around Victor and gingerly guided him towards their way home. "Does it hurt?"

Victor winced in pain, "Yah."

"Does it hurt when you breathe?"

"Yah."

"Then try not to breathe," he joked, trying to get a smile out of him. "I'm sorry for leaving like that."

Victor looked up at Eduardo. "It's OK Eduardo, they finally let me bat. I hit a line drive out past second base! Then they got mad at me because the stupid bat broke. I didn't break it Eduardo, I swear I didn't! The bat was already busted."

"I know Victor, I know. They're just jealous of you 'cause you hit the ball so far."

"You think so?"

"I know so. Now, what are we gonna tell Mama? She's going to be real upset."

"Do you want me to cover for you?"

Eduardo smiled. Brotherly love, there was nothing like it. "Will you? Tell Mama I was there, but didn't get to you fast enough?"

"Sure Eduardo, I'll do anything for you."

"Thanks squirt...and I'll do anything for you too."

Victor and Eduardo lived in that house for several more years after the incident. Rosalba believed their story and took Victor to the hospital without ever knowing the truth. Victor was sent home with only bruised ribs, which could have been worse if Eduardo continued to be selfish with his aroused girlfriend. Those boys never did bother Victor again. In fact, one of the boys befriended Victor and they've been buddies ever since.

"I need to take a vacation."

Eduardo blinked back from the daydream. "Vacation?"

The waitress approached the two men again and set down their food. "Will there be anything else?" She asked in a seductive timbre staring at Eduardo.

Victor cast up at the girl, rested his eyes back on Eduardo then shook his head.

"I think we're good," Eduardo gave back to her. He doesn't give her a second glance as she walked away and rested his eyes back on Victor who was grinning from ear to ear. "What?"

"What?" Victor said, hushing his voice down so that nearby patrons couldn't hear him. "Eduardo that chick ***wants*** you."

Eduardo shook it off. "...And?"

"...And Eduardo, you're married, remember? You've got to keep your ***palo*** in your pants now."

Eduardo choked on his food. ***No shit.*** Instantly brought to mind that burning kiss he had with Victor's wife. "Relax Victor, she's not my type."

"Not your type? That chick was ***hot.*** And she's a blonde; I thought blondes were your type."

Eduardo eyed his little brother shoving a mouthful of hamburger down his throat. Remembered the last time he'd seen Amber wrapped around Victor in embrace. "Yah well, amazing how you grow up."

Victor started to laugh. "I never thought you'd grow up Eduardo. But here you are...this macho attorney, making all this money and ***monogamous."***

Eduardo's guilty conscious overwhelmed him. "Yah, well...it was time, don't you think?"

"Yah," Victor agreed, wiping off his mouth with a napkin. "Just thought you'd be a skirt chaser for the rest of your life!"

Eduardo didn't think it was funny and actually thought it was demeaning of him to think so. "I think you were talking about taking a vacation before?"

"Yah...Amber and I were talking the other night and want to get away, just the two of us. I thought it would be fun if you and Leticia would come along. Maybe we could get Mama to watch the kids and take off to Vegas or something? Whadda say?"

Eduardo's serious expression dropped to a scowl. First of all, that remark about ***'just the two of us'*** sent him raving into another dimension, just proved to him further that Amber wasn't deliberating their chemistry nearly as much as he was. Secondly, he'd rather sit on Judge Monroe's lap sucking a lollipop than continually watch Victor and Amber embrace again. Thirdly, and most definitely last, display his lack of attraction towards his wife ***and*** pretend to be deliriously happy with Leticia when he knew he wasn't? No thank you! ***Good God, Vegas?*** Possibly share a room with the two? Maybe even get an eyeful of Amber bra-less once more under silk pajamas?

"Eduardo?"

Eduardo blinked back from another fantasy. "Huh?"

"I asked you if you wanted to take a vacation with us, nothing long and drown-out, only a couple of days."

"I'm not sure Victor," Eduardo stated, looking down at his wrist watch, "I'll have my Assistant check my calendar and let you know soon."

"Yah—no hurry, just mention it to Amber when you see her at work later and tell her what we talked about."

Eduardo took in his little brother's faith in him. It was so difficult not to exploit his desire for his wife. "I will." He barely got out and rose from his chair.

Victor went to shake his brother's hand but pulled in closer instead to give Eduardo a short fond squeeze. "Give Amber a peck for me, huh? Tell her I'll see her later. Hey, thanks for lunch, we should do this more often!" Victor exclaimed on his way out the entrance.

Eduardo froze watching his little brother exit unaware of his devious intentions. Give Amber another ***kiss?*** He meant too and soon. Not coming into contact with her was driving him to the depths of insanity. He sighed when he remembered what he'd said to Victor just a few seconds ago. ***He'd grown up,*** became this faithful husband unwavering physically, but by no means mentally. Each night since meeting that raven enchantress, he's thought of nothing else significant but how to find the opportunity to penetrate her.

CHAPTER**SEVENTEEN**

Measuring Too Close

One night Amber had an erotic dream about her brother-in-law. It was so intense, she woke up wanting more. It left her impassioned and she practically attacked Victor in his sleep, forcing him to make love to her, which he did. She was grateful for the satisfaction, but it still left a void.

Amber was totally infatuated with Eduardo now. Fantasizing about him constantly she was besieged by his effect on her. That kiss practically ate her alive. She was constantly in a haze, a daze, spinning out of control. She never met a man who simply ***loved*** to kiss. Kisses that started off slow then rose to elevated degrees, concentrated kisses that were measured and full of delight.

Amber's first kiss was when she was fourteen. Even though it was a dare, Amber still counted it as her first real kiss. The boy kept a hand on her bottom the whole time. He was sloppy with bad-breath, but she'll never forget those first initial feelings of awareness, her body twitching with glee, that 'kissing' went hand-in-hand with sensations felt elsewhere. After her first kiss there were plenty of others and after her breasts formed, boys took to her like a moth to a flame. If they could get to first base, then they could easily get to second? Right? She was just Trailer Trash anyways. French kissing, sloppy wet kisses, close-mouthed kisses, feathered kisses; nothing compared to what she felt with this ***last*** kiss. Heaven help her now that she had experienced ***the*** unsurpassed kiss she would ever come across. He grabbed the back of her neck, arched her head up with his grip so that he could maintain control. Amazing, that he felt he knew he held the power that she wouldn't try to run away. His lips, so velvety soft, kissed her passionately, with affection, wonder and interest combined. His mouth slowly opened, impulsively she unrestricted hers. His tongue moved sensuously around the exterior of hers, lunging and binding in a wondrous waltz. She has no memory of moaning in his mouth, but she recalled it now. Good Lord, she never encountered a feeling so rhythmical, so experienced and unconditionally marvelous! Instantaneously, her breasts ached for his touch and the fire between her legs throbbed to be extinguished. Completely under his spell now, anything he desired was his for the taking. She not only found him irresistible, but knowing the flavor of him affected Amber in such a way as to pine further contact.

At work, she would have to stop and catch her breath. She would be typing some brief, and then suddenly, her train of thought would escape to a daydream about Eduardo. Amber made an internal arrangement with herself that if she didn't flirt, or didn't act on her preoccupation with her brother-in-law, then she was allowed to cheat with him in her dreams. It was a good treaty, don't you think? Eduardo was safe to think about in fantasy, but she wasn't allowed to follow-through with the actual sin. Or was that a sin too?

It was difficult to work with him actually. Just knowing he was somewhere in the vast ocean of private doors on the same floor as she was nerve-wracking as hell. The Century City office was on the 25th floor of the Bank of America building on Avenue of the Stars and Amber was suddenly tossed in with all the big boys and their authority hungry secretaries. And you can't call them "secretaries" anymore, oh no, they're appointed titles like, "Lead Legal Assistant", or "Executive Legal Assistant", or Amber liked this one the best, "Executive III Lead Legal Assistant." She was considered a floater (title= "Pee-On"), latching onto whatever case needed an extra hand. But she didn't mind really, it gave her more time to escape in thought. Dream about Eduardo—who, by the way—was off mitigating a case downtown, thank God, otherwise, she wouldn't be able to even type a single word much less finish a trial brief.

There were fifteen legal ~~secretaries~~ Assistants in the office, fifteen power striving temperamental hormonal bitchy females, always griping about one thing or the other: excessive e-mail, file space, clerk wars and one office manager from hell. Never mind about teamwork, every Assistant was out for number one. Catfights were a daily occurrence at Aldridge & Watson, arguments so immense it would shape the entire staff. And Amber couldn't believe all the idle-gossip that passed through the halls at the law firm so liberally. One of the Legal Assistants was sleeping with two of the Attorneys and all three were OK with it. Who just filed for bankruptcy; whose husband/wife/child was in rehab; who just suffered a miscarriage; and, who might be pregnant, the chatter went on and on. And talk about the change in scenery! Over the hill, in the San Fernando Valley (where she used to work), workers were pretty much laid back and informal, while across the posh neighborhood of Beverly Hills, Century City mostly consisted of the material conscious work force. Men and women alike wore Prada. You had to be seen driving a BMW, Mercedes or Lexus, and if you were doing well, a convertible Beemer (BMW), Mercedes or Rolls Royce. Everyone had to own a million-dollar home or be renovating one. And your children went to private schools, the institutions that made you linger years and years on a "waiting list" with a panel of judges.

Before she got there, Eduardo was the hot topic of the past several years. His maverick outer appearance was uncustomary for a Westside defender, let alone a Harvard Law School grad. Eduardo A. Sanchez, Esq. presented himself as a class act, the dutiful worker and the unwavering ant. He mostly kept to himself while in the office, never offering information about his home life, or personal. He was aloof, mysterious, and the Assistants all wished he'd give them more time than just a passing greeting to be honest. He was the center of attention way before Amber walked through that door. And with Amber joining the pool, everyone plunged into being envious of Amber and her close proximity to the great Attorney at Law. She was considered the enemy as of late and the ladies oftentimes showed their resentment towards Amber by ignoring her. Amber was talked about constantly behind her back. She was placed on a platform for all the Legal Assistants to take pot shots at. It was unbearable until one afternoon Amber decided that enough was enough and she began to play their little game, deciding to offer little tidbits of private information about Eduardo so the witches would leave her alone. She informed them of how Eduardo looked in shorts, shirtless and even in a Speedo. ***That*** little bit of information sent the Assistants into a tizzy!

Amber was at her desk, searching for a file when she spotted Eduardo making an entrance in the corner of her eye. His office was down the hall to the right (usually out of viewing distance from her desk) but suddenly he was there, walking towards the Assistant quad.

Amber didn't dare glance up at him. Looking up at him would make it obvious to the other ladies that she was just as interested in him as they were. No, she had to make sure she was still impartial, couldn't care less.

Turned out, Eduardo was heading towards his Personal Assistant, (oh yeah, there's another title) Jackie Medina. Amber didn't like Jackie simply because she reminded her too much of Leticia. Jackie was Hispanic as well and young; a tasteful, pretty well dressed woman with short-feathered brunette hair and dark eyes. Jackie was chosen as the lucky one who took dictation and sat in meetings alongside Eduardo. Yes, Amber hated Jackie, and when Eduardo talked with Jackie, Amber fumed with jealousy.

"Jackie, where's that London file? I can't seem to find it."

Jackie stood up, walked over to the filing cabinet and began searching the cabinets 'K through M'. Meanwhile, Eduardo stood there in between four other Assistants (who by the way) stopped their typing. Eduardo's presence center stage made everyone tense, including Amber. But Amber tried to contain her enthusiasm for his intimacy and pretended to scroll for a file on her computer already bouncing away on screensaver mode.

Eduardo sauntered over to Amber's desk, knocked on the

side with a greeting. "What'cha working on?" He asked, focusing on her monitor not her body.

"Dawson versus August Executives, that sexual harassment case that Doug is working on."

"Oh," Eduardo concluded letting go a sigh.

On dangerous ground, Amber scanned him quickly. Wearing no jacket; a royal blue cotton shirt with argyle tie blasted back at her. He looked marvelous, he smelled amazing and that overwhelming sensation of grabbing that yoke and greeting his tongue took over her reason.

They didn't need conversation to know what the other was thinking. Their bodies spoke volumes. Amber was apprehensive, fidgety with anticipation. Eduardo was agitated, holding himself back from snatching her again.

"Here it is," Jackie exclaimed, breaking the unbearable silence and desperate chemistry of the moment.

"Thanks," Eduardo gave to her. He reached out for the folder and then walked away, ignoring Amber on purpose.

Amber watched him as he sauntered out of view.

"God, he looks especially yummy today," she heard one of the Legal Assistants assert.

Amber continued to gape in the direction of where Eduardo left. Two of the Assistants cast her way. Amber realized they were staring at her. "What?" Amber asked openly.

"Don't tell me you don't find him the least bit attractive," Dolores asked probing. In her mid-thirties, Dolores was a divorced mother of two.

Amber gulped. "Guilty," she maintained, holding out her palm.

"His wife is one lucky woman, what's her name again?"

Amber continued to stare down the hallway. "Amber—no, Leticia!"

Dolores started to hoot. "That's right, Leticia, what a beautiful name, she's probably drop dead gorgeous too."

Amber gazed at Dolores. "And very sweet," she added.

"Such a shame he's still not single. That man exudes so much sex appeal he should be able to give us all a sample."

Amber started chuckling, "Not when you've seen him

when he first wakes up, and believe me, he doesn't look so hot." Which was a downright lie. She turned around, and recalled her camping trip a few years back. Eduardo hated camping and didn't sleep a wink. There was no electricity in the bathrooms so his usual sleek hair was always mussed up and never bothered to comb it. He only brushed his teeth and avoided shaving all together. He was all scruffy and untidy, but he was still the most handsome man she had ever seen! Instead of being this fashionable attorney, Eduardo turned into ***laid-back mountaineer man***. Unbelievable that he could still hold quality in both margins.

Amber bore down the hallway again. No Eduardo. Her heart dropped. ***Oh how do I get him back here? Should I go to his office and bother him? What could I say? Could I ask for help on this case I'm working on, the sexual harassment case? Would he want to be involved? Would Doug care, get mad? Oh God, what do I do? What am I doing? Good Lord, what am I doing...This is crazy, insane...stop it Amber, stop it! Quit thinking about him so much...about that kiss the other day...oh God, why did he kiss me? And I'm such an idiot, I grabbed him back, you fool! Oh God I love the way he kisses...do I tell the girls*** that? ***Do I tell them that when he kisses you, it's so erotic you can't think of anything else but how to get him to hurry up and fuck you? Do I tell them that too? Good Lord this isn't funny...Oh God this is terrible, absolutely appalling...Oh God help me, what do I do?...What the hell am I doing? Oh Amber, you fool; what have you done? Oh God I want him so much. Oh God help me. Help me out of this, what do I do?***

CHAPTER **EIGHTEEN**

The Green-Eyed Monster

The firm's staff had been gathered together to wish Philip Aldridge, the partner in the firm a happy 60th birthday.

Amber had been attracted to Philip Aldridge straight away, he exuded the same traits she found so enticing in Eduardo; self-assurance, influence, and so much pride. Sable hair graying at the temples, always the most expensive suit and ties especially tailored for him. He was done with the law several years ago, should have retired ten years before, but just couldn't get the ***modus operandi*** out of his system.

"Happy birthday Mr. Aldridge, happy birthday to you..."

The various staff clapped and cheered, whistled and laughed. It was a happy carefree day. A couple of hours had been set-aside just for the occasion. Amber offered to cut the cake and passed it around to everyone. Jackie helped too, stuffing plastic forks into the cake's frosting so everyone could have a piece.

Amber grabbed two slices, walked around like the perfect little hostess and offered a piece to all the attorneys. She then handed a piece to a sitting Gordon Daggert. Gordon was equally eye-catching, but in a diverse style from Eduardo. Gordon had dusty blonde hair, blue eyes and a tanned complexion. The Assistants all swooned over him as well; Eduardo and Gordon were often gossiped about within the pool.

Gordon intentionally met eyes with Amber. "Thanks hun,"

he let go, diving in to receive the cake—he missed, and the piece went dumping into his lap.

Amber gasped, a smile embraced to her face, "Oh gee, I'm ***so sor-ree,"*** she exclaimed, making them the center of attention.

Eduardo was just a few feet away when he overheard the commotion, alarmed at the sight of Amber wiping off frosting from Gordon's center seam with her napkin.

Others around them began to express their amusement when Amber glared up and blushed at the blunder. Instantly, she stopped what she was doing and ambled away.

Eduardo looked straight at Gordon, inspected him as he surveyed Amber's derriere as she continued to walk down the hallway. Eduardo moved in. "You enjoy that?" He asked, his voice strictly indicating that he wasn't the least bit pleased.

"You bet," Gordon implied, lowering his own voice. "I often wonder to myself what'd be like to have those long sexy legs around my hips."

Eduardo fumed inside. "That's my brother's wife's ***ass*** you're staring at."

Gordon met eyes with Eduardo. "Relax Eduardo, it's not like I was going to act on it."

"Eduardo?" Philip Aldridge stepped in, obviously aware of the tension between the two associates. "Can I see you for a moment? There's a defamation case I'd like discuss with you."

Later, Amber was trying to finish up a respondent brief when in the corner of her eye; she beholds Eduardo making his arrival in the Assistants quad to see Jackie. Amber acted like she didn't see him. Turned around and took paper out of her printer and pretended to fill it with some more. She could sense that he was still within arm's reach, but didn't dare look in his direction. Heart beating practically in her ears now, she gazed up and watched Eduardo guide around her sector, avoiding her on purpose as well. His inattentiveness towards her brought moisture to her eyes.

"Amber, are you finished with that respondent brief?"

Amber looked away from Eduardo sauntering down the hall. Gazed over at Gordon, "I'm...nearly finished."

"Good, come with me to my office, I'd like to go over some inserts with you."

Despondent, Amber followed Gordon down the corridor and passed Eduardo's open door. She purposely glanced into his office to see what he was doing and found him at his desk working diligently away.

"I've been working on several new inserts that I need typed," Gordon said with authority. "Here's a tape to dictate, it's a full side." Amber reached out to get the micro cassette when Gordon consciously dropped it to the floor. Amber bent down to retrieve it; Gordon bowed down with her. "I'll get it." They both reached for the tape—both grabbed the cassette at the same time—his fingers touched hers ***deliberately***. She glanced up, his look was purely eager. She began to stand, he remained with her. Gordon brushed her shoulder with his hand. "We have to stop meeting like this."

If that wasn't a come-on line of the worst kind! Gordon leaned in to kiss her and Amber inclined to avoid his lips.

"Gordon."

Amber's head whirled around. Eduardo was standing in the doorway with his arms crossed across his chest.

Gordon retreated back around his desk. "What can I do for you Eduardo?"

"I'm here for Amber," Eduardo stated, clearly staking his claim.

Amber sensed the jealousy in Eduardo's voice. ***Good Lord!*** Did he ever look charming when he was bothered!

"Be right back Gordon," Amber said giving Eduardo a questionable glare as she walked passed him.

They met in the hallway, eye-to-eye. Clearly upset, Eduardo saluted his arm in the air as he expressed his annoyance. "He's already gone to bed with two other Assistants—are you next?"

Amber looked around them. A few of the Assistants heads bobbed up from hearing the hubbub in the hallway. Amber's mouth flew open wide. It was the drama she craved after all, the attention, the stage. Tickled with the fact that they could be seen simply ***conversing*** was stimulating beyond reason. "You've got a lot of nerve."

"You've got to be careful Amber, Gordon's a rascal, and he doesn't care who he hurts as long as he picks up what he wants."

"I can handle him; don't be so bothered with your brotherly protection over me."

"Brotherly protection, is that what you call this?" Eduardo asked of Amber now—pointing at her body then his.

Eduardo's worrying guise was simply amazing; it took Amber's breath away. But what was he trying to say? What was ***this?*** He was her brother-in-law; naturally he would look out for her, keep the wolves at bay. But Eduardo ***kissed*** her, and kissed her well, more so than a brother-in-law would ever imagine doing. Amber was still very uncertain about Eduardo and his sudden sense of compassion. She choked back tears; her tone was but a whisper now. "You're my brother-in-law plain and simple. Don't go thinking that you're anything else."

By Amber's continual inaction—and her constant pretending not to notice him when obviously she did—only proved to Eduardo further that her emotions were just as tumultuous as his. "I think we've already made that clear haven't we?"

His tone reflected a bit of sadness. It took every inch of her not to go and enfold him at that point. Amber actually saw Eduardo's broad shoulders slump. She sought to feel his body all over again; run her hands down his back and live through his hands surrounding her for a second time. "You kissed ***me***. I didn't seek that out."

"You kissed me back," Eduardo hushed down. "As I recall, there was just as much ***heat*** in that second kiss I care to remember."

"You still had no right to feel that you could just take advantage of my curiosity now did you?" A tear fell from her eye. She wiped it away, crossed her arms in irritation, in disappointment.

Eduardo noticed her eyes swell with tears; he wanted to seize her again and kiss those tears away! Good God, how much brotherly love could she resist? "I'd never take advantage of you."

What a dirty ***rotten*** scoundrel! He was worse than Gordon

Daggert playing with her emotions that way! Amber waited with baited breath. "Let's remember I'm married Eduardo—"

"***We're*** married," Eduardo corrected her, handling her shoulders now. He just couldn't help himself, not touching her ever was rendering him to pieces. And to his surprise...what a powerful certainty lie beyond that declaration. He ***did*** want to be married to her. He should have been married to her. He's never wanted to be married his entire life! It was Amber. Amber affected his train of logic. Curse the years of carrying that cross of not taking the goddamn chance when it arose years ago! He was a risk taker for crying out loud! Good God, how he'll always regret ***his*** inaction.

"Eduardo, aren't you done with that Thompson file yet?" Jackie exclaimed, not realizing that Eduardo had his hands still on Amber's shoulders.

Amber turned her back on Jackie, making sure that she didn't notice her crying. Her tears began to fall more freely at this point and the ache was so dreadfully bad. She practically ran down the hallway now, the respondent brief and cassette still clinched in her hands. ***This is not going to work. I can't do this anymore.*** Amber thought, running down the corridor. ***Why does he do this to me? Who does he think he is? Good Lord if that wasn't the purest display of jealousy then I don't know what is! Oh my God, does he feel the same way? Obviously, he must be attracted to me in some way; otherwise, he wouldn't have gotten mad so easily and wouldn't have kissed me the way he did. Maybe he was just curious. Maybe he was just acting brotherly, looking out for his sister-in-law. But that certainly wasn't a brother-in-law kiss! Oh God!***

Amber grabbed the ***pink bathroom*** key and darted out the front door. She didn't have to use the bathroom; she just wanted to get the hell out of the office. She was outside, alone in the hallway, when the door to the suite opened up. And there he was, following her again like some God damn magnet.

They stood there for a moment, Eduardo in the doorway and Amber in the hallway holding up a wall.

"You OK?"

"No."

"What do you want me to do?"

"Nothing."

Eduardo looked back into the suite, then back out at her. "Want to talk?"

"No."

Eduardo was downhearted. Amber could tell that much now. She, on the other hand was on the verge of tears. Amber turned away and began to walk back towards the ladies bathroom. Eduardo gazed back into the suite, kicked his shoe into the carpet and strolled back in.

Amber wiped away the tears that were now streaming down her face and sobbed on her way towards the bathroom. If living without him wasn't the purest form of torture, then being at work with him definitely ***was.***

CHAPTER **NINETEEN**
Passion Is Like a Drug

Amber was called into Dr. Watson's office. He was a short stocky impressive looking man in his late sixties, wise, and comfortable with his prestige and authority. "Amber, I like the way you work," he offered to her, motioning for her to take a seat. Martin Watson, who also held a degree in medicine, loved the law further and asked everyone to address him formally.

Amber was indebted, "Thank you Dr. Watson."

"Call me Martin please, Dr. Watson reminds me of Sherlock Holmes." He also ***loved*** throwing in that little joke to break the ice.

"OK," Amber smiled, appreciative of his openness.

"Amber, we were wondering if you were able to work overtime. I know you have a toddler, and we're considerate of your situation." He had an air about him that was patient and obliging.

"Yes I do, but we could use the money, so yes, I am able to work overtime." The sad truth was, Victor's hours had been cut from the waste department and they had been struggling financially for the past couple of months.

"Good, just what I wanted to hear. We'd like you to work on a defamation case, its long hours; you'd be here close to nine until we settle. The duration will take more than a year, will that be OK?" He expressed, hoping that she'd agree. It was a lot to ask of her, but she was first in line.

"I don't think that'll be a problem Martin." Amber smiled; she was offered a great opportunity. She would be able to collect over-time which paid outrageous money and Victor could stay home with the kids at night (which he never minded anyhow) and everything would work out swell.

"Good, you'll be working with Carson, Stephen, Cynthia and Eduardo. I don't perceive difficulty since the both of you are related."

Amber felt as if she just got punched in the face, or slapped—a rude awakening. "Eduardo?" She repeated off guard.

"Yes, is there a problem?" Martin regarded her empty look.

"No...No problem."

It was a defamation case. High Profile. Their client was suing a major newspaper, and Philip Aldridge assigned Eduardo, Amber and three other staff members to work on the case. It had to be a group effort, everyone involved expected to work like a machine.

Carson: A paralegal in his mid twenties, unattractive but with an awesome spiked hairdo (Amber thinks he's gay) exuded flamboyancy and worked side-by-side with Amber. He would throw in a little joke now and then to cut through the stress, and everyone would start laughing enjoying labor for a change.

Cynthia: An attorney in her late thirties was quiet, demur. A brunette a little on the plump side, sat beside Eduardo speaking quietly going over case cites. (Amber thinks she's gay too—but still in the closet).

Stephen: A law clerk in his early thirties, worked at a rapid pace. (Was he on cocaine? Amber often wondered) no one could work ***that fast***. He could read at the speed of light, run down the hallway to do Internet research, type up an outline and then back again all in the matter of moments.

"We need this copied," Carson asked of Amber.

"Sure, collated?" Amber asked back, watching Eduardo come to attention when she spoke in the corner of her eye. But she could always tell when Eduardo glanced her way—her senses began to pulsate.

"Yah, about...um, how many copies do you think we need Eduardo?" Carson asked, reaching over and grabbing the deposition out of Amber's hands.

Eduardo continued to be seated next to Cynthia. He made no effort to move. "Make around thirty for now."

"Twenty Eduardo," Cynthia spoke up not making any effort to look up from her work either.

Eduardo looked up from his brief, "Twenty, you sure? We need to serve the defendants tomorrow, Cynthia, right there we have ten companies."

"Thirty," Carson repeated handing the deposition back to Amber.

But she knew ***that***. Idiot, Eduardo was within hearing distance. "Thirty," she repeated under her breath. Amber marched down the foyer towards the copy room. Normally the firm would send out depositions to be copied, but on that night, they doubled up on meeting deadlines and there was no time to wait.

The copy room was once an office which basically looked more like a closet now with the expensive contraption, cases of copy paper, three fax machines and dozens upon dozens of office supplies located on shelves just above the machine. She opened up the face of the copier and began the long process of copying page by page. First page...her mind began to wander. Thoughts immediately drew to Eduardo. ***What are Leticia and Eduardo doing this weekend? Would they go over and visit The Family?*** Second page...***Good Lord, don't forget Victor called and asked you to bring home a package of diapers for Valentina.*** Third page...***I wonder when this project will end? I wonder how much time I'll have alone with Eduardo each night.*** Fourth page...***I wonder how much money I'll be making out of this***—Eduardo was there, in the copier room, she could smell his aftershave. Amber turned around thrilled then curious, "What're you doing?"

Eduardo just stood there—frozen—and looked at her in an undeniable way. "I'm trying to find a way around your body," Eduardo confessed, pointing up at the second shelf. "We need correction tape and I offered to get it."

Amber's mouth closed. ***Good Lord!*** She wanted to kiss him so severely. She took a step to her right and paved a way for him to reach over and grab the tape. Their shoulders brushed against one another. A blaze of sexual tension erupted and her body stiffened. Good Lord, if he didn't make her feel indiscreet! She wanted to grab his collar, feel his velvety lips on hers once more, tear open his shirt; kiss his bare chest, trail her mouth down and around his skin towards his crotch.

"Don't do that."

Amber had no way in realizing how her eyes being closed and her body so inviting caused Eduardo's self-control to topple over. Amber opened up her eyes. She doesn't remember closing them! "Don't do what?" She whispered back.

"Bite down on your lower lip like that." Eduardo expressed in a husky voice he ***never*** allowed her to listen to until now. "Close your eyes. Thrust your—" Eduardo stopped and practically ran out of that small space. Walking hurriedly towards the conference room, he cocked his head to one side and straightened out his tie trying to calm his arousal down. ***Damn her! Damn this situation! Damn it all!*** He was beginning to wonder about her working there. Before she started, he could build up the anticipation of seeing her and walk around aimlessly like a lovesick puppy. Now all she did was distract him all day long! Her hair, those lips, her body, her aroma, the way she smiled, the beautiful array of sunshine surrounding her face every...fricken'...time...she entered a room! Amber was beginning to affect him in ways ***no woman*** was ever to infiltrate, and that feat was an exalted hurdle to jump over.

It was business as usual two nights later. Eduardo and Amber kept it strictly production: typing, research, dictation, and modification. The third night was a different story. Eduardo was nervous around her—she was sheepish around him and their professionalism turned into noticeable awkwardness. The threesome finished their research early that day and went home leaving Eduardo and Amber alone in the conference room. Uninterrupted in the 20,000 square foot office suite space, it was nearing seven o'clock.

"Almost done?" Eduardo asked as he shuffled paper neatly inside a binder.

"One more paragraph."

Eduardo cleared his throat. "Amber...before you leave, do you have a moment to talk?"

Amber closed her eyes. She knew ***precisely*** what was on his mind; she just preferred not to hop through that hoop. "About what?"

"About us," Eduardo blurted out, tense and nervous once again.

Amber stopped her typing. Her heart dropped. ***The kiss...it was about the kiss.*** "What about us?"

"Will you look at me?"

Amber started typing again. Good Lord, no! His hypnotic gaze always took over her concentration. "Eduardo," she swallowed, staring straight at her monitor quickly trying to erase the grin on her lips. "What happened between us...has to remain forgotten like it never happened."

"What if I told you I'm unable to?"

That got her to turn around. "What?" She asked in disbelief.

Eduardo leaned forward in his chair, ran his hands down the front of his pant legs. "Am I imagining this…the chemistry that we share?"

He felt it too? "No," Amber confessed quietly, "But you hold chemistry with everyone."

"Not every woman," he expressed lightly.

"What are you trying to say?"

"Amber..." Eduardo hesitated, trying to find a way to be straightforward without being so ***direct.*** "...I can't stop thinking about you. Can't stop thinking about pleasuring you more than just kissing."

Amber's heart sunk. ***Good Lord!*** Talk about rascals! "Eduardo stop it—don't say anything else. Oh my God, this is ***so*** bad, this is so wrong! Just shut up."

"You're in denial."

"I am?"

Eduardo laughed, she was so cute. ***"I am.*** I'm sure you can see my carefulness when we talk sometimes."

"I notice...something," Amber voiced, her smile dwindling to a solemn gaze.

"Look at you," Eduardo determined, "Look at ***me,*** our borders are going to destroy us both."

Amber's heart was racing. She couldn't help but beam. She took his severe inquiring and turned it into silliness. "Are you trying to seduce me?"

Eduardo was deadly serious initially. Now, he couldn't help but joke along with her. "I was—is it just cause?"

Amber was enthralled by Eduardo's erotic degree. "Honestly?"

"Indeed."

Amber gathered her documents together and walked over to Eduardo's side and placed them on his workspace. She purposely caught his eyes and confirmed, "I concur counselor."

She was flirting with him now and Eduardo was no longer apprehensive and couldn't stop his mission if he wanted to. Amber began to walk away when Eduardo grabbed her waist from behind. "Can I ask you something else?"

His hands on her body sent chills up her spine. Amber rolled her eyes, "Sure."

Eduardo tediously turned her around and bore up into her stare. He was still seated but his hands remained on her waist. "You feel comfortable with me right?"

Amber looked intently down at him; she knew she shouldn't but just couldn't help herself. His green eyes were piercing, entrancing and instantly thinned her posture. "If I didn't, your hands wouldn't be resting on my hips."

Eduardo chortled, circled his eyes around her face. "We've been friends for quite awhile haven't we?"

"Yes we have," she agreed, her eyes not venturing off from his measured seduction.

"And every time I look at you, tell me what you feel."

Amber's throat closed up. She was already in love with the man, why shouldn't she know the rest?

He noted her tension, "Be honest."

"The truth?"

"And nothing but."

Amber held still for a moment and ran through all the holidays when she was not able to see him. All those long lonely days unable to visit the man she now loved. "Restraint."

Eduardo closed his eyes. ***That*** blew his mind away. All these years he'd been longing to touch her like this, yearning to kiss her lips, feel her quiver beneath him in contact, she had been feeling the very same limitations? But somehow, he knew that she felt similar deep down in his soul. He knew they'd come full circle, knew they'd make love one day. He was so goddamn sure of it; it was the insight that had been so upsetting all these years. She was ***his***, born to be his mate.

"I know you're afraid of what you feel," he said in a hushed voice, "But I sit before you already a conquered man." Eduardo conceded, his fingers digging into her torso. "I've had to restrain myself as well and I can't fight it anymore, I want to surrender to this moderation. I'm staggered by your beauty, drunk from your aroma, silenced by your mere presence in a room... Help me Amber, set me free...help us to let go."

His confession had such a weakening effect on her. Her emotions were in an uproar. ***Is this a fantasy? Good Lord, I really need to wake the hell up.*** "Eduardo," she professed, trying to find the words. "We're both married; kissing each other once should be as far as we ***ever*** go."

"Amber that kiss the other day, was me desiring to know what it felt like to finally taste you," he reasoned, removing his hands from her waist. "But that kiss didn't quite settle my greed Amber; I request to know ***all of you."***

"Eduardo," Amber softly expressed, trying ever so hard to believe every word that he said. "What the hell are you telling me?"

Eduardo grabbed her hands now; Amber was still inches apart from him and hadn't left his side. Eduardo closed his eyes and began caressing her hands within his. His heart was pounding uncontrollably; he's never wanted someone so much, never had to ***beg*** his entire life! "I want to be with you."

"I'm here now, you ***are*** with me."

He smiled, "No, not like that. I want to make love to you."

Amber now backed away and released her hands from his. "Stop it Eduardo, this isn't cute anymore."

"You think I'm feeding you a line?" He asked unbelieving.

"I don't know what you're doing, but it isn't funny...and it's downright cruel if you ask me."

Eduardo rolled his eyes, shook his head. "I've never wanted a woman more than I want you Amber. What you hear is the truth, what you've assumed and what you've heard from others is all speculation. I'm very selective Amber and I don't apportion myself with just everyone."

Apportion? Is that a fancy word for share? Amber stared at his position. ***Of course not,*** she realized***. And doesn't he look confident as he leans back against the conference room table, crossing his arms over his chest observing me taking in a deep, deep breath of paranoia.*** But then she noticed him suffering his own gulp of air. ***He wants me…I'm his selective choice. Should I allow myself to feel this special? I hold the power now with my decision. I do…me, and I can either succumb to this desire or continue to keep him…and myself…in bondage.***

He waited on her progression until her mind finished contemplating her next move. "Why is it so hard to believe that I want to be with you?" He said, holding his ground. There was still uncertainty in her eyes. If it were his decision to make he wouldn't have inquired. His commanding prurient nature would have taken over and her nails would be digging in his back in a matter of seconds. No, he was going to leave it up to her to make the decision for them. If she felt the same desire—she just admitted that she did—then she would make the first move. But if she wanted to continue restricting herself—Good God his emotions tortured his heart just thinking about it—then he would never be able to be around her again.

Good Lord, what should she do? Where was that etiquette book? The one that tells you how to act when your brother-in-law tells you he wants to make love to you? Amber couldn't say anything else her breathing was so sporadic. ***One time. No one would know. We're alone in the office; it's the perfect opportunity. A secret to bury deep for all eternity. Oh hell! Why am I still trying to be proper when all that drains me is being improper with him?***

"I wanna be with you too," Amber at last declared.

No longer at her mercy, Eduardo abruptly returned to his sexual prowess and slowly emerged her, like a wolf stalking its prey. "Do you trust me?"

"Yes."

Eduardo grabbed her hand again and led her out the conference room.

How funny, Amber thought for a second, ***to be holding hands with him.*** It didn't even feel odd or out of place, it felt natural, easy, and that scared the hell out of her! Eduardo led them down the hallway and towards the entrance of the suite.

"Where we going?" Amber halted, pulling him backwards.

Eduardo slowly turned around, "If we're going to do this right, then we're headed to a hotel."

"When is an affair ever right?"

Eduardo agreed with her smiling, "Amber, if this is my one night with you…then I want it to be a night ***you'll*** remember."

CHAPTER**TWENTY**

An affair of the Heart

All expanse of time evaporated as Amber reopened her eyes to find herself alone with Eduardo inside an unrecognizable hotel room. Where the heck were they? And when did she first realize she was there? The more she surveyed the space, the further she realized that it must have been one expensive hotel. A fireplace in a sitting area, two sofas and love seat, antique armoires with hi-tech electronics, even a small kitchen, ***no rather***, a grand kitchen, with a bar, and a 26 cu. Ft. side-by-side platinum Kenmore. A separate bedroom that housed a big bed—no, rather a massive mattress with four mammoth posts on either side made of impressive carved mahogany. The walls were even papered with some kind of silky padded fabric and there were bouquets and sprays of flowers everywhere! Fresh flowers of pink and red roses, orange Gerberas, yellow lilies, and white daisies! The room was very beautiful and oh so romantic; she couldn't stop being so incredulous over it.

"You all right?"

Under some kind of spell, Amber wandered over to the balcony area; she thought she heard waves crashing against a current. "Are we by the ocean?"

"Yah, we're in Malibu," Eduardo stated, pressing a button on the wall to light the automatic fireplace. The hearth lit up like a miniature bonfire.

Seeing the waves continuously crunch up against the rocks down below confirmed that she really was in a hotel room. She looked beyond the balcony and noticed impressions of tiny little lights twinkling beyond the horizon. "How pretty," she managed to say.

"Come back inside," he coaxed behind her.

Amber blinked out of her trance and eyed Eduardo slowly approaching. With one simple move, he smoothed down her shoulders and took her hand and led her back into the room. She tried to focus on only him and concentrated on his calmness and unaffectedness. He gently caressed her cheek, the soft dimple on her chin, circled his eyes around her face soaking up her stance and uncertainty. "Now that it's happening, I don't know what to do."

Eduardo remained composed and resumed touching her face. Amber took in every detail of his features so close up to hers. His verdant stare, the few waves of hair sticking up and around his earlobe, the tiny little scratch alongside his jaw line and his velvety lips, ***oh those lips***...she wanted to kiss those lips...

"I'll show the way," he coerced, bringing his hands up to her head.

Amber's heart dropped, ***Good Lord...what comes next!***

He gently pulled out the clip that held up her hair; the length of her mane fell decoratively around her shoulders. Amber's eyes remained with his as she watched Eduardo's face change from tender to beguiling.

Eduardo ran his fingers tenderly through the soft duration. "I promise you," he uttered while ravishing her long hair, "You won't regret it."

Yes, yes, a thousand times yes! "I won't, huh?"

"You won't," he gruffly replied, "You may even like it."

"I'll be the judge of that," Amber whispered, entranced; she wanted him just to take her already.

Eduardo entwined his fingers with hers and held her hands for a moment. He absorbed her posture and felt her shivering. "I'm not gonna hurt you," he reassured her, "Unless, you want me too."

Oh...dear...God, the man was naughty. The indecency in his eyes, followed by his perseverance smashed Amber's resistance to smithereens. Rapidly, she realized the man had walked her backwards and cornered her into a wall, his ample frame possessing her. She couldn't think straight; she definitely couldn't breathe, Eduardo's solid body had compressed against hers suddenly in a delicious, untamed way. Pressed against her privately, his leg parted hers and his erection teased her abdomen.

"Relax. Don't think...explore."

Amber continued to hold both his hands when Eduardo guided her arms behind his backside. Her chest moved up and down sporadically, she wanted him to just hurry up. She allowed her arms to extend behind his back to feel the tightness of his shoulders, ***oh God, he was amazing...***His lower hind, ***dear God and he was so solid...***she was allowed to handle him, but he wasn't permitting himself to touch her?

Eduardo didn't kiss her immediately, but gradually skimmed her neck with feather-like kisses. Closing her eyes, Amber tilted her head sideways to welcome the thrilling bewitchment. Catching her breath barely, his lips brushed hers slightly, not kissing her, but teasing her, then across her face emerging towards the back of her ear, kissing her there instead.

What a mischievous little taunt he was, she thought as she straightened out her head as he successively withdrew. Amber gleamed purposely into his eyes, lost in the deep green of them. He wanted her—she wanted him as well. She waited so long...

Amber bent forward and glided her lips across his obligingly. Eduardo wavered, held off from devouring her until he knew for certain she would surrender fully without any remorse. Her body was still trembling from nervousness; he would have to calm her down first. "Be mine," he asked compassionately, his lips back on the crux of her neck. "Just once...be mine."

His body motionless, heart pounding against heart, still hadn't allowed his hands to touch her. Instead, Eduardo left them flat on the wall behind her head and permitted Amber to roam his body at will. Allowing his warmth to comfort her, his mouth trailed sensuously alongside her neck.

With Amber's gentle fondle, she proceeded to wander his physique. Up his chest, down his legs, every caress increased her sensitivity. She rested on his erection and lightly outlined the shaft with her fingers. My God...he didn't even flinch but rather, let out a throaty groan and allowed her to handle his awakening. Hastily, Amber pulled his shirt from within his tucked trousers, anxious to feel more of him.

Feeling Amber's hands trying to nudge at his belt, Eduardo all the same set aside his arms and brought his mouth up and around her ear to allow the heat of his breath to dive inside her earlobe, twirling, infiltrating simultaneously and transporting Amber into a depth of proficient bliss.

He's an expert, Amber decided, as he left her ear for her wide-open mouth. Again, that sensational tongue of his, calling out for hers to dance, igniting sensuous fires within, she held his body tightly, why hadn't he touched her yet?

So much confidence in the way one arm remained level behind her head, while the other slid across her bottom without hesitation. Responding naturally to his commands, she spread her legs further apart while Eduardo lifted up her skirt. His hand slid beneath her underwear and caressed her bare skin, bringing her buttocks fully into him subsequently kissing and grinding her erotically.

Finally yes, oh finally, Eduardo's hands were entirely on her breasts now, kneading and tweaking her nipples through her blouse. Without breaking his connection with her lips, he anxiously unbuttoned the silky fabric grasping to get to the skin underneath her bra. Amber assisted his hands and watched in awe as her camisole and bra escaped her upper body in one clever effortless flow.

Eduardo brought his eyes down to her bosom. No longer nervous, Amber had arched her back slightly to display her tantalizing crest. Stunning even a female aficionado like him, her points were marvelous and proportionately perfect. Impulsive and oh so interested, he touched the soft under belly of her satiny mounds with his knuckles.

"You're even more beautiful than I imagined," he quietly mouthed. "I'm so attracted to you."

"You are?"

"Can't you tell?" He commented in jest, bringing her hand down to grope his heightened erection.

Amber blushed and bit down on her lower lip. That did it, hook, line and sinker. Amber had never been more aroused, her heat quickly swelled to a torrid point. He was that talented.

Sampling her kiss repeatedly, with the palms of his hands, Eduardo delicately glided over her hardened nipples. With his thumb and forefinger, he began to play with the tips of her nubs, rubbing and tweaking them in pure awe of their form and texture. The thunderous sensation caused Amber to moan as she lightly eased his face away from her mouth and down to her bust.

Amber was enthralled. His words, his manner, they were just too much to adopt...***and oh...Good Lord***...his tongue, so savage and animalistic, licked and kissed without inhibition. She gazed down at his head and ran her fingers through his nut-brown locks and watched him trying to devour every dimension of her upper body. ***Oh...dear God***...her husband never exploited his tongue the way her brother-in-law pleasurably demonstrated. Her restraint set aside; she pulled down his pants at length. Never in her life had she felt so completely willing to pleasure someone in return. She wanted to consume him—his mouth, his wonderful fingers, his enormous formation.

Eduardo's never been this stimulated by a female before. His heart raced—never been this high strung. He's usually invariant, regulating every sensation, but with Amber, Good God his sensitivity over powered him and he was out of control. He was on the brink of absolute rapture when Amber held him off for a moment. Did she lose her fucking mind? "What—what's wrong?"

Both breathing rapidly, her eyes lock with his. "Allow me," Amber confessed, placing space between them, "***...to know all of you,"*** she revealed in a soothing timbre. Amber unraveled his tie, tugged at the button of his collar and unbuttoned his shirt—exposing that firm sexy chest of his—and ***viola***—that gold chain she remembered seeing the very first day they met. A crucifix, she realized, brushing her fingers above the cross and straightening it so it hung directly in the center of his ribs. How many times had she dreamt of doing that very same thing? Hundreds upon hundreds of restless nights, tossing and turning until she woke up in a cold sweat? Amber's never desired someone as much as she did this man. She bent forward and kissed the cross, kissed his chest. Her heart was about burst as she ran her fingers up and around his muscles...***Oh God...HE was beautiful***...his chest hair, his shoulders. She gradually shed his shirt from his upper body, trying to memorize every ruffle of his rigid bronzed skin. Grazed his flat stomach first then progressively ran her fingers towards his groin, leisurely withdrawing his boxers.

Amber brought her eyes down to all the glory between his legs. She didn't know what to expect (or even believe Leticia's comment about Eduardo being ***large)*** but as soon as she witnessed his grandeur firsthand, she knew instantly that he was bigger than Victor...greater by far.

"You're," Amber whispered, bringing her eyes up from his incredible body, "Magnificent."

Eduardo was about to detonate. Amber's examination of his manhood and what he was about to extend only increased his urge to please her.

"You're the one who's beautiful Amber," he tenderly expressed, running his hand through her tresses to the base of her neck and deeply kissing her. He guided their bodies towards the bed. Amber laid down first, allowing Eduardo to kick off the rest of his clothes and pull down Amber's skirt and underwear and lie across her at last.

Eduardo pulled up on his arms and awarded Amber a sensuous kiss, delving deeper and earnest with every twist and turn of his tongue and hunger.

Her breasts throbbed, her stomach churned, the heat between her legs burned with an uncomfortable pang—all this from one incredible kiss. Within closing her eyes, Amber felt the sensitive graze of his rare expertise. Eduardo Sanchez was hers for one night, and Amber required every sensation, each and every delectable touch of his mouth, his solid muscles, the sweet taste of his skin, his masculine aroma and openly welcomed the intrusion of his ingenuity. On the verge of lunacy she desired his domination. Opening her legs wider, she awaited his invasion—where was it? Instead, Eduardo allowed his stiff cock to brush against her inner thigh, teasing and tormenting her as he continued to feast on her midriff, legs and bare side.

"My condom," he spoke short of breath.

"You don't need it," Amber quietly affirmed roaming his sinewy buttocks.

"I don't?"

His hesitancy alerted her conscious, "Unless there's something you don't want me to have," she voiced, continuing to revel at his uncommon virility and glorious pressure against her cleft.

"The only thing I want you to ***have*** dear girl is a blissful expression."

Amber caressed the stubble on his cheeks and kissed his velvety soft lips, "Then trust me, you don't."

Eduardo does trust her. There shouldn't be a reason ***not*** to trust her. Amber was in the same predicament as he was. If they got pregnant, she would be as much to blame, but he didn't want to even think about such an outcome when all that revolved in his brain was this one opportunity of being with her. Her humor, her allure, her friendship, her incredible body, he's never been more certain of a woman. He loved everything about her. Good God, what was missing?

Without variation, Amber tried desperately to entice him into her silky warmth. She bounced her hips up, she arched her back, she grabbed and pawed at his buttocks, but he didn't budge. "Eduardo," she pleaded, noticing he was ignoring her solicitation.

Eduardo leaned in and consistently fluttered over her skin with agonizing gratifying action. "Not yet."

Amber grabbed his face within her hands, "Please," she begged, looking down at him continuing to feed her insanity.

With both hands fully cupping her breasts, Eduardo positioned his mouth between her legs, blowing and tonguing the sides of her thighs. He didn't rush in, but rather unbalanced her with the sensation of a possible attack. Each subtle impact coiled her stomach causing her buttocks to buck with anticipation.

"Oh God, you don't have to do that," Amber cried,

bringing her hands up to her forehead disbelieving how knowledgeable he was of the female anatomy. "Eduardo, ***please***."

Eduardo pulled up slightly and swirled his tongue in and around her navel, leaving a wake of moisture towards the tips of her rosy peaks then engulfed them fully with his wet heat.

Wound up and scorched, Amber pulled his head away from her bosom and urged her tongue inside his mouth. Eduardo met her swallow with enthusiasm, wild and anxious, grabbed the small of her back and lifted her hips up nudging her legs wider with his knee and independently impelled his solid flesh into her. Astonished from the surprise blockade, Amber fathomed how bulky he was and let out a pleasurable moan, adjusting to meet him rhythm for rhythm. Eduardo remained pressing his tongue-wet inside her mouth, dynamic gratification; it only makes her groan for more. Feeling him practically buried to her womb, she clutched his tail end and wrapped both hands around his rear, meshing them hip-to-hip.

"Good God, you feel so good." Eduardo stressed through clenched teeth.

A wild, unfamiliar, insatiable lust surfaced that Amber could not control. The farther she explored his outburst for her, the further it was met. Amber too was on the threshold of climax. "Oh God!" She exclaimed as well, throwing her head back in stimulation, suffering an intense, ongoing climax, blooming and tingling down to the tips of her toes.

Savoring the sound of her sweet ecstasy, Eduardo strained his fit arms and searched her eyes for fulfillment. Once satisfied, he held his post for a few more seconds thereupon released the explosion that's fully plagued him.

Languidly lying back down on her body, Eduardo buried his head in the crux of her neck, kissing her throat with fluttering joy.

Good Lord...that was absolutely wonderful, Amber thought wandering the muscles on his back with her eyes back closed. ***There was absolutely no concentration on my part; he was not only an expert in enhancement, but in formula. I'm gonna need him more than once,*** Amber realized while forcing her eyes open.

Eduardo stared down at Amber as her eyes slowly opened. He couldn't comprehend what emotions were fulfilled. Was it lust? Was it a necessity? Was he...***in love?*** That, by far, was the finest sexual encounter he ever owned. Whatever the emotion he felt only increased his appetite to be with her.

Amber grabbed his face. His heightened green eyes transformed back to softness and light. He was serious...too grim. And she...well, she was overwhelmed with love. She spat out the first thing that popped in her head. "That was simply ***terrible*** Eduardo," she teased, kissing him lightly on the lips. "I thought you'd be better than that."

Eduardo tsked at her temporary insanity. "On the contrary dear girl," he playfully confessed, intimately bringing her in. "I expected more from someone I've dreamt of making love to since meeting her." He wrapped his arms behind her shoulders and tenderly kissed her on her cheek. "This counsel motions the court for an extension to plead his case," he whispered vehemently.

"We have to go home," she heard herself say.

"I am home," he quietly voiced, circling his mouth on the base of her throat.

Amber smiled inwardly and closed her eyes. Eduardo's thickness moved within her and obsession briskly flowered. Feeling secure surrounded by him, she allowed him to make love to her a second time as comfort, ease, warmth and euphoria lingered all around.

"Absolutely Mr. Sanchez," she expressed tranquil roaming his muscular backside once again, "Your motion is hereby granted."

CHAPTER**TWENTY-ONE**

In the Palm of Her Hand

"Are you avoiding me?"

Amber swiveled around in her office chair and glared into the eyes of the most handsome lover she ever had. She knew now that Eduardo's upper body was glossy silk spread over rigid muscles. His chest hair thinned downhill and lay atop a phenomenal reward. His legs strong, his tongue and mouth sinful, and when he climaxed, he closed his eyes as if in agony and the most arousing expression materialized.

Eduardo stood nonchalant with a tint of irritation spread over his raised eyebrows.

She rather liked seeing him perturbed. Amber tried to disguise her grin by biting down on her lower lip. "Whatever gave you that idea?" She teased.

"I tried calling your house," Eduardo hushed down, "Over the weekend, tried several times in fact, but I was strained to hear the answering machine."

Amber thought how convenient it was to keep Eduardo guessing by having Adrian's soccer game on Saturday, dinner out with her mother and sister Saturday night and Valentina's ***Mommy and Me*** classes on Sunday to help occupy her time. "I had things to do."

Eduardo heavily sighed. Her sturdy body posture, along with her swift attitude disheartened his certainty. "Having second thoughts?"

Amber marveled at his woebegone façade. "About what?"

Eduardo pensively looked down at the floor, "Never thought I'd be so easy to forget."

Amber smiled, "Refresh my memory?"

Eduardo met her exuberance; "You look dazzling by the way."

"You don't have to continue to say things like that."

"Attention from me is rare Amber, when you have it, enjoy it."

Amber crossed her legs mechanically and caught his eyes snagged by her allure. "Then...thank you."

"Do you wish to pick up where we left off? Or do we claim amnesia?"

Amber noted his glib temperament, gazed around them and noticed two Attorneys in the wings conversing with one another. They didn't bother to look their way. She decided to mess about with Eduardo's consideration. "Common sense tells me not to get involved with someone like you."

Eduardo laughed sickly at her comment. He gazed over at the two associates arguing. "What can I do to convince you of my sincerity?"

Amber let go a winning grin. Her flirtatious game had succeeded. Apparently, she held all the Aces and held Eduardo Sanchez by the balls.

Eduardo stood tranquilized. His restraint was unfamiliar now that he tasted her. He found a new temptation—and a keen frustration—the obstacle of not being allowed to touch her when the impulse arose. Amber was a perpetual obsession for him. He wanted to kiss her neck, her shoulders, suck in her tongue and slide his mouth over erected parts of her body. The past two days were excruciating. After their encounter, Amber said nothing else, grabbed her clothes and left without a further word. He didn't sleep a wink on Friday only to watch the sun rise and set on Saturday. Sunday he strolled around his house like a lovesick puppy thinking up lies and scenarios for reasons for him showing up unannounced at their house and had to constrain himself from driving over to his brother's uninvited. His whole disposition changed. The anticipation to get to Monday besieged him.

He looked over at Tom and Jerry still quibbling,

contemplated on how it would look if he got down on his knees—in the middle of the clerical quad, no less—and begged Amber to continue their affair. But pride held him back. He was still an overconfident male. He vowed never to allow another female reduce him to a groveling imbecile again, even if it was Amber. He felt like a helpless animal caught in a noose and humiliation surged his throat like vomit. "Well silence speaks volumes, doesn't it?" He uttered in a twisted smile. "Listen Amber I thought we were friends. I thought I'd show you some preference."

Amber giggled. "I'm flattered."

Eduardo puffed up with contempt. "By your obvious nonsensical mind-set, it seems you want me to treat you indifferent."

Amber straight away swallowed her fun.

"So here's the exit I give to all my trysts," Eduardo expressed disappointed, "Decide if you want to be on the receiving end."

Right before her very eyes, Eduardo showed her nothing but disrespect. His expression transformed from considerate and tender to cruel and glacial.

"Since sex with you was all I wanted, my time with you was enough. Last night was a mistake, so don't bother calling."

Amber's mouth slowly opened. She never, ***ever*** saw him so disconnected and inconsiderate! Amber watched in anxiety as Eduardo bent over to retrieve a briefcase and an overnight bag that he had hidden behind her desk. Amber's heart began to thump. ***He's leaving?*** All her mirth flew right out the office. Good Lord, why did she start this prank? Why did she choose to joke around instead of admitting she was happy to see him? Give in to that impulse of throwing her arms around his neck the moment he came near? Oh God, why didn't she just answer the calls over the weekend? She heard the phone ringing but never answered it in fear ***it could*** be him. The entire weekend she found herself mourning his touch, his lips, the tranquility he supplied which left her homesick. Why did she feel she had to run away from the one thing that made her feel so absolutely complete?

Tears formed at the back of her eyes, she wanted to wrap

her arms around his broad shoulders and kiss him hard till his lips swelled. "That was brutal," she voiced, blinking back tears. "I feel sorry for all those poor girls who've had to hear that."

Eduardo's unfriendly demeanor melted at the sight of Amber wiping away the wetness. He held his belongings firmly in his hands in fear he might be throwing them at the wall anytime soon.

"Where you going?"

Eduardo focused on a single tear that dripped down her cheek as she looked up. "To Sacramento to settle a case."

Amber wiped the moisture away from her skin only to feel others gushing out. "When you get back...will you hold me?"

Eduardo shut his eyes in liberation. Amber just handed him that resolution. His heart leaped with joy within seeing those tears in her eyes and the regret proved further that she wanted to be with him too. "Oh I will," he voiced huskily, "But I'll be doing more than just holding you."

*****

How can she feel shame, when it felt so pure? Amber began an affair with not one-ounce of guilt. She wanted to feel remorse, she truly did, but all she felt was love, warmth, security and an undeniable connection. She was oftentimes bewildered how well her body fit within his when they were naked, how the rhythms of their kisses were identical and the pulse of their lovemaking exactly alike. It was as if she already knew how to please that man, and vice versa. There was no guesswork involved, all she had to do was just look at him and she knew exactly what he was thinking.

Their physical attack unleashed a barrage of dormant passion. They frequented various motels up and down Sunset Boulevard who offered ***Daily Rates***. Breaking off early each night, crashing through the motel door, barely making it to the bed, it was very challenging for either one of them to be apart for too long. Their thrill for each other—on vivacity so high—it took hours to come down. They were like magnets, coming together with such concentration and force; they barely had time to think about the aftermath.

Amber was still amazed that the good-looking attorney in the office was interested in her. Amber, in spite of everything, was still very insecure. Eduardo packed full the ingredient that was missing in her marriage with Victor. Amber never felt so absolute yet still so unsure of herself.

Walking out of the hair salon with a giddy expression pasted to her face, Amber recalled her past rendezvous with Eduardo. She waited for him patiently in the motel room. He was a few minutes late, but arrived with flowers and a sensual grin that took her breath away. He threw down the flowers and grabbed her to him, nearly crushing her arms from the strength of his excitement and close embrace.

Oh how could she be this happy? Amber wanted to emerge beautiful on top of feeling that way and made an appointment at a beauty salon. She wanted to appear and undergo the part of a woman who was able to entice the likes of Eduardo Sanchez. Keeping the length of her hair, she had the stylist cut wispy bangs and several layers across the back to give it more bounce. Walking on air, she roamed the sidewalks of the Century City Plaza, searching for the perfect negligee from the ritzy boutiques.

Eduardo out of town again, had to settle a case for the firm. Amber hadn't seen him in several days and her anticipation of his return was unnerving. She felt lost without him. His full attention was like a fricken drug.

Amber purchased her nightgown and proceeded out of the doorway when Gordon Daggert cornered her.

"My-my, buying something sexy for the husband?"

Amber blushed, "Looks that way."

Gordon surveyed her attire, her new look. "You look marvelous by the way, cut your hair?"

Amber bit down on her lower lip. She was glad to see the effect worked, especially to someone as equally as handsome as Eduardo. "So you like it, huh?"

Gordon reached out and tweaked some bangs over her face. Amber's cheeks turned crimson; it was a towering feeling to experience so much admiration lately. She never received so much focus her entire life!

"I do. Where you headed for?"

"Just doing some shopping."

"Care if I join you?"

Amber thought about it. Another good-looking ladies man. She had a surplus of attention from the one that mattered, so Gordon was harmless, right? "Sure, walk with me."

They walked together down the long open-air shopping plaza. Every now and then, Gordon would lean into her and graze her shoulder. ***A display of intimacy,*** Amber realized, and that weakened her assurance.

"How's the defamation case going?"

"Ready for trial in two weeks."

"Good, then you'll be free to help me out with a case I'm working on."

Amber looked at him quizzically. "Why?"

"Because I like your company...and, I want you on my team."

Amber heard the purring in his voice. Gordon's speech turned husky, and Amber started in amazement. "Gordon, I'm married."

Gordon laughed, "I find that a challenge."

Amber rolled her eyes, "Why are good-looking men always so confident?"

He stopped and grabbed her by the shoulders, "Why, who else has been hitting on you? Tell me now so I can defend your honor."

Amber gazed into his blue eyes and giggled, "You're just as bad as my brother-in-law."

Gordon let go a meager sneer, "Ah—to be compared along the same lines as the talented attorney, then I take that as a compliment Amber. You are so sweet." Gordon brushed Amber's shoulder with his hand, still had it resting there when she looked beyond him and gulped.

Amber's heart dropped at the sight of Eduardo running towards them. ***Running?*** Look how fast he's jogging, look how fast he's picking up speed!

Gordon noted Amber's alien look and turned around; noticed Eduardo quickly approaching. "Hey Eduardo, how was the negotiations?"

Eduardo didn't stop to chitchat with Gordon. Idiot, doesn't he realize he'll never have her? Eduardo grabbed Amber away and rushed her down a nearby descending escalator. "Family business Gordon, no time to talk!"

"When did you get back?" Amber asked wondering where the hell he was taking her. She was so elated to see him, she wanted to wrap her arms around his neck and never let go.

Eduardo still had his hand firmly gripped on her forearm. "An hour ago," he gravelly expressed surveying her new appearance. "I searched for you in the office," he let go out of breath.

"But I—"

"Jackie told me you went shopping," he expressed exasperated cutting her off.

"I know I told her," Amber reflected. "The information was for you, but on the other hand, just in case for ***her*** if she needed me back."

"Good thing, but I still had no idea where you went."

Amber sensed that Eduardo was upset about something, his voice cracked with anger. "Across the street, where else would I go?" She pleaded in her defense.

"After racking my brain for nearly half an hour, I just threw my briefcase on the chair and ran across the street for no reason at all."

Amber started...he ***was*** agitated. "But you found me."

"This time," Eduardo smirked, "Imagine my surprise to see you standing in the middle of the plaza—being manhandled by Gordon no less!"

Amber was taken-back. There was now a sense of urgency in his voice intertwined with flippancy. Amber clutched her bag tightly within her hands. "He came up to ***me,"*** she uttered, suddenly back on the defensive.

Eduardo nevertheless couldn't look her in the face and yanked her off the escalator, throwing her body into the parking garage elevator. It all happened so swiftly; Amber barely had time to notice that they were alone in the enclosed space and that Eduardo arranged to pull the emergency brake.

Annoyed, Eduardo stepped away from her body and

shoved his hands down his pant pockets. "You're still mine right?" He breathed upset. "I want to be absolutely sure you're not sleeping with anyone else."

His words stole her breath. His? Amber never felt such ownership. What was he asking of her? What about her husband? She wasn't allowed to sleep with her husband? But the more she thought about it, the more she realized he was mainly talking about Gordon. He probably found Gordon as a threat, and didn't want him sniffing around. She nodded her head yes.

Eduardo swarmed her body with his arms and brought her into him, hot kisses down the side of her neck—in and around her earlobe—resting on her longing mouth. It was a passionate kiss meant to dominate. "Thank you for cutting your hair," his voice rasped, "Thank you for wearing this dress, and thank you for this..."

Eduardo pulled up her skirt. ***Good Lord,*** were they going to do it in the elevator? Anywhere to be with him, she was an eager participant. Amber started to roar when she realized how fast Eduardo was able to pull down her underwear, manage to unbutton his belt, pants ***and*** penetrate her without breaking the most sensational kiss she ever experienced. They reached climax together in a matter of moments, both breathing hard from the phenomenal encounter.

"Good God you can't imagine how much I missed you," Eduardo let go, zipping up his pants and kissing her lips again.

Amber threw her arms around his neck. She was delighted that he was finally happy. "Can't remember the last time I wanted to see an attorney so much."

He held her embrace, eyed the Victoria Secret tote in the corner of the elevator. "What's that?" Eduardo asked, grinning from ear to ear.

Amber blushed, noticed Eduardo depressing the elevator emergency brake. "What's what?" She playfully questioned in return. Amber managed to hold the tote behind her back. Eduardo tried to grab it, but Amber was too fast for him and kept the bag away.

"Com'on now...don't let me have to tickle you!"

Amber rushed out of the elevator door, still laughing and in mid-giggle when several solemn patrons ended their giddiness. They stiffened up and slowly walked out of the area.

"It's for me, right?"

Amber gazed into his darkened eyes. Good Lord he was gorgeous when he was aroused! "Of course," she replied, pulling it away from his wandering hands again. "But you can't see it till we get to the motel."

Eduardo's grin dropped. "What color?"

"Pink."

"Uh—I'm in heaven, what time?"

"After work."

"Where?"

"The Coronado, room six. I didn't know if you'd be back today or tomorrow, so I reserved both days."

Good girl. What a gratifying feeling to have finally met his mischievous match. "What size shoe do you wear?"

"Why?"

"It's a surprise."

Later at the *Motel Coronado* they lie in bed having just finished making love for the third time, worn out and content.

Amber threw up one leg in the air. She was naked, wearing only a smile and her new pink high-heeled pumps. "Thank you for these." The nighty was already off (managing to stay on for nearly ten seconds) while the shoes got the ride of their lives.

Eduardo watched Amber's leg hover up above him. "So you like your new ***fuck me*** pumps?"

Amber let go a cackle. It was all she ever did these days. "I don't like to wear high heels, but I'll wear these for you."

"Only in bed dear girl."

Amber looked over at him. Eduardo was barely covered from the waist down. Good Lord he was gorgeous naked! "How come you're so thin?"

"Sex."

Amber playfully slapped his shoulder. "No, really. Victor is starting to get a gut, how come you and he have totally different bodies?" She asked him honestly. And just like that, Amber realized what she just did. Compare brother against brother. "Good Lord Eduardo, I'm sorry," she apologized closing her eyes. The mood changed, and hot turned cold. His body tightened, he was frigid, aloof. She swore she could see the cool mist escape his mouth while he breathed. Bringing up family, their marriages, anything other than them was taboo. Amber suddenly remembered whom she was married to. "What are we doing?"

"What are you talking about?" Eduardo let out, reaching for his clothes thrown all over the floor. He began to put his pants back on. The alarm clock buzzed and he walked over to shut it off, practically breaking the darn thing trying to do so.

Amber watched him dress. "I guess what I'm talking about is continuing this affair without getting caught."

Eduardo grabbed his tie off the desktop, wrapped it around his neck in a choke-hold. "We're not going to get caught."

"Eventually one of us is going to slip, or we're gonna get caught fucking at your Mom's house in the pool." She grinned effortlessly, not realizing that she was continuing to feed the tense conversation.

He was not amused. Amber planted the seed that she was ***still*** not truly his. "We're not, because we're going to end this."

Tears swarmed Amber's eyes instantly. How very shallow of him. Here she was willing to sleep with him freely and he wasn't even warranted to talk about it? "Today? ***Now?"*** Just the thought of it made Amber shiver. She looked down at her nakedness, utterly embarrassed; she kicked off the shoes and began to get dressed.

"Leticia is beginning to wonder," he threw at her, tucking his shirt inside his pants. Now why in the hell did he have to mention ***her?*** Maybe for the same reason she mentioned Victor; tit for tat and all that good stuff.

Amber was tortured. Thoughts of their spouses swarmed her reasoning. "Maybe you're right." She let go wounded.

Eduardo straightened up his tie, nodded his head. He didn't want to be correct when he knew in his heart that he was most definitely wrong. "I'm always right," he said, shaking his head again. What the hell was he doing? This is what he's always aimed for, the challenge, the chase and the intricate girl. Thoughts of her and Gordon popped into his mind. Good God that made him ***sick.*** His heartbeat was erratic; the mere thought of losing Amber caused him to do an about-face. "I've misjudged our relationship."

Amber froze. This was it, their breakup. But having to see him back at the office or her not being able to touch him, caused Amber to tremble with such agonizing grief. "We don't have a relationship."

"We don't?"

"We do?" Amber asked hopeful.

"Amber, I'm sorry."

Amber reached the door about to exit. What did he just say? "Are you admitting you're ***wrong?"*** She had her hand firmly on the way out when Eduardo walked over and pulled her away from the doorway. He grabbed her body back and wrapped his arm around her neck. His kiss was passionate, overwhelming. Amber quickly broke apart from him out of breath.

"I'm ***never*** incorrect," he gravely uttered, "When it comes to you."

CHAPTER**TWENTY-TWO**

Thanksgiving Day

Sheila and Molly were invited, along with forty other relatives over to the Sanchez home for the family dinner. It was a big event. Rosalba and her sisters prepared for this day five months in advance. Making sure the two turkeys were basted and cooked on time, creating Mexican entrees of enchiladas, chile rellanos, beans and rice all steamed to perfection. Fabrizio borrowed his brother's dining room and picnic tables so that everyone could sit together in one colossal family feast. Kids (excited with being with their cousins) ran around the house dressed head to toe in their fancy outfits while the ladies all wore dresses and the men wore suits and ties.

Amber dressed for two men that day: Victor, her husband, and Eduardo, her lover. She knew that Victor felt proud of his wife when she dressed appropriately. When Amber decided to dress up, she often resembled a movie star or a model on the runway. Getting up an hour earlier, she curled her hair, set the hot rollers and used the curling iron, applied soft black mascara to her eyelashes, swabbed lavender eye shadow over her eyes, rubbed rouge to her cheeks and painted lip gloss to her already pink lips. She ironed wrinkles out Victor's clothes and made sure the kid's outfits hung on the doorknobs. Bought the dinner rolls the previous morning, even made sure that there was enough gas in the car so that there would be no excuses. None, whatsoever. No excuses to be late. Better not be late. She hadn't seen Eduardo in four months, and she couldn't wait to touch him. She even bought a new dress and slithered into the blushed rose spaghetti-strap dress she bought at Robinsons on sale, and admired herself in a hallway mirror on her way towards the bathroom. The dress accentuated her figure, especially her breasts. You weren't able to wear a bra with this dress. A bra would show. It was a backless wonder with criss-cross strings that tightened at the waist. She relied upon the firmness of her assets, creating cleavage to entice. She was a woman on a mission and a female prepared for battle.

Amber thought by accepting a job at Aldridge & Watson that she would be able to see Eduardo every day, but that wasn't the case. Eduardo was in high demand. He was the firms' top litigator, and he was always being sent out of the office: Sacramento, San Francisco, and Las Vegas, Washington State.

She couldn't wait for Thanksgiving Day. She knew he'd be there. Made sure she spoke to Leticia two nights before and asked her what she was bringing to the holiday. She didn't dare or ask to speak to Eduardo, the anticipation enough would send him running. Oh, she knew it was sneaky, downright naughty, but she didn't care, the volcano was about to erupt. She purposely avoided sleeping with Victor so that she'd be ready and ripe to receive Eduardo when she got him.

Arriving at the Sanchez home in the afternoon, Amber was able to explore the other cars parked in the area and found no sign of Eduardo's silvery Porsche or Leticia's sedan anywhere. Amber and Victor got the kids out of their car and proceeded to the front door. Victor opened his parent's front door, and out came the noises of the festivities. Kids were yelling and screaming, the music was blaring and the relatives who had arrived there early were already having a joyous time.

"Hey! Happy Thanksgiving..." Victor greeted his Tió Jose from Chatsworth first. Tió Jose in turn welcomed him back by throwing his arms up in the air and hugging his nephew.

Amber roamed through the relatives one by one greeting them with a peck on the cheek. She was a professional cheek kisser now, commenting on how lovely everyone looked as she expressed happiness. The anticipation of Eduardo's arrival was overpowering.

"Oh Amber—you look absolutely amazing!" Molly expressed with sangria in one hand. "That color on you really makes your eyes pop!"

Amber gave her sister a hug. "Thank you, I just bought it." She eyed her Mom standing behind her sister and was very glad that her in-laws extended an invitation for dinner to them as well. She hadn't recalled the last time the three of them were together for Thanksgiving and she was so grateful for it.

"Your father called me this morning, he's getting married," Sheila stated to Amber sort of matter-of-factly.

Amber was taken back. "What?"

"Yah, just like that, he wanted to let me know, after twenty some odd years he's finally going to marry her." Sheila's face went blank.

"Oh Mom," Amber expressed disbelieving the idea of her father marrying that woman he left her mother for. She thought he'd never get married again, thought he never ***wanted*** to be married.

"Her husband finally granted her a divorce; he's getting married next month," Sheila expressed calmly, only now with a few tears forming in her eyes.

The idea made Amber ill all of a sudden. ***He just didn't want to be married to my Mom, that's all. How awful...*** "Oh Mom, are you going to be OK?" Amber asked, reaching for Sheila for a hug.

Sheila wiped away a tear. "Oh honey, don't worry about your Mom, she's a survivor."

"Ain't that the truth," Molly agreed rubbing her mother's arm.

"Amber! We were wondering when you were gonna get here!" Leticia spat out, grabbing Amber's arm and pulling her towards the front yard. "Come here, I wanna show you what Eddie got for me for my birthday!"

Amber was shocked once again. When on earth did they get there? She kept her eye on the front door the whole time she was making her rounds greeting relatives. ***They must have been here already***, she realized. ***But I didn't see Eduardo's Porsche...***

"Eddie, come here!" Leticia yelled at Eduardo, pulling the back of his shirt. His back was turned from Amber's view—hidden from her sight barely ten feet away!

Their eyes crash together and Eduardo's mouth practically dropped. Amber looked astonishing, glamorous, her nipples rose to his attention. Eduardo looked so goddamn sexy—Amber wanted to ride him like a horse. Her favorite beige suit with maroon silk shirt and taupe tie, he personified sex appeal.

"Hi...how are you?" Eduardo asked, the three of them walking towards the parked cars.

"I'm fine, and you? How was the case?" Amber barely got out. She wanted to kiss him so desperately, she let go a huge sigh disguising it so.

"It went well—a couple million for our prestigious firm."

"Oh Philip's going to love that. You've made him a happy man thus far," Amber joked with him.

"I know I'm happy," he responded, lowering his voice, "How've you been?"

"You just asked me that." Amber smiled good-naturedly, pushing his nearing body away from hers.

"Look, look! Isn't it beautiful?" Leticia asked, making like a display hostess at a car convention.

Amber gawked at the shiny new cream Mercedes Benz station wagon. "Oh my, is this yours?" She expressed, walking over to it now.

"Yes! Yes! Isn't it beautiful? Eddie surprised me with it on my birthday," Leticia shrieked, practically jumping up and down.

"Who' she kidding, she's been hinting at me for months now. 'Gee, we need another car'...'do you like station wagons?'" He played along with her.

Amber's smiled dropped. Eduardo reached for Leticia and gave her a kiss on her forehead. Amber turned away, walked around the automobile. "Damn, this is a nice car," Amber solemnly expressed.

Eduardo noted Amber's reaction, he felt guilty for having to put on such a show.

"Where's Victor? I wanna show him my new car!" Leticia screeched, running away from the two of them for a moment.

Amber and Eduardo were left alone; unaided with the new

Mercedes Benz station wagon, unaccompanied with their strong sexual attraction, alone with thoughts of their last encounter in the motel room.

Amber shyly gazed away from him. Eduardo came in closer to her. "I wanna fuck you ***now,***" Eduardo leered down at her. "You look remarkable. That dress, I wanna tear it down."

When Eduardo was aroused, he was deadly. His lewd expression buckled Amber's sturdy stance. "Where...how do we get outta here?"

Eduardo stepped away from Amber. At any given moment he was going to squeeze her. Her body, her nipples, they were so tempting. "I don't know, but I'll find a way."

Victor came out with Leticia in a flash and eyed the car behind the two horny devils. "Man, what a great car. Damn boy, you're making a shit load of money! Maybe I should have been an attorney!" Victor joked with Eduardo, patting him on his shoulder.

"Yah—well..." Eduardo breathed, escorting Leticia away from the car and back into the house.

Victor and Amber came together and wrapped their arms around each other's waists. Eduardo glanced at Amber in that dress one last time as the couple strolled away. Amber purposely gazed back at him, toying with his enthusiasm for her.

"Pueda el reloj de Dios sobre nuestras familias. Otórguenos salud buena y mantenga alimento en nuestras mesas. Gracias Señor para esta comida maravillosa." Fabrizio expressed, passing around slices of turkey.

"What did he just say?" Amber quietly asked Victor.

"He was thanking the Lord for this wonderful meal and asked to keep us all safe," Victor expressed, kissing Amber lightly on her lips. Amber doesn't kiss him back. But Victor doesn't notice. Victor dives into the mound of food in front of him.

Amber glanced over at Eduardo. Eduardo turned his head slightly, having had to wince once again at that improvised devoted encounter.

They didn't dare look at one another other than when it was appropriate. Victor and Amber were seated on one side of the table, while Eduardo and Leticia on the opposite.

Leticia was sitting next to Tiá Gemma chatting away about church and the recent gossip about Father Rodriguez and his aide. Kyra, her daughter, was next to her, playing with some toys on the floor. Leticia kept one eye on Kyra and the other on Tiá Gemma. Eduardo was now speaking Spanish to his Tió Lamberto. Amber was thankful that evening. Thankful she held Eduardo in close proximity and equally thankful she got to spend time with her mother and sister before they left for another dinner.

Later, Victor went outside with his cousins from Orange County and Amber went with him. She knew Eduardo was ten feet away from her, she could smell his cologne nearby. He had taken off his jacket by then, his maroon silk shirt enticing her to handle. Amber playfully gazed at him and then looked away. Eduardo jokingly smiled at her, peered away. It was a cat and mouse game—catch me if you can. But the anticipation of their next meeting was unbearable. But where should they go? How do they leave without being unnoticed?

Eduardo brushed up against Amber as he approached his brother. She closed her eyes in delight as Victor and his cousin Justino laughed at a private joke. "What's so funny?" Eduardo asked them, guzzling down a beer.

Amber had a drink also. A margarita rimmed with salt. Sipping it gently she made sure Eduardo watched her lips as she brought up the salt from the edge of the glass with her tongue.

"Oh Justino was just talking about the time when we were little, when Mama and Papa took us to their house for Thanksgiving that one year. Do you remember?" Victor asked Eduardo who was mesmerized by Amber's lewd gestures.

"Huh? Oh yah," Eduardo stated, blinking back into consciousness, "When Tiá Sophie walked around with her dress stuffed inside her pantyhose?"

"Whuuuttt?" Amber chortled, realizing what they were discussing.

"Yah, my Tiá Sophie—she's back in Mexico, by the way—

we were young, you were ten, right Victor?" Eduardo asked, seemingly excited now about the distraction away from Amber. Victor nodded his head. "...And my poor Tiá walked out of the bathroom and never realized she had her dress stuffed inside her underwear and pantyhose! It was hilarious!"

"She walked around the party for almost an hour and nobody had the nerve to come up to her and tell her that we could see her chonies!" Victor concluded jovial.

They all were laughing when Leticia sprung up behind Amber. "Rosalba just asked me if I could go to the store and get some Cool-Whip for the pumpkin pie, she's so embarrassed right now, you know how prepared she was for this."

Amber stood back from Leticia's closeness. "You're kidding."

"Mama forgot the whipped cream?" Eduardo joked with her, bringing his hand to his heart, playing injured at the thought. "Whatever will we do?"

"Stop it...will you go to the store? I can't, I'm in the middle of feeding Kyra, unless you want to feed her." Leticia gave to him batting her green eyes.

"Awe Leticia, you know she hates it when I try and feed her."

"Yah—I know, I just thought I'd try. So will you go to the market then?" Leticia asked hopeful.

Eduardo gazed back at Amber. Amber finished her margarita; there was no more salt left on the rim of the glass for her to tongue. "Sure," he expressed, beginning to walk away.

"Your Mom likes 'Cool-Whip', not some ordinary whipped cream Eduardo. You'll find it in the frozen section." Leticia let out knowing perfectly well her husband would be oblivious.

"Frozen section? You know I'm shopping-impaired," Eduardo suddenly voiced upset.

"Oh heck," Leticia gave out, looking at Amber fiddling with the curls on her hair. "Amber, you know what I'm talking about, right?"

Amber looked into Leticia's green eyes. "Sure, Cool-Whip is usually by the frozen strawberries and pies."

"Will you go with Eddie then? Show him which one she likes?" Leticia freely said, oblivious to the solicitation she just presented them.

Eduardo and Amber both shot looks at each other. "Com'on Amber, give me a lesson on whipped topping," he said, waving her over to follow him.

Amber tapped her husband's shoulder, "I'm going to go with Eduardo to the store, and I'll be right back."

Victor was in deep conversation with his cousin now, nodded his head to Amber in agreement.

Amber walked away with Eduardo. Unreal. ***Unbelievable.*** There they were on the inside sinners, on the outside, angels getting something sweet.

In the Mercedes Benz they were speechless. Eduardo pulled over to the side of the road on a busy street. "We'll get the Cool-Whip first," he breathed, fingering the inside of her thigh.

Amber let go a whimper of pleasure, "I'll run in and get it."

He looked across at her again, ravishing pink dress inviting him; she stared at his maroon shirt, dying for her to tear off. They come together in unison, kissing and groping each other's bodies.

"Wait—wait –wait," he suddenly declared, breaking away from her. "Not here, not on the fuckin' street!"

Amber was crazed, "Where then? Where should we go?"

"I don't know!" He yelled back at her.

"Think of something, Eduardo! Hurry, I can't wait any longer."

The urgency was irrefutable. Eduardo pressed his foot on the pedal, screeched the rubber on the new Firestone tires and reached the market in sixty seconds flat. Amber rushed out of the car and into the store. Five minutes later, she emerged out of the self-opening doors with several tubs of frozen Cool-Whip and surveyed the area where Eduardo once parked. He wasn't there? ***Where the hell was he? Oh fuck, where the hell did he go?*** The sun had set and Amber slowly walked towards nowhere in the darkness. Then she eyed in the distance the corner of the lot. It was unlit and you could barely see the Mercedes Benz and Eduardo flashed the high beams at her. ***Why you little devil…***

She ran towards the car, threw herself in and found him already in the passenger side. ***More room***, she realized, pulling down her underwear, sitting on top of him already large and exposed. They go at it with incredible zest—it doesn't last very long, it was too quick; they were too fired up. But the end was better.

She was still sitting on him, kissing his mouth with tender ardor when she said, "Oh Eduardo, I missed you..." she cried, tears falling from her eyes. There was so much excitement, the emotion poured out of her in full force. Was it possible? Did it exist? That just one kiss from a man could make you feel utterly emptied that all you want to do is load up and repeat on kissing him? Eduardo was a powerful lover. He took her to him unlike no other. Blame it on the ***machismo***; blame it on his overconfidence, whatever it was, she wanted it entirely.

He kissed her wet cheeks, kissed her eyes. "I missed you too baby..." he expressed, moving her hips.

Amber stopped crying when she realized what was happening. He was still rock hard and she moved in for more. "Oh God bless you—"

"God Amber, I love your body—" Eduardo gushed, pulling down the straps of her dress exposing her breasts to his wandering mouth.

This time it was slow, unhurried and gradual. Everyone could wait for the topping, couldn't they? Who ate pumpkin pie without Cool-Whip? Rosalba would make sure of it.

CHAPTER**TWENTY-THREE**

Green's Her Favorite Color

"Eduardo, can you take a look at this?" Amber asked, stopping cold in her tracks. Eduardo and his Personal Assistant Jackie were very close; he (sitting in his chair) while Jackie leaned over him seductively. What an intimate little portrait! Amber fumed with incredulity.

Eduardo looked across at Amber. Saw her eyes go from wide to narrow in a flash. "Amber—"

Hands on her hips, Amber gritted her teeth, "Am I interrupting something?"

Jackie looked up from what she was doing and straightened out her blouse. Gazed down at her chemise and noticed a button unhinged and fastened it back up.

Eduardo watched Jackie do up her button and closed his eyes grasping how it came across and whom Amber would blame.

What the hell was she doing? Eduardo was still the same man, wasn't he? Being his typical immodest self and not thinking about Amber's feelings but only his own selfish needs? That was his nature, wasn't it, excessive sexual desire? Amber should have known better than to just give up her self-control and sleep with him as easily as she did. She was making this far too unproblematic for him. She thought honestly that he wasn't even sleeping with Leticia now; after all, she hadn't been sleeping with Victor! Why would she need to? After having the finest, Victor was mediocre to her now (the sad, but awful truth) and there it was. And now, watching Eduardo's guilty conscience surface on his face, she just felt the worst sort of idiot!

"Obviously," Amber spat out slamming the door behind her.

Eduardo ran around his desk leaving Jackie dumbfounded. He noticed Amber practically running down the hallway and began running after her. "I need to speak to you," he gruffly voiced, reaching up to her and grabbing her forearm from behind.

Amber yanked away from his grip causing a sight (***yet again***) in front of the clerical pool. The twosome center stage, the Assistants were at the edge of their seats with anticipation. "Then just spit out what you have to say and end it already," Amber voiced loudly, making sure to raise a plucked eyebrow or two.

Eduardo wasn't going to play her childish game when he knew full well he was innocent. But trying to convince her otherwise? "Not here," he replied, gazing around them. He grabbed her arm again and dragged her down the hallway and out the suite entrance.

Amber jerked away from his grip and dashed to the elevator fast, pressing the 'downward' button relentlessly. She crossed her arms and waited for its slow expectation.

"What's wrong with you?" Eduardo demanded, encircling her.

"I knew you couldn't be trusted!" Amber hollered, turning to look at him fully. "How can I trust a tiger that won't change his spots?"

Eduardo guffawed; it was so ridiculous, endearing the way the veins in her neck started to project. "It's ***stripes."***

"You condescending ***asshole!"*** Amber vehemently voiced, raising her hand in the air towards his cheek. She wanted to slap that patronizing smirk off his fucking face.

Eduardo held her arm firmly back. "My-my...where's this all coming from dear?"

"I'm not your ***'dear'!"*** Amber yelled back at him, looking at the elevator finally open. She walked in—Eduardo snatched her body back.

"We're not finished here!" He exclaimed, pushing her body practically into the elevator wall on the opposite side.

"Keep your filthy hands off me," Amber protested, trying to push his tight clasp away from her shoulders, "I don't want you ***ever*** touching me again!"

If he didn't desire her in the worst kind of way, he would have given her what she demanded. To walk away, end it. Normally, when a woman threw accusations like ***that*** at him, he was guilty as charged; he would leave with no reservations. But when he wasn't accountable (and this was Amber) he wanted further from her than he ever realized. "You look absolutely enticing by the way," he scoffed, both hands still pressing her against the wall.

"Fuck you," Amber fumed, "Let me go you arrogant asshole."

Eduardo did release her and waived both hands in the air in surrender. Amber's expression showed fury, but her body spoke serenity. "Meet me at *The Rose Motel & Gardens* after work."

Amber's mouth flew open wide. "You're a conceited bastard, you know that? If you think for one moment that I'd meet you after that answerable display then you're sadly mistaken!"

Eduardo watched Amber storm away and back to the office when he yelled back at her, "Room ten."

Amber got back to her desk. The nerve! Good Lord, she had never felt that much distrust in all her life!

What was it this ***passion?*** It made you feel sensations of the worst kind when the one you love was touching someone else. Amber was being controlled by emotion and fervor in full bloom. Passion was what possessed her now; it was all she could think of, want. She often read books about a character being controlled by his or her ***passion*** and wondered what the heck that felt like. ***She shot her husband in a fit of rage***...what the heck was that all about? ***He was so enraged by the sight of seeing his wife with another man; he grabbed the scarf and choked her to death***...huh? Explain that one to her! ***She stabbed her husband 106 times***...106 times? What, the first twenty didn't cut it? What emotion controlled such rage? She never felt that sensation before. She was passionless for the first ten years of her marriage to Victor and now she was being utterly controlled by the outbreak she had with his brother.

Tears swelled her eyes when she spotted Eduardo exiting the office with his briefcase in his hand. Amber needed to resolve this and solve it ***now.*** She ambled over to Jackie and threw her files on top of her desk in a loud thud.

"What the—" Jackie shockingly exclaimed looking up at Amber bewildered.

"Stay away from him."

Jackie was dumb-founded, "Stay away from whom?"

"Eduardo," Amber said, realizing that she was acting like a raving jealous bitch.

Jackie obviously mistook her suspicion for simple sister-in-law protectiveness and said, "He's my boss Amber. And besides, he's not even my type."

Amber stood back. "If that's the truth, then why did I just find you two a few minutes ago looking guilty as sin?"

Jackie started to smile. "Oh gee Amber that was nothing. I flicked my pen by mistake and went over by his desk to retrieve it. My, but you're touchy lately. He's married for crying out loud and I would never, like I said before, he's not even my type. But, if it were Gordon—"

Amber didn't even stop to hear the rest of her silly infatuation with Gordon Daggert and ran down the hallway towards her desk to shut her computer down. It was nearing five o'clock and she had to get to the motel room quick.

With his arms crossed, legs crossed, Eduardo smiled a rakish daring grin. Amber closed the door and began to unbutton her blouse.

"Does this mean you're no longer irritated?" He teased bringing down his eyes as Amber unhooked her bra.

"Shush," she whispered, ripping off his shirt, buttons darting all over the place.

"You just ripped a hundred dollar shirt, dear."

"Then it's a good thing you keep others in your car, asshole."

They make love at a hasty velocity. Amber sought his body further than she ever wanted him before and took control. Eduardo was besieged, he'd never seen her so intense. She did everything imaginable to appease him—Eduardo was in sexual heaven.

Eduardo was still breathing heavily when he exclaimed, "What got into you?"

Amber came up for air from beneath the sheets and from between his legs. "Don't tell me you oppose?" She giggled.

Eduardo laid his head back down on the bed. "No, I rather like it, someone dominating me."

Amber laid her body over his and wrapped her arms around his shoulders laying her head on his muscled chest. "No one, huh? Not even Leticia?" Good Lord, she did it again! Amber closed her eyes in disbelief. What was so intriguing anyhow? What did she want to know? When was she ever going to learn? She knew what came next. Eduardo was going to be livid.

Eduardo sat up. "Amber why do you continue to do that?" He shot out of bed. "You know this is not about them. Leave ***them*** out of this." He yanked his pants off the floor, got dressed enraged.

What the hell just happened? She was sizzling one minute, freezing the next. Amber brought the sheet up over her breasts and searched for her clothes, slowly picking them up off the floor. She was suddenly ashamed of what she was doing. What ***was*** she doing? "I will when you tell me what ***this*** is."

Eduardo ran his fingers through his hair. Good God, wasn't it obvious? "What do you want from me? What the hell do you want me to say?" He asked transforming into attorney-mode. "When we come here it's all about us—you and me—and never them. You're mine the moment you walk through that door and I'm yours the moment I see you."

Amber's hands were shaking beyond control. She was even about to throw up. "I'm sorry Eduardo; I'll try not to do it again."

Eduardo let go a quick laugh. "I'm spoiled, remember? I just want your full attention."

And what exactly does ***she*** want? Amber wanted to know how he felt without talking in circles, that's what! She wanted ***his*** devotion and ***his*** total attention too. He must care for her in some way, she could feel it in the way he kissed her, made love to her. Good Lord, or was that how he normally made love to ***all*** his women? She suddenly got sick to her stomach, brought her hand up over her mouth. "But you have ***mine...***"

Eduardo was back in his pants, shirt and tie in seconds flat. What the hell was he doing, being so standoffish? This woman meant everything to him! What was the great mystery anyhow? Why was he still acting like the old self-centered fool when Amber is whom he's hungered for? "Amber...I need to say something. Can you sit down?"

Tears swelled in her eyes immediately, it was his goodbye; she could sense the magnitude in his green eyes. Amber sat down on the bed and wrapped her arms around her stomach. "Just go ahead...go ahead and say it." She knew this day was going to happen, she just wished she were better prepared for it. Eduardo had his fill, she even went overboard today and showed him too much of her excitement by pleasuring him so.

Eduardo stepped into her…fell to his ***knees…***and laid his head forward on her lap, wrapping his arms in stages around her waist. Amber was so startled by his reaction, her arms went wide, she didn't know what else to do but downcast her hands on top of his head.

"God Amber you drive me to distraction," he said with a long pause. "...I live to make you laugh—see you smile. I love making love to you…watch your eyes light up the moment I'm inside. I love when you bite down on that lower lip of yours, makes me want to kiss you all day long…You're so beautiful; I want to give you so much more than I'm able to. I can't bear the thought of ever losing you. I've never cared so much about another person before. I'm in love with you Amber...I love you."

He actually declared it, but her doubt remained. Deep down she wanted to believe him, she really did, but Amber couldn't get passed the thought of him probably saying ***'I love you'*** to every woman he's ever been with. What made ***her*** so special? She wasn't worthy. He could proclaim it a thousand times and she'd never believe it. Amber's emancipated sobs were for her own benefit not his affirmation. "I've always loved you," she confessed, kissing the top of his head still insecure. Amber brought his body up to hers, wrapped her arms around his neck, pulling his body close, no, intimately into hers to melt within his hollows.

CHAPTER**TWENTY-FOUR**

Revelations

"Tell me about the women in your life," Amber asked, lying on Eduardo's naked chest.

"What women?" He laughed, trying to avoid the apprehensive subject.

Amber smiled, "I want to know more about you, who you've loved, broke your heart, secrets like that."

Eduardo ran his hands down her back to the curve of her waistline then up and around to the tip of her bare buttocks.

They were on a lunch break, in Room 10 at *The Rose Motel & Gardens*. Just little under an hour was all they had to share with one another. They wasted no time. Clothes were thrown all over the place; shoes kicked up on the sink in the bathroom, a tie thrown over a lampshade.

"You go first," Eduardo teased, kissing the top of her head. "What kind of secrets are you holding in?"

"I had an abortion once," Amber quietly expressed, running her finger across Eduardo's chiseled jowl.

"You did?" He asked surprised then dismal for her, "I'm sorry."

"It was awful," Amber quietly voiced, "So much happened in that day alone."

Eduardo quickly gazed at her serious face. "What?"

"During the operation the doctors found something wrong with my uterus. Sad to say, the kids were conceived with hormones. I'm having a hysterectomy next year," Amber confessed, viewing Eduardo's stern appearance melt into relief.

"Wow...I never know that."

"Now you do."

"I wish I could be there with you. You know, at the hospital when you wake up from surgery?"

Amber thought about it, "Me too. Now tell me something about you."

Eduardo gazed up at the ceiling and continued to caress Amber's hair with the arm he had curved around her body. How does he lighten up this dreary conversation? "Contrary to popular belief I haven't been with a thousand women," he said in jest, making her snicker. "Never been in love until now, no one's ever broken ***my*** heart and I'm the one who invented casual intimacy."

"No way, I'm shocked."

Eduardo kissed her forehead again, "Let me tell you how it's done. After the temporary moment of satisfaction fades, you feel emptied and isolated...compelled to search for the compensation over and again."

Amber noted he was serious. "Same like me," she added, "I was always trying to find love. I equated sex with love. I was pretty promiscuous before I met—well ***before***. You're not mad that I slept around?"

"Why should I be when I was the same way," he chuckled, scooping Amber's body into his.

Amber laughed inwardly, "Yah, having been so ***selective.***"

Eduardo let out a hoot. "You remember that?"

"Of course, I'll never forget that day. That's the day when I realized..." Amber shut her eyes, refrained from becoming melancholy.

"Realized what?" Eduardo asked anxious.

"That I had to have you..."

Eduardo brought her in closer, his body heated by merely touching hers. "We had to have each other Amber."

"Eduardo?"

"Yes?"

"I wish we could have had a baby," Amber whispered now, holding back tears.

Eduardo rubbed Amber's shoulders and kissed her forehead. "Me too," he expressed holding back his own.

"I wonder what he'd look like," Amber confessed, continuing to run her hands up his chest.

He backed away from her and lay on his side, cropping his elbow on the bed and holding his face up with his hand. "He?" He said to her surprisingly.

"Yes, he," Amber quipped at him, still running her fingers down his chest. ***Good Lord***! He looked absolutely adorable in that lazy pose! His green eyes leered down at her nakedness; she felt the urge to devour him once again.

"I always wanted a son," he expressed, brushing back hair away from her eyes. He then grabbed her waist and sat her body over his torso. His lips dart in towards her barely covered breasts. Amber takes hold of his head and runs her fingers through his hair. "I'd name him something wild like Moseley or Peyton," she expressed, throwing her head back, enjoying Eduardo's pleasurable tongue around her skin.

"Peyton?" Eduardo lets out, pulling away for air, "That's silly; my boy is going to have an ethic name like, Enrique or Carlito."

Amber snorted. "He'd look like ***me*** of course; Lord knows we don't need another little Eduardo running around."

Eduardo continued licking her erected nipple. "I'm one of a kind, and he'd have your eyes."

"Yes," Amber consented, "A combination of our hair...and incredibly delicious caramel toned skin." With saying that, she lifted up his face and presented him with a light lick on his lips.

Eduardo gently yanked at the back of her hair and controlled her kiss while desire washed over him already rising for her. She responded to him instantaneously, opening up her mouth wide to receive and appreciate all he had to offer. He lifted up her hips and glided her down on his manhood, continually running his heated kisses alongside her neck while he did so. "Good God," he revealed in a coarse voice, "I would have loved to try to get you pregnant."

"I bet you would," she optioned, trying to catch her breath.

Their bodies move at a fast pace, uncontrollable and devoted to one another. They reach climax in chorus, both panting rigorously from exhilaration when the phone rings.

THE PHONE RINGS?!

Eduardo froze and so did Amber.

"What the fuck?" Eduardo stated, rolling away from the heated encounter. "Who the hell knows we're here?"

Amber was frightened as well and reached for her bra and underwear off the floor. Who knows about them? Good Lord! Could it be Victor? Leticia? "You don't suppose..."

"Don't even think of it," Eduardo angrily maintained. He pulled up his boxers and hovered over the phone still ringing and ringing. "Maybe it's a wrong number...Shit, there's gotta be at least five other cars at this dive."

"I know Eduardo, but what if it's them? What if Leticia or Victor found out about us and are calling to catch us in the act?" Amber gazed over at the clock; they had fifteen more minutes until they had to get back to the office. With mid-afternoon Sunset Boulevard traffic it would be virtually impossible.

"What the hell? I can't believe this."

The phone continued to buzz. "Somebody definitely wants to talk to us. They wouldn't wait for the phone to ring for that long! They're obviously waiting for us to answer the damn thing!" Amber got dressed in a hurry and was back in her Anne Klein dress she bought on sale at Macy's within ten seconds. "Are you going to answer it?"

"Hell no—are you?"

"What if they knew we were here?"

"Don't get delirious Amber...***no one*** knows we're here," Eduardo declared, pulling his trousers up over his hips.

The ringing stopped.

They halt.

Finally the end.

But was it?

The thought and realization that their spouses, co-workers, ***anyone*** could find out about them created fear of getting caught.

"Did that call hurt you as much as it did me?"

"More so I imagine," he avowed, looping back his belt.

The alarm clock then began to ring.

Eduardo and Amber both ***jump.***

Amber walked over to shut the sound off. "Oh my God Eduardo, what would you do if this got out?" She asked honestly.

"Now is not the time," he rapidly gives to her.

Amber guessed he was right. She'll think about the consequences another time. Right now she had to fix her hair, apply rouge to her cheeks.

The mood changed instantly from mass hysteria down to a comfortable afternoon. Eduardo grabbed his tie that hung from the lampshade, wrapped it back around his open-faced collar while Amber walked over to aid him to make the knot straight. He gazed down at his beloved for a moment and grabbed her hands while she tried to drag away. They embrace—hug each other tightly, close their eyes at the same time and think about what just happened—or could have.

"We have to go back," Amber sadly declared.

"I don't want to," Eduardo conveyed, running his hand through her hair another time.

"We have less than ten minutes..." Amber whispered.

"So we'll be late getting back..." He murmured back to her.

Amber pulled away, opened up her eyes. "I've got a brief to type," she said in an unfortunate tone.

"I'm glad to have you Amber." Eduardo blinked back into reality. But not quite, closing his eyes one last time, he kissed her lightly on the lips. "I had fun today dreaming with you," he said, his head butting up against hers. "I would have loved to have seen what our kids would have looked like...If our situation were different."

CHAPTER**TWENTY-FIVE**

Guilt Kills

Amber nearly crashed into one of the walls when she spotted Leticia walking through the reception door. She spotted Amber through the glass window and gave a friendly wave.

Amber walked over to the reception area, "Leticia, what're you doing here?"

"Coming to see if you guys were free for lunch, are you?" She asked with drawing breath.

Amber couldn't help but notice Leticia's sexy attire. Leticia was wearing something low cut; her breasts were flat and barely raised the fabric. "I'm free, I don't know about Eduardo though," she gave to her, knowing perfectly well that they had plans to go out to lunch together. Eduardo's caseload was quiet for a change and Amber was grateful for it.

Leticia walked passed Amber and straight towards Eduardo's closed door. She waited outside for a second and then opened it up without knocking first. Amber followed her in.

Eduardo was in the middle of dictating on his hand-held device. His Italian leather loafers crossed on top of his desk. Startled by Leticia and then swiftly Amber behind her, he dropped the piece of equipment as if it were on fire. "Leticia! What're you doing here?"

"Came to see my loving husband, and my favorite sister-in-law...ask you both out to lunch."

Eduardo composed himself and eyed her clothes. "New dress?"

"You like it?" She asked, twirling herself around, thrusting her breasts out for viewing.

Eduardo couldn't help but gawk. "It's nice."

Eduardo goes in for a hug while Amber stepped back behind them embracing. She's hurt, jealous isn't the word for it—she's downright injured. Amber turned around and headed out the door. She was in mid-hallway, about to scamper away, when she heard Eduardo's voice ringing through the passage.

"Amber!"

The sense of urgency in his voice brought awareness to the other Assistants who all looked up from what they were doing.

He composed himself instantly and trotted down the hallway, grabbing her forearm, forcing her into an empty office. "Where you going?"

"She wants to have lunch with you, go ahead; I've got work to finish anyhow," she expressed, deeply, deeply suffering.

Suddenly, and on cue, Leticia appeared behind them. "Amber, what's wrong? Com'on let's have lunch, I'm not able to do this very often, let's go, whadda say?"

Amber looked deep into Eduardo's eyes. He nodded slightly. She raised an eyebrow. "OK, if there's not a crowd..."

They sat down at an outdoor café in the Century City Plaza. Leticia wrapped in her new outfit, Amber wrapped in her remorse. Eduardo, feeling uncomfortable himself, fiddled around with the food on his plate. Leticia watched his every move like a hawk. "Eddie honey, can you do me a favor and get me a Café Vanilla Frappachino from Starbucks before I leave?"

Eduardo gazed over at the line for refreshments. It was long, about ten people out. "Are you sure?"

Leticia let out a deep sigh, "I'm sure."

Eduardo grunts and walked over to the line.

Amber watched him saunter away. Now alone, face-to-face with Leticia she was truly dreading the moment. At the Sanchez household at least she had relative reinforcements.

Leticia caught Amber's eyes and her own filled with water. "I think...I think Eddie's having an affair." She whimpered softly, wiping away the tears that fell from her eyes.

Amber swallowed hard, "You do?"

"He's been coming home late, later than usual. He constantly has this mysterious look on his face, and once I thought I smelled another woman's perfume on his shirt." Leticia tried to contain herself but it was too late, the tears kept on flowing.

"Oh God Leticia, how could you tell?" Amber let out; hoping and praying Leticia's next words weren't about them, about her. What the hell were they thinking anyhow?

"He doesn't want to touch me anymore," Leticia whispered. "Lately, he's been too busy, too wound up, too tired to make love."

Amber held her hand. "We've been working hard on this defamation case, we're going back to court again, and we're trying to make a deadline." She reported.

"Have you noticed anything unusual about him Amber? I mean...has he been giving any special attention to any of the Assistants here?" Leticia asked, searching in Amber's eyes for some sort of proof.

Amber brought to mind the night they made love on his desk, all those important documents flying in the air as soon as their bodies reached the surface. "No—no, I haven't noticed anything different."

"How come I don't believe you?"

Amber almost expired at that moment—the conviction stabbing at her heart. It was so strong; she felt she needed to confess. Just then, she spotted Eduardo coming back towards them with the iced coffee in his hand. Amber froze. Eduardo took note of it. His head tilted for an odd second wondering what the heck was going on.

Leticia noted Amber's eyes and then stiffened up, disguising herself wiping away her tears.

"What were you two girls talking about?" He asked curious, sitting down.

Amber coughed away her humiliation and stood back up, strolling away from the table. "I've got to head back to the office, I forgot I have discovery to type. Thanks for lunch Leticia." She stated, abandoning them.

Amber rushed back into the suite with heated fury. What the hell was she doing? Why did she feel so incredibly dreadful about hurting Leticia? Lying and deceiving her just now. It pierced her heart in the most horrible unimaginable throb. Amber reached her desk, surveyed her files piled high on her desk. She doesn't want to work at the moment, couldn't, can't. She wanted to ***throw up,*** felt the need to and stood back up. Eyed in the distance Eduardo entering through the suite's doors. He immediately spotted her, but was captured momentarily by another associate. Eduardo looked impatient while talking to the other attorney. Amber made her move and escaped but was suddenly cornered by Jackie.

"Are you still working on that Howard file Amber? I can't seem to find it in our cabinet," Jackie expressed, smiling as she viewed Eduardo quickly approaching them. "Hey Eduardo, nice lunch?"

Amber turned to face him. He was fuming with that same rage mixed with jealousy. But he contained his anger for Jackie though, disguised it so well, she doesn't know the difference.

"Yah—thanks Jackie...you need me for something?"

Jackie took a few steps backward. On second thought, maybe she did feel his hostility. "No…I...was just asking Amber if she had a file of ours. The Howard files."

"I have them," Eduardo expressed to the quick. "They're under a pile of magazines I was gazing through, on the right side of my credenza, you'll find them there."

Eduardo waits till Jackie disappears before he noticed that Amber has left the conversation as well. ***Damn her!***

He practically runs down the hallway, peeking through doorways searching for Amber. His heart was racing, no, it's about to jump out of his chest!

Amber was hiding in the copier room. Began to take out reams and reams of paper and opened up the copier to put them in. Eduardo reached her at last and slammed the door behind them.

"What the fuck was that all about?"

"You need to keep up appearances." Amber related to him, crossing her arms out in front of her. She wasn't about to let him bully her; she knew exactly how to handle him. A kiss on his lips should do it.

"And who decided that!" He continued to yell.

"Me."

"You?"

"Yes, me."

"And what makes you think I want to be near her? I see her every fuckin' night! Isn't that enough? She wouldn't talk to me after you left. What else is going on?"

"She thinks you're having an affair," Amber let out finally.

"Did you tell her?" Eduardo asked, heart pounding.

"No."

"Are you gonna tell her?"

"No."

Eduardo noticed the tears in Amber's eyes. In a flash, his anger halts. He wiped away one of them. "Then what's wrong then?"

Amber walked away from him, his body, and his gaze. She knew him all too well to know what came next. They'd be at it on the copier if she didn't toddle away. "Do you still have sex with her?"

Eduardo's jaw practically dropped. Does he tell her the truth? Does he lie? "Why?" He asked instead.

"Images Eduardo, that's what I'm talking about. What do you feel when you touch her?" She asked, her arms still crossed.

Eduardo grabbed her hand and tried to unravel her tight grip away from her waistline. "Amber, I don't want to hurt you."

Their eyes lock and hold.

"You do, don't you?"

Eduardo closed his eyes. Amber let go of his hand and stepped away from him. "I still have sex with your brother," she confessed, watching his body grow weak. "We both have to continue being married to keep the impression we still care about them."

Eduardo doesn't want to hear anymore and cursed a few profanities before leaving Amber alone.

Amber wants to run after him, but doesn't. Instead she falls to the ground and starts to weep. She hated for having to face the ugly truth today, but really, how far could this go? Ask for a divorce? Would it be accepted? His brother's wife? Having to see Victor after the divorce? Her kids calling Eduardo dad? HUH? This was so stupid, incredibly insane to comprehend. How do you rationalize any of this? Secretly meeting each other, lying to their spouses; feeling totally awkward every time they bump into one another publicly, when privately they're unable to be pulled apart.

And then one night, one lonely evening at the in-law's, Amber knew it would never be the same. She wandered around the house aimlessly, wondering what the hell Eduardo was doing with Leticia. ***They were married***, she kept reminding herself. Leticia was so in love with Eduardo, she doted on him in the same way Victor pampered her. ***It was weird***, she realized. ***I may have married the wrong brother. Leticia could have married Victor and she would have been perfectly happy. Both cherishing each other, living in a world full of saccharine.***

Passion was what Amber realized was missing in her marriage to Victor. She was intensely in **"*like*"** with Victor now. They had a brother-sister kind of friendship and could talk for hours. He was her Father Figure, and all she wanted from him now was his continued support in raising their children. But the children were playing second fiddle at the moment, oftentimes forgetting to pick them up, unable to show them her love and affection. She was being managed by Eduardo's mesmeric force. It was like her life with Victor was a dream world, floating around, not being able to exhale, experience emotion or pain. She was numb with him, isolated within her own household. And on the contrast, Eduardo at work was her real life, alive and breathing with him, exploding at his touch, wanting him constantly, day or night. She was too far-gone, a human being unable to breathe in life.

CHAPTER**TWENTY-SIX**

Listen to Experience

"Mom?"

"Hi, Amber."

"Can I come over? Are you busy?"

"Amber, everything OK? What's wrong, sounds like you've been crying..."

Amber ***had*** been crying. For the past several days she'd been crying a lot. Tucked away from the sound of the shower, behind the sound proof glass of her Volvo, in the garage muffled away by the rumbling of clothes being tossed from the dryer, wailing so loud, Amber had no control over it. She was in agony, on the verge of a nervous breakdown. Amber was so madly in love with Eduardo, she couldn't see straight. She was far passed the point of no return and wanted to be with him constantly and walked around aimlessly thinking of nothing else but how to be.

Tears fell down her cheeks the moment Amber arrived at her mother's front door step.

Sheila opened up the door. "You look like shit, what happened?" Sheila joked, trying to put a smile on her daughter's face, but unable to.

"Oh Mom," Amber gushed, bending down to wrap her arms around her neck. "I don't know what to do, where to turn..."

Sheila escorted Amber into the house and onto the couch in the living room. "My goodness, what could be so bad? Are the kids OK? They're not sick are they?"

Amber nodded her head. "No Mom, it's nothing like that."

Sheila grabbed her daughter's hand. "Then what is it Amber?" Sheila asked in her stern motherly voice, "Just spit it out it'll make you feel better."

"I'm in love..." Amber confessed.

"I know..." Sheila agreed, thinking she was starting to say something about Victor, and then noticed Amber's bizarre expression on her face. Then she knew. Amber's frown on her forehead confirmed that it wasn't with her husband. "Who with?"

Amber swallowed hard. "I can't tell you, but I've been in love with him for a very long time."

Sheila shook her head in disbelief. "Oh baby, what happened?" Sheila knew from her own past, and through friends of hers, that having an affair meant something was lacking in the marriage. People who usually had affairs meant that they weren't receiving emotional support and went elsewhere to obtain it. Sam left her for that very reason alone. He wasn't happy…wasn't happy with her, so he sought out another who could make him happy. "What's been going on with you and Victor? Did you two have a fight?" It was always the couple that you thought never fought, or had the greatest of marriages that had the most problems.

"No Mom, we don't fight," Amber expressed honestly.

"Everyone has a little spat now and then...Is that why you felt you needed to stray?" Sheila inquired.

"Stray?" Amber stopped crying all of a sudden. "Didn't you just hear me a few minutes ago? I've been ***in love*** with this man for the past twelve years!"

"Twelve years? But you've been with Victor for nearly that long. My God Amber, what're you doing?" Sheila was in shock, but shock wasn't the word of it. It was a slap in the face.

"...And I want to be with him forever, Mom. Night and day, he's all I ever think about."

"And what? Are you thinking about leaving Victor, about leaving your kids?"

"I don't know Mom, that's what's driving me insane; I don't know what to do."

"Twelve years...oh baby, you're gonna hurt that Sanchez

family, please reconsider."

The Family? Amber looked across at her mother now. An incredulous look washed over her face. Could it be? That Sheila Thomas was living through her ***own*** marriage? That her mother could prevail this time knowing that her own flesh and blood could hold onto a marriage longer than the two year mark, like it was her own accomplishment? "The family Mom? What about ***me?*** Your daughter? Aren't you concerned about me?"

Sheila positioned herself across from Amber and surveyed her daughter more closely. Oh how could she have missed it? Amber's physical change...Her gradual transformation from dowdy tomboy to full-fledged sophisticated woman? Amber's cheeks flushed softly with a pink hue. Her eyes decorated with soft black mascara. Hair cut and curled to perfection. Her attire so elegant, so updated, so ***not her***.

"I'm in love with Eduardo Mom, Eduardo ***Sanchez..."*** There, she said it. The truth finally let out. It felt ***so*** good to express her aspiration for him out loud and not within her own conscious.

Sheila was taken back. Her eyes round with trauma. "Your ***brother-in-law*** Eduardo?"

Amber looked down guilty. "...Yes."

Sheila stood up from the couch and ran her hands down her pants, through her hair and then covered her mouth in uncertainty. "You're not pregnant are you?"

Amber looked away intense. "I can't believe you asked me that, you know how hard it is for me to get pregnant! I'm in love Mom, ***in love..."***

"My God Amber, how did this happen? This is ***so wrong***. Did he force you? How did this happen? No, I don't wanna know what happened...oh Amber, this is ***so wrong.*** How could you have allowed this to happen? How could you ***ever*** make this right? You'll never be able to, you know that don't you? Oh God Amber, you're definitely going to rip that family to shreds!"

"Good Lord Mom, forget about ***them*** for a change and start thinking about me!" Amber bawled, suffering a throbbing so unhealthy, she doubled over in pain.

Sheila went for her daughter and pulled her face up from

within her knees. "Oh baby—I'm sorry, I can't imagine the pain you must be going through. I just can't help but think of all the sorrow Victor and the kids are going to experience if this affair ever gets out."

Amber continued to sob. "Oh Mom...I don't know what to do. I can't leave Eduardo. I don't know ***how...***"

"I can't believe you did this."

"Of all people Mom...I thought ***you'd*** understand." Amber threw back at her. "You've been through more relationships than I care to remember. Falling in and out of love faster than you change your pants! I've at least been devoted to the man for the past twelve years!"

Sheila took a step away from her daughter. That was contempt in Amber's voice. A buried scar meant to sting. "I guess I deserve that." Sheila agreed stopping in her tracks. Oh God, this sounded all too familiar. She recalled the day Sam asked for a divorce. He was in love with another woman. Sam should have been the one she got old and gray with. She was devoted to ***Sam,*** but no one could ever know that. Sheila was still in love with him after all. He was ***her*** Father Figure. So tall, such handsome features. The outlaw rogue she so craved in a man. Sam left Sheila for a married woman. She would have forgiven him in a heartbeat, but Sam confessed he was in love. In love with that married woman. . .

"I'm obsessed with him Mom. I can't think of anything else ***but*** him. I'm gonna ask him to divorce Leticia." Amber blew her nose on some tissue she had stashed away inside her purse.

Sheila shook her head at her, "He's no good for you." She tried to find reasons for Amber not to react just yet. "He's conceited and arrogant; you've never been into those types before. He's just using you for your body you know that. Those types always seem to think they can have any woman they want and a wedding ring or being one's sister-in-law isn't gonna stop them."

"Mom...Eduardo is not like that."

"He's quite the charmer, isn't he? He knows exactly what to say to a woman to flatter her, coerce her into doing something she's somewhat not sure of?"

"He's educated, that's all. Underneath it all, he's just another man."

"Are you so sure...has he told you that he cares? Has he said he loves you?"

"Yes, he's said it." Amber quietly mouths uncertain.

Sheila noted her daughter's somber reaction. "But you don't believe him do you? I bet he hadn't even suggested leaving his wife for you, has he? He can't possibly be devoted to you as you are to him. Otherwise the man would move heaven and earth to be with you."

Oh...Good Lord she's right. Amber closed her eyes and threw herself on the side of the couch in agony.

"This is so wrong Amber..." Sheila said, trying to explain away the own hurt in her voice.

"I don't care; I just wanna be with him..." Amber cried, caressing the fabric on the couch, "...I don't wanna hurt the family, or my kids, or Victor, but I can't see any other way around it...***Someone*** is gonna get hurt... I hate causing pain. I hate confrontations."

Sheila sat down next to her daughter now. Yes, she did know that. Amber hated arguments. Whenever Sam and she would fight over the phone, or in person, Amber would come between them and try and stop it. And after six divorces, Amber saw her share of heated arguments with all the men in her life, six different relationships, with six completely different men, all of which walked out that door when they couldn't stand the intensity.

"Amber...I think you know what to do. I think you've thought about it more than once. There's really no other solution."

"Then what do I do?"

"You're a smart girl Amber, I think you already know."

"No, I don't know Mom, please help me."

"Just don't see him anymore," Sheila simply expressed.

Not see Eduardo? ***Could she do it? Is she that strong? To walk away, quit her job, die every time she saw him at her in-laws...with Leticia. Is she that secure? No. Never. Not being with him would kill her.***

Amber let out a terrible cry and her emotional outbreak

overwhelmed Sheila to tears.

Sheila sat down next to Amber and held her body over hers. Amber intuitively laid her head down on her mother's chest and continued to shell out emotion.

"Sometimes," Sheila said softly, stroking her daughter's hair. "...We have to do things," she expressed, fully crying with Amber now, "***...things*** that make us ***unhappy*** in the moment...but ***content*** in the long run."

Like marrying a man you do not love.

CHAPTER**TWENTY-SEVEN**

Misery Eats at Your Soul

The arrangement was far too convenient. A secret affair would simply be a rendezvous she would have to conceal. They could meet up occasionally and she could differentiate between her secretive days and her marriage. But her affair with Eduardo was borderline approval. That was the reason why it was so hard for Amber. It was so appropriate when she could see him regularly. With them at work, meeting him at family gatherings—he was just so damn accessible! And the more time she spent with Eduardo, the more she didn't want to spend with Victor. Running away, out of the house, making excuses to go to the mall, get her nails done, and continually using her endometriosis as an excuse for him not to touch her.

She oftentimes found herself bawling her head out. Curling up in ball in the shower and crying like she never thought she could or realize. She was so madly in love with him now; she couldn't quite remember when she ***wasn't*** in love with Eduardo. When did she first realize…The day she met him?

Oh God, it was nearly fifteen years! In a blink of an eye, she had managed to deceive, mislead, betray, and be disloyal towards her family, Victor. Her own mother asked her to leave him, but she didn't listen. Oh, she should have…she should have! But the very next day, she saw Eduardo at a family picnic and was not capable of doing so. He was so adorable that day, playing with his cousins, nieces, nephews and daughter, dressing up as a clown, making everyone laugh. Amber couldn't help but fall head over heels for him.

Everyone, especially the ladies, fell in love with Eduardo that day; he just seemed to hold that persuasion on the female heart.

Amber closed her eyes and stared at the fixture on the wall. Jesus hanging on the cross. Inside a church, The Family was heartbroken. Tió Lamberto had passed away.

Rosalba was crying uncontrollably while Fabrizio tried to calm her down. Lamberto was her older brother, and she wasn't the only one who was going to miss him. Victor was crying as well and Amber reached over and grabbed his hand.

Amber's heart filled with anguish at that moment. Seeing Victor in so much pain made her realize that leaving him would be devastating. She just couldn't do it, won't, will. But then, as she watched Tió Lamberto's casket being rolled down the aisle, she eyed Eduardo pushing the casket along. An intense expression so unbecoming of him, she knew in her heart that she couldn't leave him as well.

The Family was outside, soothing one another when Victor suddenly grabbed Amber and cried on her shoulder. It was a distant feeling she had towards him. It was odd; he was like a stranger to her now and she tried to feel something by wrapping her arms around his neck and pulling him closer to her chest. Over his shoulder, she eyed Eduardo watching her as tried to console his brother.

They walked together towards the gravesite. Hand in hand, dressed in black, engrossed in sorrow, women were crying hysterically while the men disguised their grief by wiping their noses on their sleeves. Children laughed and played amongst the headstones, unable to fathom the realization that they would never see their loving Tió Lamberto again but in the clouds or in their dreams of Heaven.

Leticia walked over to Amber and held her hand within hers. "You've known him longer; did you know he was sick?"

Amber felt peculiar holding Leticia's hand; an overwhelming sense of remorse entered her heart. "No—I...I think Victor did though."

Leticia wiped mascara around her eyes. "This is all very

sad, my grandfather died a couple of years ago and we never had this much family come to his funeral."

Amber swallowed hard. She's right. She looked around them, so many family members, nearly one hundred, two hundred, maybe even three hundred people; trucks and cars lined up around the block, more even entering through the cemetery gates.

Victor came up behind them, took Leticia's other hand and held it. "I'm so glad you're here Leticia, our family wouldn't be the same without you," he smiled, presenting a weak smile for his wife as well.

That was a very nice thing to say, Amber thought as she noticed Eduardo walking towards the three of them. With his hands down his pant pockets; he ambled over, his look no more uplifted than theirs. "God, I'm gonna miss him," Eduardo suddenly burst out, choking back his tears.

Amber set out towards her brother-in-law first unaware that she was doing so. Eduardo saw her approaching and his arms went wide to receive her. Victor headed towards him first however, as Amber deliberately stepped back—grasping what nearly took place? Eduardo veered towards his brother instead and closed his eyes realizing what just happened unconsciously. Eduardo embraced his little brother back and brought his body near.

"I love you Eduardo," Victor expressed, squeezing him tight.

"I love you too squirt."

Amber nearly died at the sight of Eduardo displaying affection towards Victor. ***"Oh God!"*** She cried out loud, releasing Leticia's cold hand and running away.

Victor disengaged from Eduardo and eyed his wife running away. "Amber—"

Amber doesn't look back. ***I can't leave! Eduardo won't leave! Leticia's gonna get hurt, Victor's gonna get hurt! This is so wrong! This isn't right! What the hell am I doing? What the hell!***

"Amber, ***wait,*** Amber!"

Eduardo stood frozen. Eyed his sister-in-law running away, wanted to dart after her as well...wanted to...but couldn't.

Good God what absolute hell! With his family all together, all he could do was wonder why. Why was she crying? What the hell was she doing? Where the hell was she running off to?!

Rosalba grabbed her son's hand and squeezed it tight within hers. "Mehió, you have to go back to the office soon?" She asked letting go a weak smile.

"No Mama, I took the day off," he gave to her, continuing to watch Amber run further and further away into the cemetery lawns.

Rosalba couldn't help but glimpse towards the area where her son was staring. Victor was running after his wife. Amber reached the mausoleum and dashed inside. Victor followed her in.

"It's a good thing he has her, I don't believe he could handle this if he didn't," Rosalba relayed, walking away from Eduardo at that moment with Leticia's hand. "Leticia daughter, come with me and greet some relatives of mine from Mexico."

Eduardo was left alone and detached with his deep concern for Amber. Does he make a complete ass of himself and run after her as well? What the hell was she doing running away? What the hell was going on? He took a step forwards then backwards again. Does he let his brother handle the situation? Does he allow himself to refrain? Good God he wanted her so much it tore him to pieces too!

Victor reached Amber crying uncontrollably on a marble wall filled with plaques. Goes over to her body and lifted up her face. "I didn't think you cared so much for Tió Lamberto," he asked honestly.

Amber continued to cry…sobs so loud… she fell to the floor accepting her role and anguish.

CHAPTER **TWENTY-EIGHT**

When it's bad, it's Ugly

It had been four months of being apart. In the middle of the calendar year when there were no holidays for The Family to draw together. No funerals, no weddings, no birthdays; no open excuses for them to see each other outside of work. Eduardo was constantly being reprimanded for continually being late, for handing in jumbled briefs, he was constantly being sent out of town. Amber too, never concentrated during work hours, her time was spent thinking about Eduardo, where he was, and how The Family would accept them as a couple.

It was in the afternoon, on a Wednesday. The sunlight streamed through an opening in the motel curtains at *The Rose Motel & Gardens* making the sordid ambience almost beautiful. They said nothing...they didn't have to. Amber knew exactly how to gratify him; Eduardo was obliging, knew specifically how to please her. Hands roaming nakedness, mouths expressing pleasure, they were both on the same wavelength towards the identical finish line.

Back to front, Amber was straddling Eduardo in a chair. She leaned forward first and allowed his substance to plunge inside her vagina. His hands instinctively inch their way down through her soft curls, and rubbed her sex as she continued to ride him slickly. She arched her back to lean on his chest as Eduardo brought his hands up and around her breasts. Instantaneously, their mouths weld, tongue to tongue, his hand still on her sex, her torso rapidly brought him and herself to culmination.

They pulled apart for a moment, bodies breathing heavily trying to wind down from euphoria. Amber wanted Eduardo no matter what and wanted him in her life period. She loved him so much; she would do ***anything*** for him. Amber decided she would leave Victor first. Cast everything away, her marriage, her children, would Eduardo do the same?

Sighing heavily, Amber would have to say it now or die from constant suppression. "I'm leaving Victor."

Eduardo opened his eyes. Did she just say that? The announcement he wanted to avoid at all costs? "What?" He asked wanting affirmation.

"I'm leaving Victor…I'm going to ask him for a divorce," she expressed, standing up from his sitting body.

"I'm not leaving Leticia," Eduardo stated roughly. After he said it he wished to God he hadn't. Amber's shocked glare made his heart sink.

"Did I ask you to leave her? No, I just said I was leaving Victor, I'll continue to be your mistress."

Eduardo closed his eyes in astonishment. "Do you realize what you're saying Amber? If this ever gets out?"

Amber was furious now. ***Good Lord!*** Did he just ***agree*** to that part of being his mistress? She just wanted him to contend that he'd do the same, leave his wife for her! Amber was livid, upset wasn't even the word. She wanted to have ***her way,*** throw a tantrum, whatever she could to try and sway his actions into agreeing to react.

Eduardo leaned down, pulled his clothes off the floor.

Amber noted his angered feedback. Why did he always do that? Show his inner-spoiled brat by getting dressed in a hurry? "Eduardo ***please,*** I can't do this anymore," Amber said, pleading her case.

"Can't do which part?" He shouted back at her. "Sleep with me? Meet at motels? Work? What!" Eduardo stood up—reached for his shoes—throws one by one, furiously against the wall. "Good God Amber, we just had the best sex ever and you start up this shit?"

Eduardo's remark made her feel like an idiot. Amber expressed desperation now. "You don't love her...you never have...you love ***me,*** don't you want to leave her for me?"

Eduardo's muscles tensed up. "Amber, we can't. It would ruin what we have now...it would ruin ***them***."

"Them meaning your parents...***your family,***" Amber mocked their existence now, something she thought she'd ***never*** do.

"Do you know what it would do to my family if they ever found out about us?" Eduardo gave to her, instantly remembering the day of the funeral.

"Do you know what it's doing to ***me*** every time I'm not in the same room with you?" Amber cried, pulling her clothes off the dresser. "I love you so much but I'm forced to be without you!"

"Amber calm down. This isn't that easy. My family...it would be a scandal. They would be ashamed. After Tió Lamberto died, everyone united. The bond is tighter than ever...do you even realize that? I won't do that to them, I just can't. Can't." Eduardo zipped up his pants, searched for his undershirt.

"Can't...***won't...***is more like it," Amber quipped. "I'm scared too Eduardo, I'm going to hurt Victor, and I don't want to hurt him."

"I don't want to either. I love my brother," Eduardo expressed looking away in agony. He closed his eyes in frustration. Why was this happening? Why did she have to bring them up again? What the hell was she doing?

"We've been sleeping together for three years Eduardo, and not once have I woken up in your arms. I want to have breakfast with you; hold hands on the beach. Go to Vegas, Europe, and Mexico—just go away, anywhere—together. We always sneak around...make love in a hurry. Don't you want some sort of normality?" Amber paused and waited for a response from him but doesn't get one.

Eduardo continued to shake his head and combed his fingers through his hair. "It's not that easy..."

"I know you could do it...it's not that hard...please leave her, Eduardo." Amber held up a nearby wall she was nearly out of breath watching Eduardo stubbornly pace the floor out in front of her.

"Why can't you fathom the outcome?"

"Why can't you realize I would do anything for you?"

"I do realize that, but why are you starting this now?"

"Damn you, Eduardo! Damn you!" Amber yelled back at him, he wasn't listening to her; he was only listening to common sense. "I don't want this to sound like an ultimatum," Amber let out suddenly, still standing her ground.

"Don't you dare," he avowed, staring her down.

"But if our situation doesn't change, then I'm leaving," Amber asserted. "How much longer do I have to wait for you?"

Eduardo was stubborn, worse than that; he's been spoiled far too long. He was used to getting his own way, and his way wasn't arriving fast enough. Her condescension was a direct hit to his behavior. The Bitch just turned him into an Ass. "Fuckin' Amber!" Eduardo shouted back at her. "It's not that simple!"

Eduardo grabbed his shirt and buttons up crossly. Amber continued to cry as she watched him fully getting dressed. A wave of disappointment flushed through her. Her last attempt at begging didn't work and her scorn served no purpose. If those two radical demands were not going to work, then nothing would. Amber then realized that maybe her mother was right. That all these years all he ever wanted or needed from her was sex. He ***lied*** to her and misrepresented himself adequately. They never really had any kind of future. She was ***already*** his mistress. Telling her that he 'loved her' was just a device to get her to continue the affair. What a fool she was, falling for his continual charm! How could she have been this naïve? ***Wake-the-fuck-up, dammit!*** She's been caring for him for so long she continued to believe everything that he said. She was even prepared to throw her entire marriage away for him! And Eduardo wouldn't even do the same? His marriage was in ***name only***; he's never even cared for his wife! Good Lord, what the hell was she doing? "Move heaven and earth," her mother said. Eduardo would move heaven and earth to be with her—was he doing that ***now?***

Amber felt used, discarded, ashamed and unwanted. Her Father Figure didn't want her anymore. She was being left alone again, waiting for her father by the window. Dressed in her special outfit, shiny shoes and all, waiting for Sam Fitzgerald to come and pick her up. Waiting and expecting her Daddy to show, but never did. Her Daddy didn't want her...never wanted a daughter...Eduardo doesn't want her...never wanted her to begin with. Her Father Figure was rejecting her and Amber was frantic. Her commitment to him suddenly became offensive and her passion for him panicked her and she wanted to escape! Amber was beside herself; her body shook as she tried to get dressed. If she couldn't leave Victor...and Eduardo wasn't going to leave Leticia...then ***no one*** would win.

The alarm clock ***rang.***

It was that ridiculous device that she absolutely ***hated.***

It told her it was ***time.***

Time to break ***apart***.

Time to go back to ***work***.

Go home.

Amber reached over for the alarm clock then chucked it clear across the room. The alarm clock continued to buzz until silenced against the wall. Amber was hysterically incensed now, so impassioned, and knew that there was one thing left that her lover hated most of all...mentioning sex with another man.

"It's over Eduardo," Amber callously uttered. "I'm going home to make love to my husband. Prove to him that I'm still his...I'm gonna stick my tongue down his throat...offer my naked breasts to his mouth in the shower...and, ***fuck him*** all night long."

Eduardo's throat closed up. Amber couldn't have said anything more malicious to him than that. She knew full well that mentioning sex with his brother injured his very soul. Eduardo felt like he'd been kicked in the gut. "Why you little bitch—" Eduardo proclaimed haughtily, desperately yanking her body back into his. "You know you belong to ***me."***

Amber pushed him away. "No I don't! I never did! This is over—"

Eduardo grabbed her back. "No, it's not!"

"This is one time you're ***not*** getting what you want!" Amber screeched, slapping him across his face.

The burning sting only made him angrier. Eduardo bound his muscular arms around her body; Amber tried to get out of his wrap, yanked at his arms, scratched at his collar until she felt his gold chain being yanked away from his neck. She watched it as it gradually slid down his pant legs then onto the rug.

When it's bad, it's dreadful, she was riled up, distraught, drowning and unhappy…something clapped inside her head; ***she*** would be the one to break his style, teach him a lesson he would never forget.

"...Are you going to calm down now?" He asked exasperated, arms still around her body in a tight grasp. He wasn't going to let her take off yet, not until he gained his way.

Amber was breathing heavily, she wanted to compose herself, she did, but relaxing would only mean to continue the misery. ***"Please leave her,"*** she asked one last time.

He was worn out with the subject and closed his eyes in disappointment.

His silence only fed her decision. She could either go on through life the way she was living, or she could end it, no longer feel the pain.

With all her might she pulled away from him and pushed his unreceptive body into the wall. Amber ran out of the doorway and hiked down the narrow hallway—ignoring his calls for her return from the staircase above.

* * * * *

Call it intuition. A mother's inner voice…but Sheila knew somehow, her child was hurting. Sheila got sick to her stomach; her body became nervous, anxious. She called Amber's cell phone, knew she would answer, but didn't. Called her daughter at work, they said that she hadn't come back from lunch yet. Lunch? It was nearly four o'clock in the afternoon! Thought about her being with Eduardo, he would know. But how would she get a hold of him? Where was Amber? Oh God, she couldn't get passed that distressing feeling!

Sheila had to think quickly. Amber told her about their affair. Sheila dispensed her opinions that Eduardo was taking advantage of her but knew Amber wouldn't listen. Her daughter was fragile at times, always wanted to be desired, wanted and loved. Sheila did the best she could; spoiling Amber with affection but Amber always craved extra attention when she was a little girl. Sheila tried to do her best, but Amber was oftentimes short changed. Trying to accommodate her new husband and showering her daughter with attention was oftentimes daunting. Someone was always being left behind. If it wasn't her new husband, then it was Amber and Molly. And when she felt the girls were content, her husband was not. It was an endless tug of war between her children and maintaining a relationship, and she loved her girls, and oftentimes not so much her husband and it was easy to let the man go.

Sheila got into her car and started to drive. If Amber was with Eduardo, then they were at a motel. Amber gave her addresses to three of the motels they often went to just in case of an emergency with Valentina or Adrian. ***Just in case,*** she told her mother. Just in case at times like these? Times when she felt something horrible had happened? She couldn't shake off that awful feeling.

She parked her car at *The Rose Motel & Gardens*. Got out of her car and ran around the parking lot searching for Amber's white Volvo or Eduardo's silver Porsche. They weren't there, but did that mean she wasn't there at all? Sheila still had that unpleasant ache.

Sheila got back into her car and drove down two more miles towards *The Ocean Front Motel*. There was no ocean around the vicinity and Sheila laughed sickly at the sight of the seedy baby blue motel. Again, she got out of her car and ran through the few cars that were parked there in the parking lot. No trace of Amber or Eduardo's vehicles.

Sheila closed her eyes in frustration. Was she just imagining it? Was she just wasting her time? What was it? It was a dreadful, terrible feeling deep down in her gut that kept her in pursuit. She finally reached *The Motel Coronado*.

Oh my God! Sheila found Amber's car. Sheila ran around it

and into the motel and yelled at the manager, "Where's my daughter!"

The office manager looked up from his paperwork. "Uh? What? You need someone missy?"

Sheila was out of breath and was on the verge of delirium, "My daughter, her car is outside; I know she's here, I need to see her!"

"Now ma'am, please calm the hell down, you know I can't give out any information on who's staying here, it's against procedure and against the law."

Sheila pounded on the counter in front of him, "Listen idiot! My daughter is in trouble so if I don't find her now I will have every biker here on your doorstep demanding free room and board for the next twenty years!"

The office manager doesn't like that word ***trouble*** and ran through the roster of names and offered the frantic woman a few room numbers filled with single women. Sheila sighed when she realized there were only three rooms to visit. "Thank you."

Sheila stopped over the rooms one by one. Knocked on the first door and woke the woman from a deep sleep, a prostitute obviously, looking for her next 'John'.

The second, a battered wife with a bruised face. Oh God, Sheila realized, what kind of dives did this asshole take her too?

Sheila finally reached the last door. Knocked, no answer. She had that horrible, frightful mother's perception slapping her in the face again. She banged on the door. Tried for the knob, it was locked. Goes to her purse, searched for a bobby-pin, tried to pick the lock. And by some miracle (the marvel that she was even there) forced the door to unlock. She threw the door open and noticed the bathroom light on. She called out, "Amber?" No answer.

Sheila quickly scanned the room. There were her clothes, her purse, and the cell phone taken apart on the floor. There were three letters left on the dresser. Oh my God! The three letters were all addressed! Fear spread throughout her body.

OH MY GOD!!

Sheila ran towards the bathroom and gasped at what she saw. Amber's lifeless body had sunk underneath the water in the tub making it red as a rose. Blood apparent on the tiled walls, it dripped over the edges and trailed onto the floor causing the white linoleum crimson as well. Sheila reached for her daughter's body.

"Oh my God!"

Sheila managed to pull Amber's unresponsive body up and out of the water to hold her to her chest. Her life was gone…her spirit…her heart, her will to live. "Oh Amber, why? Oh baby, please...please wake up, please? Oh God, not my baby….oh God please, ***Amber no!***"

CHAPTER **TWENTY-NINE**

If You Eat It, You Will Choke

Sheila sat alongside her daughter's comatose body. Amber was in a coma caused by lack of oxygen to the brain coupled with extreme blood loss. A few minutes more, a centimeter deeper, she would be burying her daughter rather than hovering by her bedside. Sheila then focused on the surgical wrap around Amber's left wrist. It was an obvious display of what had happened. What would possess her daughter to do such a thing? A suicide attempt? What a horrible awful insight. Her once sane daughter...her normal daughter, the one she always believed was more practical and stronger than herself?

"I'm gonna kill him," Sheila conceded, "Or at least make ***him*** bleed."

Molly tugged at her mother's sleeve. "Make who bleed Mom?"

Sheila forgot that Molly was in the room. Forgot about a lot of things. Sheila was so distraught, unrecognizable.

Sam Fitzgerald came as soon as he got off the phone with Sheila. An intimidating sort if you weren't friends with him first, he was a tall thin leather-wearing biker with coal black hair pulled back with a band and hazel eyes under dark sunglasses. Sheila closed her eyes at that moment and wished to God Amber could see that her father still cared about her and that he never did abandon her completely.

"Will she be OK?" Sam asked quizzically, walking over to Amber's side.

"She's in a coma Sam..." Sheila whimpered.

Sam goes for her. Wrapped his large arms around her body and held her close. "I'm so sorry," he apologized now for deep-rooted regret. "I should have been there for her."

"I know...I know you are." Sheila gave back to him. "But you're here now," she expressed.

"I hope it's not too late," Sam said, still holding Sheila in his arms.

Molly goes for her father as well, gives him a hug. "Thanks for coming Dad, I know it would mean a lot to her knowing that you were here," she said clutching him close too.

Victor suddenly entered the hospital room. Walked over to his wife, surveyed her body lying there. Disbelieving what she'd done. "Sheila . . .Sam?" He asked in a defenseless voice.

Sheila broke away from Sam and viewed Amber's unconscious body, nodded her head in disbelief. She knew in her heart what to say, but didn't quite know how to express it.

Victor grabbed Amber's motionless hand and stared down at the bandage on her wrist. Never a clue...Nothing was wrong. It was life as usual. She was stressed from work, but who the hell wasn't? He was never demanding, never forced her to do anything that she didn't want to do, or asked to do. She was always allowed to go anywhere she wanted. Free to go shopping, to the movies, get her nails done, and work late, out to see her friends, Leticia. He loved this woman, he showered her with affection, comforted her when she wept, felt lonely. What did he do? Why did she want to end it all? The kids...him, what was ***so wrong?***

Eduardo rushed into the hospital room out of breath. It was Eduardo alone detached from Leticia. He was always with Leticia, and there he was...solo. Victor looked his brother up and down. Why was ***he*** here anyhow? How could he have known? He didn't call him, why would Sheila call? Eduardo was so concerned about Amber. Victor watched his brother as he slowly staggered over to Amber's bedside; inspecting his wife, practically dying at the sight of her in slumber.

"Eduardo?" Victor barely got out.

Sam raised an eyebrow at Sheila. Sheila's stone face and tight lips were all he needed to validate that these two men adored his daughter. Sam walked over to a nearby corner, crossed his arms and enjoyed the show. Molly went with him.

Sheila sat silently back down. She knew this day would come eventually. But she never thought, ***never dreamed*** that Amber would do something so drastic to make it all come forth.

"Is she…all right?" Eduardo expressed, holding back tears. "Is she gonna be OK?" He demanded from Sheila at that moment. "What do the doctor's say? How much blood did she lose?"

Sheila gazed at Victor's quizzical expression and forced herself up to escort his brother out of the hospital room. "Eduardo, you're making a scene," she let out shoving his body against the wall in the hallway.

"Is she gonna be OK? Will she be all right?" He repeated.

"She's in a ***coma***," Sheila started to cry, releasing tears of sorrow. "We don't know yet if she'll regain consciousness."

"Good...God," Eduardo expressed, rubbing his hands through his hair. He's going to throw up; he never felt emotions so terrorizing. He closed his eyes and found a nearby water fountain, splashed water on his face. Turned around—

Sheila slapped Eduardo across his cheek. "Damn you! Look what you did. Amber told me what happened, what's been going on, how could you do this to her?"

"I—I, couldn't help it." Eduardo managed to get out.

"You dirty cheat. You ***used*** my daughter and played with her affections for years now...you're so God damned selfish!" Sheila began shouting, "Get outta here! Go away! You don't belong here!" She didn't care that Victor was within hearing distance; all she cared about was Amber—to protect her daughter from further harm. Eduardo was the damaging influence now and Sheila wanted to shield Amber from any further pain. What kind of man would allow his loved one to self-destruct? Sheila slapped Eduardo across his face again. Wanted to kick him in the groin when—

Victor suddenly appeared, eyed his mother-in-law hitting his brother, his face drawn—in shock. "Eduardo—Sheila? What the hell is going on?"

Eduardo shot a look at Sheila…Sheila managed to reach Victor's side; caressed his shoulder then let out a huge sigh.

The truth had to come out one-way or the other. She just couldn't believe that ***she*** would be the one who would liberate the infidelity. In a calm voice, she allowed herself to say, "I'm so sorry Victor, but the reason he's here is...is because they were having an affair."

Victor's face went vacant. Eduardo gulped, looked beyond Sheila—***froze.***

Sheila wandered out of the moment and does a double-take at Amber's in-laws: Fabrizio, Rosalba—their faces white with shock.

OH HELL!

She didn't mean to let The Family know as well! Victor, Eduardo, Rosalba and Fabrizio were all in disbelief now.

Eduardo? Did she just say that Eduardo was sleeping with their daughter-in-law? "Que?" Rosalba let out, shaking with trauma. "Usted hombre ***estúpido!*** What were you thinking?"

"Su hijo de esposa, Leticia, don't you love your wife?" Fabrizio asked angry.

"You're the devil Eduardo, ***el Diablo***, hurting your brother this way." Rosalba cried, crumbling in her husband's arms.

"Look what you did to your brother Eduardo, look what you did to his ***wife."*** Fabrizio stated, sadly unable to look at his son.

Eduardo walked away from his family; he doesn't worry about what they think of him...

Good God...he doesn't care?

With his head down he contemplated his next move. How to get back in to see Amber, how to wake her up, how to tell her he's sorry, how to tell her to ***hold on***. "But I love her."

Sheila thought she almost missed it, like a whisper from one of the nurses down the hall. "What did you just say?" She could not believe it. Maybe didn't want to allow herself to believe when she heard those particular words.

"I've always loved her," he replied, staring at Sheila's doubtful gaze.

Sheila scanned his attire, all business-like...so fashionable, with the best coat and ties, the fancy shoes, hair all neat and combed, so unlike Victor. "And when were you planning on telling her that?" She threw at him, a laugh still in her words. Sheila was wise. After all the husbands and lovers, and ***men***, she had to be shrewd. It was armor she wore well. A medal she cherished and was proud of.

"She knows I love her," Eduardo confessed honestly. "I tried to make her come back. To tell her that I was sorry...I was going to leave my wife."

Sheila started to express amusement. "You are a piece of work, you know that? Keep shoveling those hearts and flowers out you bastard, but it's still after the fact now isn't it? ***She almost killed herself today!"***

"It's the goddamn truth!" Eduardo angrily yelled back at her, the harsh attorney now emerging. "I've always wanted to take care of her, Sheila, always wanted to be ***near*** her. I'm the one she should have married," he motioned, pounding his chest. "I'm the one who should have fathered her children. I love her more than anyone ***here*** could ever imagine!" Eduardo shouted back at Sheila in addition to everyone in the hallway. The Family heard everything that was hollered. He didn't need to be so complacent about it. They all nodded their heads in shame. Rosalba crying uncontrollably, Fabrizio tried to calm her down. Disbelieving his brother's proclaimation, Victor ran out of the glass doors nearby.

"Eduardo, even I don't believe you...When Amber wakes up I don't want you near her. I want her as far away from you as humanly possible. You're going to have to live with your guilt. Amber was going to sacrifice ***everything*** for you today, her marriage, her children, and her life...because ***she loved you.*** It's obvious to everyone here you didn't love her; she wouldn't be lying unconscious if you did...I hope you're in ***hell*** right now, a special kind of hell."

CHAPTER**THIRTY**

Making Things Right

"We're going to send her to county," the doctor stated. "It's a good facility there; she'll be tended to well."

Sheila eyed Amber's body. Amber was still in a coma. It was going on four weeks now with no relief in sight. Hospital bills were mounting and Amber's HMO denied any further benefits directed to an uncontracted hospital; she would have to be moved to another hospice where her insurance could cover an all-inclusive residency. "Anything, I just want her well."

"I'll have it arranged."

It was the only solution really. Sheila didn't have the resources; neither did Sam after spending practically his life savings on getting remarried in the Bahamas. Amber needed a full-time nurse and the watchful eye of monitors and medications.

Two days later, Amber's body was wheeled away into a transport van ready to be sent to the county building. Sheila was by her side...but the Sanchez family was nowhere in sight. Amber had been abandoned once again. The family she once loved, cherished had suddenly turned their backs on her. In a sudden rage, Victor had gathered up all of Amber's belongings and stuffed them into suitcases and plastic bags, banishing them to the garage for Amber to pick up when she awoke and was out of the hospital.

"You her mother?" The medic asked Sheila, who was standing near the ambulance door.

"Yes," she replied concerned.

"You can follow me if you'd like. We're just transporting her to another location," the medic stated, properly shutting the rear doors and getting back into the driver's side.

Sheila turned away. It was raining. It was appropriate. No crisp sunny days for her little girl. Amber would hereinafter be thought of as unsound...unstable even around her own children, forever having to explain the scar on her wrist when she woke up. If she ***ever*** woke up. That comprehension overtook Sheila with emotion as she opened up her car door. She was just about to get in when Eduardo reached for her as she tried to sit down.

Sheila rolled her eyes, choked back tears, "I told you I never want you near her again."

"I can't Sheila," Eduardo broke down in front of her crying. "I know I don't have to continue to justify myself to you...but that's ***my wife*** in that van."

Even in the rain, Sheila witnessed the redness in his eyes. She permitted tears of her own when she actually felt his grief. She covered her mouth with the understanding. "Let her go," she breathed through heart-rending sobs.

Buckling over in pain, Eduardo went for her body and grabbed her into him.

Sheila cried a few more seconds within Eduardo's arms—then suddenly pushed him away. As much as she truly wanted to loathe the man, she was so grateful that someone other than herself sincerely cared enough to be there for Amber's transport.

"How is she?"

Sheila gazed over to the back of the van. "She's still the same."

Eduardo choked back more sorrow. "I miss her so much, what are you doing with her?"

Sheila wiped the water away from her face, away from her eyes. "I'm taking her to Valley Hospital."

"A ***county*** hospital?" Eduardo expressed delicately, a bad taste in his tone. "What about her insurance? Victor's insurance? There are no other possibilities? Goddamn it—this can't be right!"

Sheila couldn't believe it, but Eduardo's dominating presence shot through her entire body. It was an electrifying response, his authoritative tone. She could see why Amber was so drawn to him. Sheila herself was suddenly being pulled in by his magnetism. "What can I do? They won't cover her stay any longer; I have no other choice but to send her to a public facility."

Eduardo eyed the van again. He just couldn't grasp the fact that Amber was half-dead in that back cargo. "Keep me informed of her recovery...will you do that for me please?"

Sheila noted his sincerity. "Sure."

"I mean it Sheila. Amber's not going to be there for very long. I'll make sure of it."

She nodded her head just to get away from him. Sheila then opened up her car door and finally got inside; honked at the van that was waiting for her patiently in the rain and drove off.

Eduardo pulled himself back together and ran his hands through his wet hair, watched as the van pulled away while Sheila followed directly behind it. What absolute terror; his future bleak, driving away to a county hospital no less. Sheila asked him to let her go. Let her go? Impossible. He wanted what was his. He would never abandon Amber. ***Never.***

* * * * *

"Daddy? Will you tuck me into bed?"

Eduardo stared down at his little girl. Round green eyes, long black hair tied together in two ponytails, she was the illusion of her mother.

He lingered for a moment before responding. Amber consumed his every thought lately. He had no time for Kyra. "In a moment sweetheart, Daddy's had a rough day."

Leticia suddenly appeared behind the doorway. Subtle, introverted, she had a wineglass in her hand. "Kyra honey, go to your room for a moment, Mommy wants to talk to Daddy alone."

Kyra stretched out her pajama top and flipped it up over her face playfully exposing her skinny frame. "OK Mommy."

And she ran out of the room.

Eduardo then eyed his wife. "Don't start."

"Start what?" Leticia asked, sipping her chardonnay.

"I don't want to talk about it."

Touchy subject, Leticia gulped. "I just wanted to know about Amber, that's all. I spoke to your Mom earlier, but everyone's so hush-hush about it all…how's Victor? Have you spoken with him yet?"

Eduardo searched her eyes...Good God, she doesn't know? All these weeks and his family hadn't relished in the justice of telling her? It was up to him, he realized again. They wanted ***him*** to confess his infidelity. He wasn't in the mood. He would keep her in the dark a couple more days. He didn't feel like having a heart to heart with her, especially when his heart was somewhere else. "No."

Leticia took down a long gulp of her wine, "I can't believe Amber tried to commit suicide. What would make her do such a thing? I thought she and Victor made such a sweet couple; they made such a great pair. I feel so sor—"

"Enough!" Eduardo yelled at her with all the grief he was feeling at the moment.

Leticia's mouth closed up. "What's the matter with you?"

"Leave me the hell alone—"

He pushed passed her and stormed out of his study and found himself inside his bedroom. The moment he arrived, his clothes were ripped away from his body. He threw his coat clear across the room, his jacket was tossed across the bed, his tie yanked off and thrown at the nearby armoire. He was incensed, exhausted and utterly at Amber's mercy. Without her...without being able to talk to her daily, see her smile...feel her touch...he was reduced to nothing. Nothing! Nothing he could think of would come close to the equivalency of Amber in his life. How could he have been so stupid? How could he have been so blind? He was such a smart man. Intelligent, quick-witted, admired, respected among his peers...how could he have allowed the woman he loved try and take it all away? Why couldn't he just bow down to the companionship he had with Amber? He kicked himself for not being more experienced in holding together a relationship. Good God, he practically dictated connection with a jury, but he couldn't comply with one simple request? Good God...what did ...he do?

Eduardo finally sat down on the edge of the bed and bent over clasping his hands behind his head before setting free his penance for being so gluttonous in need. He would push and prod until he found his answer; after all, he still possessed tenacity.

CHAPTER**THIRTY-ONE**

The Truth Stings

After several long weeks Eduardo finally heard from Sheila. He couldn't believe it, but even the mixed up County of Los Angeles seem to lose tract of her. One week she was at one hospital, the next week she was moved somewhere else. It made him pale the way the county mistreated patients. He was going to defend her to the death, whatever it took.

Assisted by his crutches and dressed in a camel coat over head-to-toe finest suit apparel, Eduardo looked fashionably out of place as he went down the corridor towards the information desk. Various nurses and staff members all stopped to watch him hobble by.

All around him were lunatics, drug attics, transients, and God knows what else they let roam in those halls. He felt sick to his stomach. Eduardo couldn't believe that Amber was there. Amber was too good for this. If she was going to go to an extreme, then he was going to follow her lead. Amber was going to go to a private hospital, a place where they displaced compassion ***daily.***

Within reaching the reception desk of the district rest home, he said, "I'm here for Amber Sanchez."

The intimidated medical Assistant nervously looked up at him. "Who sir?"

"Amber Sanchez."

"How do you spell that?"

Eduardo rolled his eyes, "You're kidding right? S-A-N-C-H-E-Z," he said sarcastically gazing down at her name tag that shouted the last name "RODRIGUEZ".

"Um-yes, she's...oh my...just a second, I'll have a nurse escort you, mister..."

"Sanchez," Eduardo stated, not looking directly at her.

The Assistant continued to gape at him. "It'll just be a second Mr. Sanchez; a nurse will be here shortly to take you to see your wife."

Eduardo now eyed the medical Assistant who was still staring at him. He doesn't bother to correct her. Felt weak within for not making Amber his wife years ago.

Thirty minutes later, a nurse led Eduardo to another section of the hospice. A silent quarter. You could hear a pin drop in this wing it was so quite. The nurse opened up the door to a three-part room partitioned off by two thin curtains. She strode over to the last section and pointed to Amber's expired body.

Eduardo choked back tears. ***Good God!*** She looked asleep, but she wasn't. ***Wherever*** she was he wanted to be with her. "I want her out of here today, do you hear me?" Eduardo demanded, caressing Amber's unresponsive hand.

The nurse stepped back. "Yes sir, I'll inform the administrator."

"Do it ***now,***" he ordered. He couldn't take his eyes off Amber. He waited until the nurse was out of his peripheral view when he let the tears advance. "Oh...God," he sobbed, wrapping his arms around Amber's body, crying on her chest. He rubbed her body down; smoothed out the hospital sheet that barely covered her waist and chest. "Amber, please don't leave me…I love you... oh God...please come back, I'm ***so*** sorry...I get it now, I should have agreed to leave her…I'll take care of you Amber, I promise, ***please***...please honey wake up, please wake up."

While Eduardo continued to shell out emotion atop Amber's insensate person, he recalled the past several weeks. He finally told his wife. Sat her down and disclosed the whole affair. He was back to his ole self that day, the detached and heartless Eduardo Sanchez, trying to let down another clinging female with his not so subtle lack of sympathy. ..

"…How could you do this to me?"

Yes, how could he? How could he ***not?*** It wasn't really a temptation, how could he explain it? With Amber he found his soul mate, the love of his life. With Leticia he felt like her roommate, a prisoner contracted to a piece of paper and a stupid band of metal.

"I've been the ideal wife for you," Leticia related heartbroken. "You don't touch me for several months at a time and I'm OK with it."

"Haven't you ever wondered ***why?"***

Leticia stood defeated. "We look similar except for my...except for ***my,"*** she expressed looking down at her upper body, "I'll get breast implants if that's what you like."

Eduardo could not believe the insensitivity in his own voice, but he honestly never loved this woman. "If you think that I'm that superficial just proves you never really knew me."

"And I suppose she knows you more than I?" Leticia screamed back at him. "When I'm the one who's cooked and cleaned your house, washed your clothes and taken care of your child all these years!"

"It's over Leticia; listen to you, you sound like you could have been my maid."

"That's what a wife does for her husband when she loves him!"

"Face it," he heartlessly testified, "You were just a substitute and a device to further my career. You were a buffer with my family and a reason to get closer to ***her."***

"...But you ***love*** me."

"I've never loved you. We got pregnant. I asked you to get an abortion, but you cried that I compromised you and forced me into a marriage I never wanted in the first place!"

"You never wanted to get married?"

"No. What the hell ever made you think that I was the marrying type? I loved being single! I loved playing the field and meeting new women."

"But you gave in."

"My heart ***always*** belonged somewhere else, Leticia. You were just a replacement."

"But when we make love," Leticia rationalized, "The tenderness that I feel from you, that can't possibly be fabricated."

Eduardo scratched his head, "Gee, another item I'm good at, simulating compassion."

"You're a heartless bastard!" Leticia shrieked.

"That's right, I am a bastard. But a ***conceited*** one, and spoiled rotten. I know what I want, and what I want is not you."

Leticia fell to the ground weeping, her last chance to win him back. "I was going to tell you next week, but you'd better know now—we're having another baby."

Eduardo felt a lump in his throat. "You're ***not*** pregnant."

"And I'll tell your mother," Leticia voiced, noticing her husband's body questioning. "She'll make sure you don't leave while I'm expecting."

Knowing women as well as he did, there was something about Leticia's posture that wasn't quite right. She was either telling the truth or she was an incredible liar. "You're not pregnant Leticia," Eduardo continued to deny. "How could you be? I haven't touched you in several months, and even then, we don't have sex unless I wear—"

"I took a sewing needle to all your condoms," Leticia disproved. "It was only a matter of time...I am Eddie...and since ***I*** don't sleep around, you ***are*** the father."

Eduardo wasn't scared of her threats. Worse than that, he definitely didn't like being placed in a vulnerable situation especially by someone he barely tolerated. "I'm still not staying," he explained, trying to bring himself back to monopoly. "Don't worry; I'll take care of the child. I always take care of what's mine."

Leticia was crushed. She loved her husband with all her heart! All her hopes and dreams discarded in a matter of moments. "Please Eddie, please, I love you, I'll do anything for you, anything you want, please don't leave me...please leave her."

Please leave her.

Please leave her...

That same exact instrumental statement was the catalyst of Amber's repercussion. Those words were more potent to him than a judge's proclamation of ***'you're in contempt'*** affected him more.

"By the way it's ***Eduardo***, and I want a divorce," he soullessly uttered to her. "If you ***are*** pregnant, then you'll begin to show in the next few months." Eduardo watched her expressionless as she crumbled back to the floor. He grabbed his suitcases already by the door and shoved them outside in the rain. "Your crying just proves my theory," he grins patronizing. "I want to see my daughter every other weekend, I won't fight you on physical custody, I know she's better off with her mother than an unstable father like me right now. You'll be hearing from my attorney soon." And then he shut the door. The next thing he heard was glass shattering from a vase being thrown at the door behind him. But he loved his daughter, doted on her constantly, and treated her with respect; he just never loved the mother.

Two days later, Eduardo went to talk to Victor. But Victor would have nothing to do with him. He came out of the house swinging a baseball bat in his hands. Eduardo made every attempt at trying to calm his brother down, but the scene was so overwhelming he felt he almost needed to be thrashed.

"You stupid asshole—fucker –son-of-a-bitch! You betrayed me!" Victor shouted, swinging the bat aimlessly. "You can get every fuckin woman practically ***alive,*** but that just wasn't enough was it? You had to see if you could get mine! You stupid mother-fucker!" Victor swung the bat, missing Eduardo's face by inches.

"Victor let me explain," Eduardo pleaded, his hands up in the air admitting defeat. What the hell could he possibly say? He knew deep down it was nonetheless, unexplainable.

"There's no explanation for what you did Eduardo, no excuse for it." Victor bellowed, taking a swing at Eduardo's head. "You took my wife ***dammit!*** I thought if she weren't a blonde, at least I'd have a chance. But noooo...you took my wife's attention away from ***me,*** from our kids, she tried to commit suicide because of you!" He took another swing at his brother's head.

Eduardo's reaction was quick enough to duck, but just barely. He felt the wind of the bat graze against his back shoulder. "Victor please, stop swinging that bat before you kill me!"

"That's my intention you fuckin' wife stealer!" Victor swung again, only this time got Eduardo in his knee. Eduardo chopped down to the ground in ear-splitting agony.

Victor was ***his brother***. He really truly loved his little brother. "Victor no more," Eduardo cried in pain, flinching on the ground from the sight of Victor up above him ready to take aim at his other leg. "Victor, please—I'm in love with her!"

Victor hesitated having had the realization sink in. He lowered the bat, choked back furthering tears. "You better be," he demanded pointing the bat to his face. "Because if I ***ever*** find out that you were just...you were just," he expressed disheartened, fully crying now, "...***using her to feed your ego—*** Oh God, I'm coming back and bashing your fuckin face in!"

So many fond memories dashed inside Eduardo's mind when Victor spoke to him for the very last time. "You're no longer my family Eduardo, mi hermano...you're no longer my brother!"

That declaration injured Eduardo mentally, rolling over on the lawn, he wanted to die.

Eduardo was already separated from his parents for quite some time, going to college, getting his degree; he became independent from their emotions a long time ago. If it wasn't for Amber and wanting to be ***near her,*** he would have never spent so much time with his family and at their house. His mother was the matriarch of the family, and when Rosalba called for Eduardo during the middle of business hours, did he wait until his work was done? Hell no! He ran to the Sanchez house so fast his co-workers saw his exit as a blur. Rosalba wanted to hear with her own ears from her son's mouth that he had had an affair with his sister-in-law.

The moment they see each other, he falls to her feet and cries at the base of her legs. Rosalba's heart broke at the sight of her son in torment. She loved her little boy and caressed his hair as he continued to shed his heart-felt tears.

"Mehió...so it is true."

"Sí Mama, lo siento. I'm sorry," Eduardo confessed, looking up at her.

"Do you know what this is doing to your brother?" She asked, holding his head in the palm of her hand.

"Hago...I do know Mama."

"And you did it anyway?" Rosalba asked; disbelieving the conversation even existed.

"I fell in love with her, yo la adoro."

"Eduardo mehió...you could have any woman. You had Leticia, a loving companion. El compañerismo y adora. Why her? Why your brother's wife?" Rosalba pulled her hand away and wiped away her own tears that were falling down her face.

Eduardo stood up, took a seat next to her and grabbed her hands within his, "I didn't know I was in love with her until she married Victor. I tried to make my feelings for her subside, but they wouldn't go away. Era tan duro, it was torture for me every time I saw her. I tried to forget her with another woman, hide my feelings, live my life, but she still kept haunting me...***ah Mamá de dios***, she's the ***other half*** of me. Tell me who can turn away from that? I thought I was a strong man Mama, I've always been arrogant, always knew what women wanted, but Good God Mama, I ***never*** knew she felt the same. All those years I wished she had met me first, Amber adoróme también."

"Ah mi hijo pobre, Victor," she cried for her other son. Rosalba wanted to sympathize with him—she really did—but she couldn't get passed the reality of Eduardo hurting Victor. It was son physically harming son, and Rosalba was in deep distress.

Would he ever be allowed to come to family events again? Only time will tell. He was given a life sentence, only allowed visitation rights on good behavior. So was it all worth it? Alienating his brother, parents and Leticia? Worth all the torment, the lies, the deceit, just so that he could continue to be with the woman he loved? He was determined to find out. He wasn't going to go through all the heartache and not receive a reward.

Eduardo was signing paperwork in the administration office. Amber would be relocated to the Palm Desert

Treatment Center as soon as possible. Eduardo was going to pay for her care. He wanted to keep her from further harm and the Palm Desert Treatment Center came highly recommended.

He was just finishing up the formalities when his cell phone rang. He grabbed his crutches and dismissed himself from the office for a moment and hopped outside to the hallway to answer it. The administrator followed him and reminded him that he needed to "shut his phone off immediately." Eduardo shrugged the fellow off and the cell phone rang again and Eduardo had no other choice but to hobble outside the hospital to answer the call. It was Aldridge & Watson, they needed his assistance there. He needed to go back to work as soon as he was done. He had to go back to Century City or else. ***Or else what?*** As soon as they heard that Amber tried to commit suicide (and that Eduardo and Amber had an affair) Philip Aldridge put Eduardo on probation so fast his head spun. Eduardo created his ***own*** reputation and reserved his own good character as the city's top litigator, so if they were going to threaten him with being fired, then they would have a lengthy wrongful termination lawsuit on their hands, no doubt about that.

Eduardo was determined to see that Amber was transferred safely. He didn't want to leave, but had no other choice. He gave instructions to the hospital administrator one last time and went back up to Amber's room to say his goodbye.

How could he say goodbye? Farewell, so long? It was unimaginable. He would see her again. He felt so in his heart.

It was dark in her room. The curtain was still drawn, but Eduardo could hear someone mumbling behind the sheet. Could it be? He got excited. Was she finally awake? He could tell her now how much he loved her, and how everything would be all right.

Eduardo gasped when he saw a large African-American orderly fondling Amber's breasts as she lie inanimate in her coma.

"What the hell!" Eduardo shouted at him. "Get your fuckin hands ***off her!"***

He grabbed the man's arms away from his beloved, shoved his awkward body into nearby monitors and machines and the man shuffled along the linoleum trying to get to his feet to escape but was unable to as Eduardo held him down with the blunt of one of his crutches and kicked the man repeatedly with his one good leg. "Get the fuck outta here!" Eduardo protested, ***"Get the fuck out!"***

The impulsive uproar echoed down the corridor. A nurse in another room heard the commotion and came pouring up the hallway and into the room. "Sir? What's wrong? What's going on here?"

Eduardo tried to catch his breath. Wiped down his attire. He couldn't believe what just happened, what he ***saw***. It was appalling—it made him nauseated. Disgusted thoughts ran through his head. She was in this hospital ***how long?*** A week, eight days at the most? God only knows what went on behind the curtain! Good God, he had to get her out of this place!

"Tell that fuckin hospital administrator of yours that he's gonna have the most expensive lawsuit on his hands...If I have to carry her out her myself, ***Amber leaves now!"***

"I will...I will Mr. Sanchez," the nurse continued to assert, her hands stopping his egress, "But before you leave..."

Eduardo looked down at her hands halting his exit. "What—what?"

"I might get fired by telling you this, but there's something else you should know..."

CHAPTER**THIRTY-TWO**

A Year and A Half Later

Eduardo departed the plane and found himself amidst other travelers at the Ontario Airport. Heading towards the booth to pick up his rental car, he recollected his routine.

Amber was transferred out of that disreputable district infirmary and into the Palm Desert Treatment Center the very same day. With the aid of Aldridge & Watson and the nurse testifying on his behalf, Eduardo sued the Los Angeles County, the hospital, and their staff for a considerable amount of money for mistreatment of a comatose patient, and he prevailed. Aldridge & Watson succeeded by having it broadcasted on every prime time news cast, magazine and newspaper and acknowledgment and praise soon followed. Eduardo was taken off probation, given a promotion and Amber's fees were compensated.

Every weekend for the past sixteen months he's made this journey. Eduardo would stand vigil by her bedside...hoping and praying...for her healthy recovery. There was so much to share with her, why hadn't she sprung to attention by the sheer sound of his voice? He loved her so much, hated seeing her motionless and unresponsive from just holding her hand. Eduardo was not used to Amber not clutching his body in return. Why hadn't she responded to his contact? He missed her so much—he's never been so in love. The one instance where he could prevail in his perseverance did not hold credence in his motivation to get what he truly wanted. So, where were the magic words?

Amber came out of the coma eleven months later. What happened? Why was she unconscious for so long? He often thought she didn't want to recover, want to be alive again, never wanted to ***see him*** another time. He was so relieved, elated, wanted to see her the moment she awoke.

Eduardo punched Dr. Hayward in the jaw when he refused to let him see Amber. ***He*** paid for her keep, even salaried Dr. Hayward. Why couldn't he see her? Dr. Hayward acted against it. Amber was distraught, depressed—it wasn't a good time. Eduardo didn't give up though, how could he? Dr. Hayward was now in control, and Eduardo had to accept the rule. He complied with the doctor's orders as his punishment for what he'd done. For what ***they'd*** done; caused two divorces, ripped The Family apart. A family that was once happy and thriving with love and happiness was now torn and beaten, scandalized. He would wait for the day Amber asked to see him. Wait with expectation, wait with his remorse.

Eduardo shoved the receipt for the rental car in the glove compartment and began his descent towards the center. His days were nothing more than solemn of late. Work was employment; it helped him pass the time, coming home late at the dead of night with hollowness in his heart and an ache that no one else could stop but Amber. Good God, however it began, he was lovesick over her! It was so hard to be forced to walk and breathe when all he could think about was being with her.

She refused to see him? Why? He'd been rejected? What was that all about? He's never been cast aside, never! He was devastated. Crying in the shower, listening to heartrending music, sitting alone in the dark, drinking. The only thing that kept him breathing was past memories...and what joined them together ***now.***

He had the chance and should have taken it. The day the two met...Amber, so young and naive. He could have seduced her away from his brother, before they got married, had their son, bought a house and made another baby. He did it before...***twice***, in fact. He robbed two other girlfriends' of Victor's, and neither their mother nor their father or family took notice or cared.

One girl was all over him the minute Victor was out of the room. Octopus hands roaming everywhere, it was Victor's first girlfriend at the tender age of thirteen. She was fifteen and ***very*** persistent. A dirty blonde, practically straddling him in their pool when Victor was underwater diving for rocks. It was all very innocent. They only stole a few kisses, but Eduardo still felt guilty and Victor was so heartbroken.

The next girl wasn't so easy to evade. Victor had been dating her for several months, another blue-eyed blonde, but not that exciting elsewhere. Eduardo didn't even say the word ***boo*** to the girl and she likewise ignored him until one night. Victor and his parents were out of town and left Eduardo in the house alone to finish studying for a college exam, when a tap on his window startled him. It was nearly two o'clock in the morning, and whoever it was, was being inconsiderate. Eduardo stormed over to the window and to his surprise; it was Victor's girlfriend—dressed in a fancy prom dress of sorts. He opened the front door and she explained to him that she just left her sister's wedding and had to use the bathroom. ***Bathroom?*** Well, he was tired from all the studying, and thought the excuse was worthy, so he let her in. The next thing he knew she was in this incredible sexy garter belt with silk stockings and a lace bra that he just couldn't seem to keep his eyes off of! She suddenly had this hot little body, and one thing led to another and they had sex on his bed. And wouldn't you know it, the girl confessed to Victor to make him jealous, and Victor was so impaired, he didn't speak to Eduardo for nearly six months. Lucky for Victor, Eduardo rented an apartment off-campus while attending UCLA and hardly ever saw his little brother and the girls he further dated.

Eduardo began to unwrap his sandwich he purchased just before he rented the car and began eating it. Chicken salad on sour dough bread toasted slightly, his favorite. He was a practical man, an intellectual...an educated male. He graduated from Harvard for ***crissakes!*** Working for top rated Aldridge & Watson producing seven figures a year. A long-established bachelor by choice, he never allowed himself to fall in love. If you wanted to spend time with him fine, but don't go hinting at love, relationship or marriage. He ran away from commitment and never batted an eyelash or gave an excuse as to why. He was always up front with the women he dated. It was clear not to believe in silly nonsense like love at first sight, or a thunderbolt of devotion drawing two people together. It never happened to him, so why give credence to it? It was some cruel joke God played on him when Victor presented Amber to his family for the very first time. Amber was so mysterious he couldn't keep his eyes off her. He always looked passed brunettes (especially women with black hair) but with Amber peeked singularity. Her hazel eyes pierced through his heart like a sheet of lightning. His perfect woman, she was everything enhanced; body, personality, friendship, consideration and undying love for him. The chemistry they shared was so intense, he oftentimes found himself running away because he was so over-whelmed with guilt just thinking of what he wanted to do with her. His brother's girlfriend. It was shameful, distasteful. Out of respect for the previous two times he stole what was Victor's, Eduardo felt he had to withdraw himself from the race. He would step back. Give his little brother a present. Watch with jealously, as Victor and Amber kissed and shared their dedication to each other, that acceptance of their love, their admiration for each other. Fall back from what he felt in his very soul could have been true happiness for the rest of his miserable presumptuous life.

Never in his life would he have believed that Amber felt similar. At that very moment in time, when they first laid eyes on each other, if the devil himself would have enlightened him that he would be sacrificing so much to be with her, he would have laughed his fucking head off. ***That's insane! No woman would make him do that!*** He ***was*** insane, totally and undeniably in love with his brother's fiancée.

He honestly didn't realize how much he loved her until the day of their wedding. Victor presented Eduardo with Amber's ring. Eduardo was Best Man. He was supposed to hold it until the exchanging of rings during the ceremony. Eduardo held it in his palm for so long; he thought it might have melted into his skin. It was a plain platinum band. It was faultless, simple, like her and he left it in his wallet in the dressing room never intending to give it to Victor. He wanted to grab her on that altar and whisk her away; present her with the ring he bought—and make her his eternally. Amber was gorgeous that day; he wished he had said something then. Once again, he had an opening, purposely strutting in front of the bridesmaids, pretending to be lost on his way to the groomsmen. And when he saw Amber, dressed head to toe in her wedding dress that should have been for him; all he could muster up was the word ***wow.*** She took his breath away. Grabbed his heart, twisted it so tight, he felt such anguish; he couldn't see straight the entire ceremony. The days after were filled mostly with emptiness. He went home alone, while Amber and Victor made love, it pained him physically just thinking about it. Oh, how he wanted her for himself, envisioning her in bed with him, his wife for all eternity. Days turned into years of yearning for his sister-in-law and wishing fantasy would mutate. He was totally unbalanced when he finally met Leticia.

Leticia was like a breath of fresh air. She filled up his time, his concentration, the moments he ***did not*** think about the woman he now loved. He was lonely, and constantly dreaming of Amber, that one night he practically attacked Leticia. In his eyes, as he tore her clothes away from her body, she ***was*** Amber. He wanted to make love to her, feel himself inside her. Leticia satisfied the moment of compulsion, he never intended on marrying her but her family came from a strong Catholic background and she had been a virgin and he had no other choice but to put a ring on her finger when she announced that she was with child. She was merely a stand in for the person he really wanted. And oh how he always felt guilty for having sex with his wife! He felt like he was committing adultery (which was totally absurd) and should have been diametrical. It was forever daunting trying to keep up appearances with Leticia too, forcing to show affection towards her in front of his parents and family, continuing to have intimate relations when he really couldn't stand the sight of her. He was in love with Amber the first day he met her. No other woman would suffice.

He was so grateful for all the little incidences he had with his sister-in-law when she initiated them. Amber constantly sought out his friendship and it fulfilled the need of wanting her for himself. Sitting on the couch, joking at the dinner table, daring each other to swim laps in the pool, unimportant moments where he could have her full attention. And when he decided to see if she felt equivalent, he would purposely walk out of the same room, absent from her view, talk with someone else or simply speak with Leticia alone. He knew he'd sparked some kind of interest because Amber would always follow him. Until one day Eduardo couldn't take the torment any longer and decided to be so bold as to taste her lips. He needed to satisfy that constant craving of feeling her skin and, Good God; the desire was never quite fulfilled. Damn he was reckless, sleeping with his brother's wife. Amber was everything he's ever wanted and he found himself brutally sexually attracted to her (and if he had his way) they'd never leave the bed.

She was constantly driving him to distraction at work too. He couldn't believe all the cases that got settled in those years; how on earth could he have concentrated so much on legal effort when all he wanted to do was passionately kiss Amber all day long?

Come to think about it, Eduardo realized, with all the places that they did make love; someone should have definitely caught them. In the car, at the park, bathrooms, restaurants, elevators, even once at his parents' home. Good God, how that was exhilarating! The thrill that they might get caught caused them both to get excited...in the garage of all places! His father's 60th birthday no less! All his relatives were singing Happy Birthday when Eduardo pulled Amber aside to steal a kiss. He should of known from the start that one kiss from her would lead to pulling each other's clothes off. They ran towards the garage, it was the only place they could think of that wouldn't be occupied. With the lights off, it was perfect. Dark, sheltered and quite. Voices with song rang through the stillness as he entered her. It was crazy, it was breath taking, it was so, so immoral. But if felt **so** right.

Merging onto Interstate 10, trying to ease into the fast lane within traffic he thought about what Amber did to have everything come to pass.

He apprehended Amber within his arms. She pushed him away with all her might. She was strong, tougher than he expected and released her body slightly, only to have her push his size against the wall. Amber raced towards the door and ran down the hallway. Down the long corridor towards her car, he shouted down at her, but she refused to hear his failed attempts at doing so. Her car screeched away...What the hell was she doing? Was she ***really*** going to end their affair? Was she really going to leave Victor? Where the hell was she going?

He panicked, called her cell; she didn't answer. He called again, only this time she responded. He knew something went terribly wrong when Amber yelled at him for the last time. Being on the other end of that conversation, listening to the love of his life in anguish, in pain, tore his heart out. The phone went dead. It was cut-off in mid-sentence. She said she was going to teach him a lesson? A lesson in ***what?*** What was he supposed to think? He called the cell phone carrier; they told him the cell was deactivated by the possessor. The possessor? Good God, what happened! She was driving in her car hysterical; she lost control and caused an accident? Bleeding and dying on the pavement somewhere, he was impaired himself. He had to find her wherever she was. Thinking like an attorney more than a lover, he called up the one person he knew that wouldn't hesitate to help him out in a bind. Being employed by a five star firm had its advantages. Aldridge & Watson had access to private investigators up the yin-yang (really, really good PI's) like former FBI Agents called 'Joe.'

"I need a cell phone traced Joe, it's urgent." Eduardo recalled the conversation with him.

"You got it," Joe volunteered.

"Here's the number," was all it took. And honest to God, not twenty minutes later, Eduardo received a call from Joe telling him that Amber was being rushed by an ambulance to Cedars Sinai. Eduardo went cold. It was a nightmare. He was going to ***lose*** her?

Seeing Amber in that hospitals bed unconscious did he realize what an absolute self-satisfied asshole he really was? Instead of agreeing with her justification to seek a divorce, he forced Amber to make a harrowing decision. She wanted to die? She'd rather remove herself from the cause than face a future without him? She couldn't bear to live with his brother anymore than she could tolerate their relationship. That was her message to him. It was a memo sent loud and clear. ***Good God if he'd only yielded!***

The drive was nice, breath-taking in fact. The immense mountainside shaded the desert like a grandfather over its descendants with palm trees, white sand...a beautiful oasis of modern motels, restaurants, golf courses, stores and casinos.

Eduardo reached The Palm Desert Treatment Center within two hours. It was peaceful there, pleasant, upscale and professional.

CHAPTER **THIRTY-THREE**

Time Heals the Heart

Amber sat up. Wiped the sweat away from her brow and looked down and noticed her shirt damp and moist from perspiration. Recalling in detail, her vivid nightmare, the recollection infuriated her—enraged her enough to become visibly distressed. She threw the pillows off the couch then removed her shoe, flinging it at one of Dr. Hayward's dubious plaques on the wall. The picture comes sheer off, glass shattering into several million pieces.

"Now—now Amber, why did you throw your shoe?" Dr. Hayward expressed containing ***his*** hostility.

"Because you keep asking me to rehash my depression," Amber exclaimed, remaining on the couch. "Over and over, I can't do this anymore! ***I hate you!*** You evil vile man!"

"Amber this is part of your therapy. You've come so far, you're doing so well."

Amber didn't look at him, she was so overwhelmed with anger she just couldn't see straight.

"Let's calm down now. Only one picture today," Dr. Hayward quipped, tsking at the sight of his treasured doctoral degree lying on the ground. "That's a good sign."

It was a gigantic office, bigger than most for a clinical psychiatrist but Dr. Dirk Hayward had a big ego, and considerable psyche's required immense quarters. He was mostly proud of his bulky comfortable couches and oblong daybed. The divan his patients could conveniently position on (or what most employees thought) conducts sexual acts on top of. He was a curt, bald, stocky man in a rich community of other specialists, nurses, orderlies, Assistants, security and resident staff. He was never sympathetic to others, he treated all his patients callously, all but one—Amber Sanchez. She wasn't considered mental or even had a psychological problem; she was just a woman troubled. But oh how he loved being in the same room with her. She was a natural beauty, exotic appearance, silky raven hair that fell across her shoulders, blushing pink lips, tone voluptuous figure, he loved staring at her while she thought he was listening...

Amber laid her body down on the brown tweed couch and gazed up at the smooth white ceiling above her. She was a ***space case***, whatever that term meant. She oftentimes heard that term floating around the halls of the Palm Desert Treatment Center perfectly located within the serene desert of Indio County, California. She was a momentary guest (until she felt she was well enough to check out) at the final destination of the mess of her life. Slashing her wrist didn't help. Amber was so uncertain, constantly crying, deeply depressed...and the days past quickly inside. In a blink of an eye the days turned into sixteen months incarcerated. Her kids grew up without her. Coming to visit for thirty minutes at a time, but Amber was so low, no visible life in her face, her mother would gather them up, and say politely, "Well, we'd better go, mom looks tired." And off they went.

Never mind what she thought might be happening in their lives. Her son Adrian was turning twelve, her daughter Valentina, getting so tall. What they thought about their mother living in a mental establishment was incomprehensible. Never mind what her own mother thought and the reason she was ***there*** in the first place. It didn't matter; she didn't care, because Amber found an ***O-U-T***. She found the ideal way of not facing the actuality, what reality was and where her mind and body lie. It was perfect really. Not being able to confront the faces that respected and loved her so, trusted in her, relaxed with her easiness, never making waves in their little group. It was simple, an exact answer to all the endless questioning. How to get out...how to avoid Eduardo...how to avoid Leticia...how to face the facts...how to face responsibility...how to face her husband...to encounter his relatives...all the questions of how, where, when and why! She would be considered irrational. The reaction of hate would turn into sympathy. She would no longer need an excuse; the defense was mapped out for her. She was now just an opinion inside everyone's heads, instead of the obvious, the source of his or her gossip. She would be set free, let go from all the attention, and she would be shielded, defended of her irrational behavior. And after spending several months with Dr. Hayward, Amber realized it stemmed from not having a father. That void of always trying to be the ***good girl***. Daddy's wanted to see their good girls. They don't leave good girls behind, just the bad ones. And good girls face their responsibilities and Amber thought the solution was to not face the responsibility of what happened, therefore, she was a bad girl. She was forever trying to please everyone, hating confrontations, avoided them at all costs. This too, stemmed from not having a father, Dr. Hayward would point out. Amber's behavior was immoral, and to make sure her Father Figure stayed awhile, she was pleasing to him. Agreeing with everything Eduardo asked she didn't want him to leave. But he did leave; he had his own agenda, and according to Dr. Hayward, Amber's prognosis was ***'fear of abandonment'.***

Amber closed her eyes, on the verge of a pleasant sleep when Dr. Hayward's voice came ringing through her peaceful climate. "Let's talk about your brother-in-law, let's talk about Eduardo."

Amber let his name sink in.

Eduardo...

Eduardo A. Sanchez, Attorney- At- Law.

Memories flood her heart, her brain. Just the mere mention of his name sent Amber over the edge of compulsion. "I'm ready Dr. Hayward."

Dr. Hayward was confused. "Beg your pardon?"

Amber arched her back, tried to get comfortable. Her bosoms stretch out the fabric on her T-shirt. "I think I'm ready to see him now."

"You ***think*** you are?" Dr. Hayward gazed away from his pencil and writing pad and surveyed Amber's profile lying on his comfortable couch. She's beautiful, unique. Her indigo hair draped off the side of a square pillow, so silky, so touchable. He sat up straight, noticed Amber curving her back to get cozy again. His intentions are devious; he knows this to be true. He's a sick individual. Demented. No, not sick in that sense, enough to be a patient of his, but infected in the way he lusted after Amber constantly, calling her into his office for no reason at all but to smell her. Amber's affair was enthralling; her description of it intense. He loved to hear her explain the reasons behind it all, oftentimes keeping her away from other sessions. "Amber," he let out clearing his throat, shuffling his legs around, trying to calm his feeble erection. "I can call him today if you'd like."

"The sooner the better," Amber expressed with anticipation.

"Good, 'cause I'm afraid I can no longer continue to make excuses for you not to see him. He's a very stubborn man." He gave out exasperated feeling his sore jaw. Even though he loved ogling her, she was still a patient—a sufferer who was mulish as hell. Amber arrived in an unconscious state. She was unaware of the occurrences of even the past year. The Behavioral Health Department determined that she wasn't a threat to society or even to herself. So when Dr. Hayward felt it was time for Amber to leave, she fought against it. It was Amber who felt the need to remain in the realm of safekeeping. To be fed, bathed, consoled, harbored, protected, concealed and looked after. This was a private treatment center, with well over five hundred staff members willing and able to come running to a patient's beck and call. Who was he to complain? Her stay here was paid for—and the facility didn't come cheap. No, Amber had a rich benefactor, someone who loved her deeply enough to sign the monthly five-figured checks.

Dr. Hayward placed down his pencil and writing pad again, clicked on a nearby voice recorder. Put it in position to start recording. "Eduardo has something to tell you...it'll be good for you to face him."

Amber's whole body froze. He has something to tell her? Good Lord, what could it be? Does she truly want to come face to face again with the man that forced her there? Tears began to pour down her eyes.

Dr. Hayward took note of the misery streaming down her face. It was a dissimilar reaction to what he'd been used to. Amber was known to throw such fits of anguish; tossing everything in sight she could get a hold of. The orderly's would be called and she would have to be sedated, placed in a harness and barreled out of his office. No, Amber was releasing this time. This was a definite sign of improvement. Finally, she was beginning to accept her past, embrace her demons.

But what was this? Amber's tears turned into huge sobs of torment. She rolled over into the crevice of the couch and cried her heart out. "It's been over a year and half," Dr. Hayward expressed vigorously, "Meeting Eduardo will be a definite sign of recovery."

"I'm not recovered," Amber cried out suddenly, sitting up straight. Dr. Hayward began slowly putting some of his breakable items back into a nearby box. Amber clutched her hands around the pillow puncturing the tight fabric. "Dr. Hayward...I changed my mind."

When she gave him that ***expression*** it caused him to dampen his pants. He was mush around her. He wanted to gather her body up and rock her sometimes, console her, cuddle her anxiety away. "No," he chuckled, "You can't agree to something then do an about face. I'll give him a call, he'll be glad to hear from me finally. I'm tired of having to send him away. He's beneficial to your stay here, and as your doctor, and mostly as your friend, it would be a good idea to finally meet with him."

Amber wiped away her tears. Her rage subsided. Dr. Hayward served as the strong figure in her life and she did what she was told. And just like that, she felt her head nodding confirmation.

The following day, Amber sat quietly outside waiting for her visitor along with the other patients. Unlike most treatment centers, Amber was allowed to wear her own clothes. She never dressed up, always wore what was most available and soft, sweats and a T-shirt.

Amber was tense, nervous, and kept eyeing the glass patio doors while other patients around her visited with their loved ones, unintentionally clouding her view. What was she going to say to him? She hadn't seen him for over a year and a half. Sixteen months and fourteen days to be exact. The exact day of the motel room. ***Oh God,*** she just thought about it again, she didn't want to, but it just happened. Amber brought her hand up to close her eyes. Now why did she think about that? It just slipped right in. The motel room, Eduardo and her are making love. ***Oh no,*** it happened again. ***OH NO! Not again, go away, make it go away.*** She had been safe for so long, coming out of the coma into a safeguarded world, going through her daily routine with ease. Not wanting to talk to anyone if she didn't want to or feel like it; only talking to Dr. Hayward, who, in his own way, was a sheltered haven. He could have been a priest, a teacher, her boss, ***or her father***. He was helping her come out of a bad situation, and she respected him.

And then she saw him...

Her brother-in-law entered an area like no other. Her heart saluted at just the mere sight of him. Sauntering down the sidewalk...dressed in a dark brown suit, beige tie and cream-colored dress shirt. Her favorite colors on him. He knew that, he did, ***damn him***. Amber felt her throat close up the moment his eyes met hers. Looking into that man's face always seemed to weaken her restraint.

A nurse showed him the way towards the outdoor visitor's courtyard, and Eduardo began, which seemed like an endless walk, towards Amber. Along the way were splendid views of the landscape and facility beyond. Individual one-bedroom one-bath bungalows set amongst grassy fields of Sego and King Palms, a tropical array of desert terrain, with patios of cobblestone concrete and stone waterfalls. A personal domain for each patient, and that warmed his heart. He came in closer, sat down next to her and gently grabbed her hand.

Oh God, don't touch me! Her heart yelled out, but her body didn't react that way, her flesh wanted more. ***More, more, MORE! Oh God...please, pretty please...oh God please...no more.*** Her heart dropped into her stomach, tears swelled within her hazel eyes, she bit her lower lip trying ever so hard to make them subside . . .

CHAPTER **THIRTY-FOUR**

Hello, Remember Me?

Eduardo's legs nearly buckled from underneath him the moment he reached her side. Instantly he noticed she had cut her hair, but it endured a silky black. Wearing no makeup, dressed in a plain white T-shirt and light gray sweats, she was the most radiant creature God ever created.

Eduardo reached for her hand and gently grabbed it. Just the slightest touch sent electricity throughout his entire body. Tears swarmed his eyes at once, remembering when he came into contact with her he would soon forget how to let go.

He brought her palm up to his mouth, gently kissed the scar on her wrist. "Amber, ***I'm sorry***...please forgive me," Eduardo confessed wholeheartedly choking back further agony noticing her tears. Amber slowly wrapped her arms around his neck. Simultaneously, releasing huge sobs of relief, they clutch each other fierce and cry from the anticipation of seeing one another again—bawl from the realization of what brought them to that point.

"I've been a so selfish," Eduardo confessed, wiping the moisture away from his eyes. "I wanted to mask our affair, I know now what I demanded came with a price. Seeing you dying in the hospital, you taught me a lesson." Eduardo brought her palm up to his mouth and kissed her scar once more. "Wherever you were, I wanted to be with you. I've never been so petrified in all my life. I know I shouldn't be telling you this, Dr. Hayward asked me not to, but I think you should know that I ***was*** going to leave her. I know how to seduce a woman," he snickered, rubbing her hand. "I know how to break-up without any complications, but when it comes to maintaining a relationship, I'm still a trainee. I just needed a shove...and when you left, you ram me down. I was going to make us legitimate Amber—you're all I ever wanted and Good God, I never thought you'd do what you did." Eduardo kissed her palm over and again; tears rolled down his cheeks instantly. "I've been at your bedside since I brought you here and prayed each night that you'd be healthy once you awoke and that you'd still love me. Seeing you now and those tears in your eyes, I know that you still do. I don't need my family Amber...***I need you...***You were meant for me and I always take care of what's mine. We're going to wake up in each other's arms, eat breakfast in bed and hold hands on the beach. I've been in love with you since the day we met." Eduardo kissed her scar for the last time and turned her hand over to slip a 3-Carat Radiant Cut diamond solitaire on her finger. "I want you forever Amber and we're flying to Vegas this weekend to make it official."

Amber was still in awe that his body was even sitting next to hers! A weak smile embraced her face while tears continued to run down her cheeks. She finally gazed down at the ring and spread her fingers out to admire the precious stone.

"Do you know how long I've owned that ring?" Eduardo beamed at her. "I bought it the day before you married my brother."

Amber returned his happiness and giggled. It had been a long time. Eduardo Sanchez had been the man in her dreams. When Dr. Hayward told her who paid for her support, made sure she was comfortable, she knew she would never forget this wonderful human being. Throughout all her therapy, both pleasing and unfavorable, she probably never would. Sessions so arduous, other patients around her were so engrossed. Had it not happen to Amber she would have never believed it was true. That a couple like them would endure that long, worship extensively; desire to be with each other ***even now.***

Amber continued to shed tears. Eduardo reached for a nearby tissue box and tore one away and gently wiped the misery aside.

"I don't need diamonds Eduardo," Amber spurted, grabbing his arm moving in closer to him, "I only need you."

"Good God…just hold me," Eduardo mouthed, embracing her body. "Now do you believe me when I say I love you?"

"Yes," Amber expressed, breaking apart from him.

"I love you to extreme," he gushed, holding her face within his hands. "I want to be with you until one of us draws our last breath. Do you hear me? You were put on this earth for me and I will ***never*** abandon you."

Eduardo couldn't withstand his mania any longer and lightly drew his mouth towards hers. Amber kissed Eduardo foremost with sweet impulsiveness before long returned his frenzy tenfold.

Eduardo forced himself away; he wanted to make love to her right then and there! He whispered in her ear, "You ***are*** going to marry me, right?"

"Yes."

Still aroused, he voiced, "Good, 'cause there's someone I really want you to meet."

Apprehensive all of a sudden, Amber brought the ring up to her face and continued to dab her eyes with Kleenex. What did he just say? The range of emotions he divided, giddiness was now mixed well with skepticism. ***Someone?*** What does that mean? What happened to him while she was unconscious? ***Who*** did he meet?

Eduardo waved at the windows beyond. Amber watched him as he stood up and became removed from her. She wanted to grab him back—why was he withdrawing? Her heart jumped out of her skin. She was just offered the most comforting words of encouragement to finally feel steady enough to walk out of medical care when Eduardo selfishly plucked the solace away?

Amber was startled by the sight of her mother entering first and didn't notice Sheila leading a small hand out the glass doorway. Amber brought her eyes down towards the toddler and practically exploded.

Good Lord, who was that!?

Eduardo knelt to the ground and rested his torso on top of his heels. Amber went pale with shock as Eduardo opened up his broad arms and invited the little boy into them.

Once the boy was within Eduardo's clasping, Amber gazed up at her mother skeptically. Amber didn't know what was going on, she was utterly confused and was trying to catch her breath.

"Oh baby," Sheila exclaimed, reaching out for Amber and gathering her body in for a hug. "I'm so sorry for having kept it from you. We asked Dr. Hayward not to tell you until the timing were right."

Amber went motionless—she was stunned. She eyed Eduardo again; he had scooped the little boy up within his arms and held him tenderly confined.

Amber wanted to be glad for him, she did, but she felt nothing but heartache. Did Leticia have another child when she was in a coma? Thank God Eduardo made sure to soften the blow by offering to get married before...***before...***Good Lord, he introduced his son. Amber could tell the boy was his. The toddler had Leticia's coal black hair and unmistakable green eyes like the both of them. He looked just like Kyra when she was little. The toddler was obviously at ease with his dad; the youngster laid his head on Eduardo's chest and bore right into Amber's eyes sucking his thumb.

"Amber, you OK?" Eduardo asked, concerned that Amber's face went pale.

Sheila continued to caress her daughter's hair, "Baby, you feeling all right?"

Amber shot looks at the both of them. No, she didn't feel all right, no, she wasn't OK!

Eduardo and Sheila both glanced at one another.

"Maybe we should hold off telling her," Eduardo expressed dejected.

"Maybe you're right," Sheila agreed, continually caressing Amber's tresses.

"Just go ahead—say it, tell me what you're trying to avoid. I promise I won't overreact to your son," Amber confessed, feeling her throat close up. "Anyway...he's adorable Eduardo, you must be very proud."

Eduardo gulped. Another distinct gaze at Sheila. Sheila turned her head in dismay.

Amber noticed that the toddler suddenly fell asleep on Eduardo's shoulder. He was angelic-like with his dark eyelashes shut.

"Amber...your mother had no other choice but to transfer you out of Cedars and into a county hospital. Your care was oftentimes unethical—"

"I know all that Eduardo," Amber cut in, "Just introduce me to Leticia's son..."

"He's not hers," Eduardo reciprocated, caressing Amber's cheek with his hand, "He's yours."

"He's...***what?***" Amber stood up immediately and backed away from them.

This is why Dr. Hayward insisted they hold off telling her so quickly; Eduardo realized swiftly watching his beloved cover up her mouth now in skepticism. "He's yours Amber, he's your son...you can hold him if you'd like."

Amber felt this incredible urge to do just that and took the little boy away from Eduardo's warm clutch. The child continued to rest and curled up within Amber's cynical arms. She scanned his little body in uncertainty. Hers? "H-How?"

Eduardo wrapped himself around mother and child. Stroking the back of Amber's hair, he expressed, "It was unprecedented—although not uncommon for a woman to be pregnant in an unconscious state. The doctors were in disbelief...your past medical history proved without a doubt any possible way for you to be expectant. My heart sunk when I first found out, I thought you might have been raped. I demanded an ultrasound the minute you arrived at Palm Desert. Your mother and I were with you when they did the procedure; we wanted to know ourselves how far off you were. We were overjoyed the moment they told us the fetus was a four-month gestation."

"Oh God," she cried, holding the boy tightly bound. Good Lord he ***was*** a miraculous angel!

"Relieved that you weren't assaulted, I went to see Victor to share the good news. I thought this would make him happy...bridge the gap between us. But when we discussed the pregnancy, he threw the divorce papers in my face."

"He didn't even want to know?" Amber uttered through tears. "But Victor loves children."

"That's just it...the look on my brother's face when I told him, it made sense."

"What made sense?"

"That you hadn't been sleeping with him. That the conception couldn't have been his...but mine."

Amber began to fully cry now and buckled to her knees. She glared down at the child who was still within her grip. He was a perfect mesh. He had her hair color, her mouth and long fingers, Eduardo's skin-tone, nose, dark eyelashes and green eyes.

Eduardo bent down with her and eased her body back up. "You had a C-section at seven months, the baby was under stress and they performed a hysterectomy at the same time. After that entire trauma on your body, the doctors said you'd probably never wake up," he cried, butting his head up against hers. "***But you did***...I knew in my heart that you would and Sheila and I were elated and asked the facility not to tell you just yet prior to knowing that you were sound enough to handle the truth."

Amber kissed the boy's forehead, "He's...magnificent Eduardo."

"You created life Amber, not me. We watched him grow inside your belly while you had no knowledge. I thank you for giving him to me."

Amber looked across at her mother and smiled. Sheila in turn beamed back at her daughter. "I love you baby."

"I love you too Mom."

Eduardo gazed over at Sheila himself, "Your mother's been staying with me by the way; she's been an angel taking care of him while I go to work. Without her support, I don't where I'd be."

Sheila burst into tears…Eduardo had been sincere. Since the birth of her grandson, she watched Eduardo transform from a self-centered maniac into a patient parent and coddle that boy like there was no tomorrow. "Dear God, I know this would be hard—"

Eduardo reached over to his future mother-in-law to caress her shoulder. Amber observed her mother as she patted Eduardo's hand accepting his touch. ***So much has happened!*** So much to sink in! She had another son. A son with Eduardo! Her mother and Eduardo were friends. They cared for one another! Good Lord, Dr. Hayward never told her, made sure she was solid enough to deal with the reality. She must have been sane enough to handle the comprehension, a potent sense of happiness sunk into her heart. She not only had Eduardo's complete devotion, but the little boy...***Good Lord;*** the child created a family with the man she never stopped loving.

Amber giggled, and then kissed her son's forehead once and again. "What's my son's name?"

"Peyton."

Printed in the United States
137115LV00002B/4/P

9 781432 732752